LOVE GROWS *Wild*

OTHER TITLES BY WINTER RENSHAW

THE NEVER SERIES

Never Kiss a Stranger

Never Is a Promise

Never Say Never

Bitter Rivals

THE ARROGANT SERIES

Arrogant Bastard

Arrogant Master

Arrogant Playboy

THE RIXTON FALLS SERIES

Royal

Bachelor

Filthy

THE AMATO BROTHERS SERIES

Heartless

Reckless

Priceless (a Rixton Falls crossover)

THE P.S. SERIES

P.S. I Hate You

P.S. I Miss You

P.S. I Dare You

THE MONTGOMERY BROTHERS DUET

Dark Paradise

Dark Promises

THE PAPER CUTS SERIES

Hate Mail

Yours Cruelly

Dear Stranger

STAND-ALONES

Single Dad Next Door

Cold Hearted

The Perfect Illusion

Country Nights

Absinthe

The Rebound

Love and Other Lies

The Executive

Pricked

For Lila, Forever

The Marriage Pact

Hate the Game

The Cruelest Stranger

The Best Man

Trillion

Enemy Dearest

The Match

Whiskey Moon

The Dirty Truth

Love and Kerosene

You or Someone Like You

Fake-ish

PRAISE FOR WINTER RENSHAW

"Winter Renshaw crafts the best romances! She always delivers it all—angst, emotion, and humor. Her books are a true delight."

—Adriana Locke, *USA Today* bestselling author

"Passion. Drama. Angst. Renshaw nails the romance trifecta with her perfectly paced office love affair."

—Deanna Roy, *USA Today* bestselling romance author of the Forever Series

"If you're looking for stories that are thought provoking, wildly sexy, and unputdownable, you'll never be disappointed with Winter Renshaw!"

—Jenika Snow, *USA Today* bestselling author

"The queen of contemporary angst knows how to curl toes while breaking hearts! A perfect romance for two imperfect lovers!"

—Sosie Frost, *Wall Street Journal* bestselling author

WINTER RENSHAW

This is a work of fiction. Names, characters, organizations, places, events, and incidents are either products of the author's imagination or are used fictitiously. Otherwise, any resemblance to actual persons, living or dead, is purely coincidental.

Published by Montlake, Seattle

www.apub.com

EU product safety contact:
Amazon Media EU S. à r.l.
38, avenue John F. Kennedy, L-1855 Luxembourg
amazonpublishing-gpsr@amazon.com

ISBN-13: 9781662523731 (paperback)
ISBN-13: 9781662523724 (digital)

Cover design by Eileen Carey
Cover image: © Regina Wamba of MaeIDesign.com

Printed in the United States of America

To the farmer who watered me and put me in the sun
so I could bloom again.

PROLOGUE

Wren

"You sure you want to do this?" My best friend, Reese, frowns from my doorway. She comes bearing cardboard boxes, moving tape, Sharpies, and a wistful expression on her face.

"It's not optional." I sip my iced chai and scan the lofty downtown Des Moines condo my son and I have called home for the last four years. Twenty years ago, I left my hometown of Colton Valley—a blink-and-you-miss-it Iowa farming town, got a generic college degree, and somehow along the way stumbled into a career as a romance novelist.

Everything was going well . . . until life happened.

Turns out it's impossible to write—or at least write well—when your personal life goes up in flames. One of the worst feelings in the world is having a story to tell that refuses to come out. The flashing cursor on a blank white page is a visual that haunts my dreams on a nightly basis.

"You're sure you're not doing this because of he-who-shall-not-be-named?" Reese sighs. "It's just that everything is so fresh, and this decision seems so . . . sudden. I just hope you're doing it for the right reasons and it's not some knee-jerk impulse reaction. Don't let that asshole run you out of the city you love."

"I'm not running from anything—or anyone." I tuck the flaps on a cardboard box. "And you can say Nick's name. It's not forbidden. He doesn't get to leave me at the altar and still wield that much power over me."

Reese sits straighter, satisfied with my answer. While it's been six months since Nick left me the morning of our wedding day, and the aftershocks of that rug-pull are still shaky, the love is gone.

I don't miss him.

I don't wish things had been different.

I just wish I could write again.

I have overdue contracts, and I feel like I'm letting everyone down. My die-hard readers. My agent. My editor. Myself. My son and the life I was building for us . . .

Two months ago, Atticus found me sobbing over my laptop in the middle of the night. He brought me a blanket, his beloved teddy bear, and a glass of water, and then he scampered off to grab his favorite book, telling me I needed some inspiration.

Inspiration was exactly what I needed, just not from between the pages of *Goodnight, Goodnight, Construction Site.*

"I can't live here without you." She sets the boxes on the dining room table and sinks into a chair, half pouting.

"Then come with me. It's only forty minutes away," I say. "It's a cute little postcard town. You'd love it."

"I'd hate it," she counters.

"True. But you hated sushi until I made you try it," I remind her. "Now it's your favorite."

The day I left for college, I vowed to myself I'd never move back home. Not that there's anything wrong with that quaint little Hallmark town. But for me, it wasn't about that. Leaving home meant pushing myself out of my comfort zone and into the unknown. I was convinced that would be where my life would truly begin. And it did . . . until it started to feel like it was ending too.

Reese uncaps a black Sharpie and takes a whiff, grimacing. "Why do I both hate and love this smell? Make it make sense."

I tape a box of paperback books and label it **OFFICE**.

"I just can't picture you living on an acreage. In a *farmhouse.* You've been a city girl ever since I've known you. You have this modern industrial loft with these huge ceilings. You eat at the best restaurants. You travel all the time, and you're ten minutes from the airport. And Atticus goes to that cool preschool over on Walnut. I bet they don't have schools like that in Colton Valley. And how many restaurants do they have? One? *Two?*"

I chuckle. "Four, actually. Five, if you count the bar that serves frozen pizza by the slice. I've been wanting to learn how to cook more anyway. And their elementary school is one of the best in the state, believe it or not. Atticus is really excited for kindergarten this fall. Plus, my mom works there, so he'll get to see his grandma every day."

"Good for Atticus. But *you're* going to hate it, and you're going to be calling me up asking me to pack you up again, and I'm just going to say I told you so."

"Just wait until you see the property. Cute little white farmhouse. Wraparound porch. Tree-lined driveway. Room for a food garden. The yard backs up to the river, and there's even a little gazebo. Oh, and there's a red barn with a little corral. I was thinking of getting one of those adorable mini cows—or maybe a pony for Atticus? And a dog. I should get a big dog."

She pinches the bridge of her nose. "I love your enthusiasm, but as your oldest and longest friend, I'd like to remind you that you've never kept a single houseplant or goldfish alive, so it worries me to hear you talk so casually about growing your own food and raising large animals."

I snort. She's not wrong, but I think this could be good for me.

I need to refocus.

I need to get out of my funk.

I need a change of scenery.

I need nature and purpose and to be closer to family—to my roots.

I need inspiration . . .

My god, do I need inspiration.

"I'm excited for this new chapter," I tell her. I don't want to devote more energy to Nick than necessary, and while I'm not angry at him anymore—he personally did me a favor—I'm still struggling to forgive him for the giant hole he left in my son's heart. That's what hurts the most. He promised to raise and love Atticus like his own—same as what my stepdad, Will, did with me. Nick and Atti were inseparable—until Nick's ex-girlfriend reached out to him the morning of our wedding, and that was all it took. "Atticus has had a hard year, and so have I. I miss seeing him smile. I miss writing. And I need to see my family more often. This place is beautiful, Reese. Once you see it, you'll understand why I couldn't pass it up. Here. I have pictures."

I pull out my phone and open one of the first images my mom sent me—the little white two-story house nestled among thick green trees under a blanket of clear blue sky. It's the perfect size for the two of us, and with all that space, Atti can actually touch grass instead of growing up in a concrete jungle.

Reese studies the image before letting out a long breath, her head cocked and her eyes softening as she hands my phone back.

"It's cute," she says. "But I worry you're romanticizing it."

"I'm a romance author. I romanticize everything. It's kind of what I do . . ."

"Okay, fair." She uncurls her shoulders. "But I also have another concern that you probably haven't even thought about."

I sniff a laugh. "What's that?"

"Pretty sure they don't have food delivery in Colton Valley."

She's not wrong. And it's a valid concern, given my robust DoorDash reliance. But it's a sacrifice I'm willing to make if it means being able to write again.

"All razzing aside, I'm happy for you," she adds, leaning close to wrap her arms around me. She squeezes me longer and tighter than she ever has, and I breathe her in: a mix of her musky vanilla perfume and the comfort of best friendship. "If anyone can jump without looking and land on their feet, it's you."

Last month, when I was crying on the phone to my mother about my writer's block and feeling stuck in life, she proposed the idea of me moving back to my hometown, mentioning there was some man they knew who was thinking about selling his forty-acre farmhouse plot by the river.

After she told me the price—which was a fraction of what I paid for my downtown loft—and rattled off all the other reasons I should make this move, I couldn't stop thinking about it, couldn't stop envisioning spending endless days enveloped by the gorgeous landscape of this farmhouse retreat, slow mornings sipping coffee while watching deer graze in the meadow, writing next to open windows with gauzy curtains, curling up with a good book on the front porch swing, midday walks along the riverbanks under a warm sun, Atticus skipping happily by my side as birds chirp around us.

In the strangest way—one I still can't explain—the moment I saw that photo, it instantly felt like home.

1

Hunter

The tractor hums beneath me like a living beast, all steel and muscle and diesel breath. I've been out here since before sunup, dropping blades into dirt that smells like home and every decision—good and bad—I've ever made. Autosteer's doing most of the work, but I sit up straight, one hand on the armrest, the other on the throttle.

I've never been good at sitting still for too long.

I glance down at the monitor. Eighteen point three acres an hour. Not bad. If the rain holds off and nothing breaks, I might get this north section done by nightfall.

Sky's a little darker than I'd like today, so I won't hold my breath.

I take a swig of lukewarm coffee and scan the rolling hills of the horizon. The ladies at the coffee shop this morning were buzzing about some writer who grew up around here who's now moving back. I didn't catch her name, but they sure seemed excited. Based on all the stars in their eyes, a guy would've thought they were discussing a local celebrity. Can't blame them, though. We don't get much for excitement around here, so every little thing quickly becomes the talk of the town.

But an author? Don't think we've ever had one of those before.

Can't recall the last time I cracked a book. Had to have been my university days, but at forty-two, college was a lifetime ago.

My phone rings, and I take the call over my headset.

"Truitt," I answer.

"That planter at the Everly farm's acting up again." The frustration in my farmhand's voice tells me this is exactly what I didn't want to happen today. If we're lucky, we get ten good planting days a season. It's the second half of April, and thanks to all the rain we've had this month and the time it took for the fields to dry out, today's our first one.

Not ideal.

"You check the vac pressure?" I ask. I've got two full-time guys—Cal and Truitt, each about a decade younger than me. Solid guys who aren't afraid of the long days and even longer nights that come with this kind of job. Not everyone's fortunate enough to have a good right-hand man, but me? I'm lucky enough to have two.

"Yep." Truitt sighs. "Called the mechanic too. Still waiting to hear back."

I picture him out in the field, pacing and muttering to himself, likely more upset about disappointing me than having to fix a broken planter during planting season. Truitt's work ethic is rivaled only by his people-pleasing tendencies—at least when it comes to me.

Over the past ten years, I've become his boss, his best friend, his mentor, and his big brother all rolled into one. Letting me down is always the last thing he wants to do, but no matter how many times I remind him that this is farming and things happen, he still gets worked up when things don't go according to plan.

I've never seen the point in letting these kinds of situations get the best of me. Not when I have more important things to focus on—like running my operation and buying more land. My guys always joke that I might as well be married to the place, that I've never needed a woman because farming is the "love of my life."

They're not wrong. They just don't have all the backstory, and it's not worth my energy to give it to them either. It's none of their business, and I don't see the point in mucking around in the past anyway. Doesn't change anything.

"And you checked all the seed tubes?" I ask.

"Sure did." His voice is flat. It's Friday. The last thing either of us wanted was to deal with a breakdown, but machines don't give a damn what day of the week it is.

"And you bled the lines?"

"Of course." Even in his frustration, Truitt's still respectful.

Cal would've answered me with something like "Got any more stupid questions for me, boss?"

"All right. Give me a few. I'll head that way. We'll figure this out," I assure Truitt before ending the call.

I bring my tractor to a stop, then kill the engine before climbing out and trudging to the edge of the field where my truck is parked.

I'm pulling onto the road a few minutes later when a black Audi SUV blazes past me in a trail of gravel dust. No sound other than the tires crunching on the rocks. Must be electric. Electric cars and luxury imports are a rare sight in Colton Valley and an even rarer sight out here in the middle of farm country, where the miles between towns and houses stretch on forever.

When it zipped by a second ago, I caught a flash of pale blond hair, long and glossy, the kind that looks like it costs more than a month's worth of diesel. Her taillights glow cherry red through the brown-gray dust, and she crawls to a stop when she reaches the bend in the road at the end of my section.

My stomach knots. Something about this feels disruptive.

I remain in my truck, my right boot jammed against the brake and my left hand gripping the top of the steering wheel, observing through squinted eyes.

Maybe she's lost. It's not uncommon for people to get turned around out here, especially if they're not from the area. Willing to bet Blondie's not local.

She's parked in the road now, climbing out of the driver's seat and walking toward the gate at the end of Rich Sanders's place—the only parcel along the Colton Valley riverfront not owned by me. For eight long years, the man's been claiming he's going to retire and move south, and he promised he'd let me know when he's ready to sell. But every year, he tells me "maybe next year."

As someone who's negotiated dozens of land deals, I know firsthand you can't act desperate or you lose the upper hand. He knows I want it—he doesn't know how badly I want it or why I want it—but he knows I'll pay him cash, and that's all he needs to know.

I've negotiated dozens of deals over the years, and I'm used to playing the long game, except we're going on eight years of this now and it's getting ridiculous.

I'm a patient man, but lately mine's running paper thin.

I want that land.

I *have* to have it.

I scratch at my temple as she fusses with the rusty orange cattle gate at the end of the dirt driveway that leads to Rich's farmhouse. It takes her a second or two, but she finally figures out the latch, swings the gate wide, and returns to her Audi.

I bet she's a real estate agent.

But that doesn't make sense. Rich said he'd sell to me, that we'd do a private party deal. I even promised to give him 10 percent above market value in an attempt to eliminate any competition.

In twenty years, I've amassed nearly ten thousand acres of farm ground. My personal home rests on a secluded piece of four hundred of those acres, my house sitting at the top of the hill overlooking it all. It's a million-dollar view—best one in the county. Trees. River. Rolling hills. Stars for days on a clear night. Privacy on top of privacy. The ultimate luxury. No neighbors for a solid five miles in any direction. The freedom to let people into—or keep them out of—your world is priceless. It's a piece of ground that's mine and mine alone, space to think and breathe and be alone and unbothered with my thoughts at the end of a long day.

It's my fortress of solitude—minus having Rich as a neighbor.

But more than that, I've got personal ties to that property, to that house and those grounds and that section of river. I made a promise to someone a lifetime ago, someone near and dear to me, and I'll be damned if I break it.

Blondie disappears down Rich's driveway.

I don't usually make a habit of being nosy—in this town you don't have to because everyone talks to everyone and things always trickle down eventually. But that woman's definitely not from around here, and she's sniffing around *my* land.

Pulling out onto the road, I take a right and head to Rich's.

Only, the second I do, Truitt sends me a panicked text asking if I'm on my way yet.

I am.

Just not in the direction I should be headed.

2

Wren

The key turns with a satisfying click.

For a second, I stand frozen—my hand on the doorknob, my son bouncing at my side, and the weight of everything that brought us here pressing down on my shoulders. But beneath that weight, there's something else too.

The faintest flicker of hope.

The buzzing undercurrent of excitement.

The thrill of the unknown.

"Can I go in first?" Atticus asks, practically vibrating. He's been patient for the entire drive, even when my phone's GPS lost signal halfway down a gravel road and I had to wing it like some pioneer mom in a black Audi.

"Go for it." I hold the door open wide.

He darts inside, his thick, sandy hair bouncing as his sneakers thud against the old wood floors. The place smells like cedar and dust, warmth and love, and a lifetime of other people's memories. Yet at the same time, it smells like home.

I follow him in, eyes sweeping the open space—the whitewashed walls, the exposed white oak beams, the warm glow of late morning light filtering through sheer linen curtains.

It's smaller than our downtown loft but cozier, grounded in something real. It has depth and charm and character. If these walls could talk, I imagine they'd have stories for days.

I'm feeling inspired already.

There's a spark in my chest, a nudge, a niggle in the center of my stomach that gives me reassurance that this was the right move.

"Mom, we have a real fireplace!" Atticus shouts from what I assume is the living room. "And the floor creaks when I jump! Listen! Can you hear it?"

"Just try not to fall through it," I call, smiling despite myself. I leave the key on the entryway table, where someone left a little ceramic dish shaped like a horseshoe. A welcome gift or a forgotten knickknack—either way, I'm claiming it. Besides, horseshoes are supposed to symbolize luck, and lately I've been running low on that.

Atticus barrels back into the foyer a minute later, already winded. "Can I go outside now?"

"There's five acres of backyard and no one to yell at you for running too fast. Go wild," I say, waving him off. Thirty-five acres of this forty-acre purchase consisted of rentable farm ground—which I'm told will bring in about fourteen thousand dollars a year in income, among other tax benefits I had no idea existed. Not only did I find a property that belongs on a movie set, I'm being paid to own it too.

Mom always told me sometimes things fall apart just so they can fall back together when the time is right. She's never wrong about these things. She was right about my ex-fiancé too. Her first impression of Nick was that he seemed "fickle." I told her he was probably just nervous, but deep down, I wondered the same about him. He was notoriously indecisive about everything, from the color of his button-down shirt for work each morning to the drink he was going to order at a restaurant we'd been to a hundred times before. I used to tease him about it, never thinking he'd one day be indecisive about *me*. I suppose sometimes it's easier to see what we want to see, to believe what we so badly want to believe.

Atticus tugs his little red Converse sneakers tighter, then pauses at the glass-paneled back door, eyes squinting toward the sun-dappled barn.

"We should get a pony," he says, not for the first time. "And I'm going to need cowboy boots and a cowboy hat."

I chuckle. He's been asking for a pony for years now, ever since he went to a birthday party on some hobby farm outside of Winterset.

"We'll see," I tell him. "But we have to unpack before we can talk livestock, little cowpoke."

"'Kay, Mom, I'm gonna go check out the barn." The door slams behind him, and I'm alone with the echo of his excitement.

I wander deeper into the house, touching plaster walls, brushing dust from windowsills, opening doors like each one holds a different version of the life I'm trying to rebuild. There's a small dining room with gossamer-thin curtains, a galley kitchen with navy blue painted cupboards and butcher-block countertops, and a mudroom that smells faintly of the outdoors. Every room whispers stories of whoever lived here before—but none loud enough to drown out all the ones I hope to write now that it's my turn.

It isn't until I reach the front of the house again that I find it—*the* room.

Not sure how I missed it before.

It's tucked just off the main hallway, all warm wood floors and quiet charm, with a wide bow window that arcs out like an invitation. The view from here is something out of a storybook: a winding dirt driveway accented with soaring hundred-year-old oaks, sunlight cutting through the branches like gold ribbons.

I sit on the window seat, dust motes dancing in the air around me like whimsical fireflies. For the first time in a long time, I don't feel suffocated by silence. I feel . . . still.

And then I see it.

A white truck—big, boxy, and gleaming with chrome. It rolls to a slow stop at the edge of the drive, then idles for a moment, like it's deciding something.

I squint, shielding my eyes. It's too far to make out much detail, but I catch a man's figure. A hand tapping the steering wheel. Other than some dark hair shoved under a ball cap, I can't make out much else.

Not being neighborly in a small town is practically a crime, so I retreat from the window and trot to the door to introduce myself, only by the time I set foot on the front steps, the truck quickly accelerates, leaving nothing but a trail of dust.

Weird . . .

I watch until it disappears around the bend, a little frown tightening between my brows. Maybe someone just missed a turn. Or maybe they were thinking about turning in to say hi to the former owner and changed their mind when they saw my car.

A nosy neighbor?

A friend of the seller?

"Mom?" Atticus's voice breaks the quiet. He's standing in the hallway again, cheeks flushed, dirt already on his knees. I didn't even hear him come back inside. "Are we staying here tonight?"

"Yes," I say, standing and brushing off my jeans. "The movers should be here in an hour, so you're heading to Grandma's for the day while I get things settled, then you'll be back tonight. Sound like a plan?"

He shrugs, half disappointed he can't stay and pal around the acreage, but the glimmer in his crystal-blue eyes tells me he's excited for a day at Grandma Trish's. Besides, he has all summer to explore everything this property has to offer. There are endless adventures to be had . . . once we're unpacked.

"You'll have plenty of time to explore, I promise," I assure him, quietly relieved at how well he's taking to this place already.

Atticus scampers off to finish surveying our new digs, and I head up the creaky stairs to the second floor, where three large bedrooms with light-soaked panoramic views await me.

With the office on the main floor and the two of us only needing two of these rooms, maybe I'll turn the third one into a playroom—though I'd prefer Atticus to do most of his playing outside.

He's spent almost his entire life—a whopping four, almost five years—doing mostly inside things. As a single mom, technology has been a godsend more times than I can count. But deep down, I worry that he's not bored enough.

When you're bored, when you have time to be alone with your thoughts, when you have room to breathe, that's how a person really figures out who they are.

I want Atticus to know who he is. I don't want his past—my past—to write his story for him.

Moving here wasn't just for me.

It was for both of us.

3

Hunter

I never come to the store this time of day if I can help it.

Even in a town of two thousand, the predinner rush packs this little grocery store with too many people any given day of the week. Too many carts clogging the aisles and too many neighbors wanting to catch up like I've got all day to talk about the weather and speculate on grain prices. But I had a hell of a time getting that planter fixed earlier, ended up skipping lunch, and spent the rest of the afternoon daydreaming about a juicy rib eye. Didn't even get a chance to call Rich Sanders about that property.

Now here I am.

Shoulder to shoulder with the other locals—on a Friday no less, the worst time to grocery shop.

I've got no one to blame but myself, so I suffer in silence, as one does.

I'm standing at the meat counter, arms crossed, waiting for Britt Collier to finish wrapping the couple pounds of sirloin ahead of me, when I catch a flicker of movement out of the corner of my eye.

Blond hair. Navy leggings. Oversized canary-yellow Iowa State sweatshirt. Pristine white tennis shoes that wouldn't last a day on the farm. Shopping cart filled to the brim with enough food to stock a bunker. She looks like she got hit by a long day and backed over by it twice. Her hair's a mess—some kind of bun situation piled haphazard on top of her head—and she wears a tired semblance of a smile, like she's trying to make the best of it. I've never seen someone so exhausted yet somehow so distractingly gorgeous at the same time.

In fact, this woman turns no less than five heads as she makes her way through the produce aisle. Three men. Two women. All of them just as curious as I am because we don't have anything like her around here.

It takes a second for me to realize how badly *I'm* staring, but something about her holds me captive for longer than I'd care to admit.

She's a pretty little thing.

No, not just pretty—stunning. Messy hair, slightly smudged mascara beneath her eyes, and all.

I turn back toward the meat counter, but not before she sees me.

She stops a few paces behind me and releases an audible exhalation. I'm certain she's about to say something about my staring. But she doesn't. Just parks her cart and waits her turn like everyone else. Only now I can't help but notice how the air seems to have shifted—like the electric heat of a late spring storm moving in close behind me. Except this air smells like berries and almonds: sweet and clean and wildly out of place in a town where most of us smell like dirt, grease, and a hard day's work.

"Hey there, Hunter," Britt says, drawing my attention back to the counter. She gives me that syrupy smile she's been practicing since 2017 when she took over as head butcher at her daddy's meat counter. "The usual?"

"Two prime select rib eyes," I say, keeping my eyes on the cuts of meat in the case to make sure she picks the best ones. She usually does, but it's Friday, there's a long line, and she's looking at me with those hungry eyes she gets every once in a while.

"You should come over and cook those on my back porch later," she says with a little wink, like it's the first time she's made that joke and not the hundredth. "I'm off in an hour. Just saying."

Per usual, I don't laugh. I remain stoic. I don't want to be a jerk, which is why I can't give her false hope. Britt's not my type for a myriad of reasons, but mostly because I don't have a type. Not anymore. I've got a list of priorities a mile long and dating is dead last on it.

Her smile fades, and I feel like a jerk anyway. But it's for the best. She only wants me because she can't have me. If she had me, she'd stop wanting me real quick. That's usually how it goes.

"Your smoker's nice," I say to soften the exchange, "but I like mine better."

Out of the corner of my eye, I notice the blonde watching us.

Britt clears her throat, trying to reclaim her pride. "You ever going to give me that recipe you use? That spicy marinade you always talk about?"

"Nope." It's a secret family recipe—not that I have much family left these days. At least not around here. But very few things in life are sacred and special, and I'm keeping that one for myself.

She laughs like I'm flirting.

I'm not.

I never am.

I miss the days when her father ran the show. He didn't inflict any kind of small talk on anyone. He wrapped their meat tight, called "next," and kept the show on the road like a good butcher should. That, and he sure as hell didn't try and flirt with me.

I take the wrapped steaks once she hands them over, nod to thank her, and turn to leave—only to meet the blonde's eyes—deep blue and hypnotic—locked square on mine.

My breath hitches, but I tell myself to pull it together. She lifts a single brow and wears a knowing, tight-lipped smirk on her rosebud lips, like she fully understood the nuances of that little exchange. The whole thing lasts maybe a second or two at most, but in that time my boots refused to leave the ground and I'm pretty certain time stopped moving.

"Who's next?" Britt calls out before motioning at the blonde.

I step aside, still transfixed, not quite wanting to leave her aura though completely confused as to why.

People don't tend to have that effect on me.

Well, people generally don't tend to have *any* effect on me—which is exactly how I prefer it. I'm convinced that being unbothered is the secret to life. But something about Blondie bothers me—I'm just not sure why that is yet.

I think of the black Audi at Rich's house earlier and the blond woman. Then I think of the rumors of some big-city author moving to town. This has to be her, but her connection to Rich is the part that doesn't make sense. Is she living there? Did he rent out his place? He's a lifelong bachelor with no family, at least not around here. Not much for friends either.

I need to call the man—immediately.

"Could I please get a pound of the grass-fed ground beef?" Blondie asks, her voice sugar sweet.

I press my lips flat, willing myself not to say something. I shouldn't care. I shouldn't waste my breath on someone who thinks buying grass-fed is somehow superior, but I also hate to see someone pay a 20 percent premium for meat that tastes like hot garbage.

Against my better judgment, I lean closer. "You know, the whole grass-fed thing is just a marketing gimmick."

She turns toward me, her brows knitting in confusion as she half laughs. "I beg your pardon?"

"It's not actually healthier," I say. "And most of the time, the cattle might be grass-fed but grain-finished. True grass-fed beef doesn't have as much marbling. It's dryer. Not as tasty. The cows tend to be older too. Takes more time to fatten them up. You're paying extra for old, tough cow."

This is the most I've ever spoken to a complete stranger before, but something is compelling me to not shut the hell up and I'm strangely powerless about it.

She squares her shoulders with mine. I bet she also believes all the propaganda about corn products being the root of all health issues and cage-free eggs being more nutritious.

"But there are more omega-3s in grass-fed than grain-fed," she protests through blinking, baby doll eyes that give off an innocent vibe I don't quite buy.

"If you enjoy eating dry, flavorless beef, then by all means, get your omega-3s."

"No one has ever called *my* beef dry or flavorless," she says with a teasing tone as she looks me up and down. "Maybe you're cooking it wrong?"

I don't know whether to be amused or annoyed or a little of both.

Is she flirting with me? Or trying to prove me wrong?

She walked in here all pretty and polite and has this innocent look about her, but there's something more behind those intense deep blues of hers, like she notices more than the average person.

And I certainly didn't peg her as being quick-witted.

A pretty face, yes.

Wiseass? No.

We linger for a moment too long, both of us looking like we have something more to say but whatever it is just isn't making its way to either of our lips.

"Here you are, sweetheart," Britt hands over a pound of grass-fed ground beef wrapped tight in brown paper. "And I hate to say it, but Hunter's right."

I fight a satisfied smirk and nod at Britt while keeping my gaze trained on Blondie. "See? Straight from the butcher herself."

The blonde thanks Britt before playfully rolling her eyes at me. I've got at least a solid foot of height on her, and the playful way she looks up at me just now sends a strange tightness to my chest that I don't quite know what to make of. The second she pulls her attention off me, I find myself immediately missing it, wishing for another minute or two of that sweet sass that gets me frustrated and fired up all at the same time.

I head to the checkout. Five minutes later, I'm climbing into my truck when I notice the shiny black Audi SUV parked a few spots down.

That was definitely her in there—the same girl I saw going to Rich's earlier.

Judging by the amount of food she was buying, she must be sticking around for a while. Rich has been a bachelor as long as I've known him, in his mid-sixties, about as tall as he is wide, and his main hobby is playing the penny slots at the casino three towns west of here. He couldn't land this woman on his best day.

On my way home, I finally call Rich to figure out what the hell is going on.

It goes straight to voicemail.

4

Wren

The back hatch of my Audi beeps open, and a bag of tortilla chips makes a slow-motion tumble to the ground.

"Perfect." Crouching to grab it, I brush off a thin film of driveway dust. People who say the city is dirty have clearly never experienced country life.

I've unloaded half the groceries when the rumble of a familiar truck engine growls from the road. Mom and Will must be here to drop off Atticus.

"Mom! Guess what?" he calls, sprinting across the gravel a minute later.

"What?" I ask, standing just in time to catch him in a half hug.

"Grandpa let me drive his lawn tractor. And Grandma made waffles for dinner. *Waffles.*"

"Steer," my stepdad, Will, corrects him. "I let him steer it, not drive it. Big difference, bud, but we'll get there."

"You lucky duck." I brush a curl from his forehead. "You gonna help me put all this away?"

He wrinkles his nose. I let it slide this once. Normally we're a team, but this is a special circumstance—and I need to figure out where everything's going to go first, otherwise I'll find a box of cereal under the stove and a bottle of ketchup in the freezer.

My mother's already making her way toward me, arms open, warm and smiling. Pretty sure she hasn't stopped smiling since the moving truck arrived this morning. She took the day off work specifically to help take Atticus off my hands while I handled the movers.

"Hi, sweetheart." She's beaming, dragging in a literal breath of fresh air. "Wow, look at this place."

"Come on in," I say, gesturing her and Will inside as I grab another couple of bags. "It's still a disaster. And we'll be eating Tony's frozen pizza for the next three days, but it's starting to look more like home than some old farmhouse."

Inside, my mom makes a beeline for the kitchen, already unpacking without asking. It's her love language—acts of service disguised as mild bossiness. My back is on fire and I can barely keep my eyes open, so I accept her help with a tremendous amount of quiet appreciation.

"Atticus, show Grandpa your new room," she calls as she tears open a bag of Gala apples and dumps them into a ceramic bowl on the counter.

"I was going to give you the official tour," I say, handing her a box of pantry items. "But Atticus probably knows the property better than I do. I haven't even ventured to the outbuildings yet."

The movers finished early this afternoon, and I spent a few hours unpacking clothes and other essentials before running to the lone grocery store in town.

"It's all he's been talking about all day," Mom says. "I don't think I've ever seen him so excited about anything in his life. Did he tell you he wants a pony?"

I chuckle. "One of the first things he said."

She tilts her head to the side, eyes crinkling and warm. "You know, one of our neighbors down the road has a little Shetland. Got it for their grandkids years ago, but the grandkids grew up, got too busy for pony rides. It'd be perfect for Atticus. Want me to ask if they'd sell it to you?"

"Sure." I don't know the first thing about pony ownership, but how hard can it be? I've got a barn and a corral and some fenced land. I'll figure out the rest. Besides, Atticus needs some chores. Real chores. Not just unloading the dishwasher.

Upstairs, the sound of Will and Atticus's footsteps make the place creak and moan. Mom stocks my fridge, making sure all the labels face out the way she always does. The house feels warmer with them here. The kind of warmth that has nothing to do with the thermostat.

"I'm setting up my office in that little room off the front hallway," I tell her as we unload the last of the groceries. "The one with the bow window."

"Oh, Wren, I love that one. You'll be able to see when someone's coming up the drive."

"Exactly. I can be nosy and productive at the same time."

She grins. "Just like Grandma Betty used to. That's where you get that from, you know."

We move from room to room, and I show her everything—the unfinished sunroom off the kitchen that I'm dreaming of turning into a reading nook, the barn I haven't dared venture into yet, the spot in the backyard where I want to plant lavender and tomatoes and zucchini—and probably kill them all, though I'm hell-bent on proving Reese wrong about my black thumb.

"It's weird being back," I admit as we circle back to the kitchen. "Everything looks familiar but different at the same time. And the grocery store was filled with strangers. The hardware store too. I saw my old English teacher, Mrs. Crest, on the square and waved. She waved back, but I could tell she didn't recognize me. Gosh, she was the whole reason I got into writing in the first place."

"You've been here *one* day," Mom says, head cocked in sympathy. "And people haven't forgotten you."

I raise a brow. "I wouldn't blame them if they did. I've been gone almost twenty years."

Despite coming home to visit on a regular basis, it's not the same as calling this place home again. There was never an attachment to it, never a second thought, never a single care about what had and hadn't changed over the years because it never affected me.

Grabbing the wrapped ground beef out of the next bag, I think about the handsome yet grumpy guy from the grocery store today. I felt his gaze land heavy on me before I approached the meat counter, but once I got there, he was stoic, uninterested, and unbothered. I might as well have been invisible—until I requested grass-fed hamburger.

Hunter—I'm pretty sure that's what the butcher called him, though my mind was going fifty different directions and firing on all cylinders, so I could be wrong.

He looks like a Hunter, though—all stoic and rugged.

"Call Natalie Dinsmore," she says, snapping her fingers like she's just remembered. "You two were joined at the hip in high school. She's still around—runs that little boutique on the square. She'd love to hear from you."

"I haven't talked to Natalie in over fifteen years." Last time I saw her was at a house party some summer right after college. We had a blast, just like old times, and exchanged numbers, but neither one of us followed up. Alcohol-and-nostalgia-fueled promises tend to play out like that.

"Which means you'll have *lots* to catch up on." She nudges my shoulder.

I lean against the counter. For the last five years, I've only been forty minutes away, but it might as well have been across the country some days. No one besides family ventured my way too often. If they did, they were shopping or seeing a concert or show. And other than visiting my parents, I had no other reason to come back to Colton Valley.

"We've missed having you close by," she says softly.

I exhale, smiling, but a little guilt creeps in. I let life get too busy. Too loud. I forgot how grounding this place could be. How easy it is to breathe when people know you. And how good it feels to be home.

Really, truly home.

"Thanks for helping with Atti today," I say as she wipes her hands.

Will calls from the foyer that they need to head out.

She cups my face, her eyes full of hope and sanguinity. "We're just glad you're finally home—where you belong. I always had a feeling you'd come back."

***

Later, when my son is shower-fresh and tucked into his new bed, I sit cross-legged in the middle of my office, surrounded by unopened boxes and tangled cords.

The faint scent of old books and pine cleaner fills the air. There's a soft whoosh that glides through the opened window every time the wind rustles through the trees. The chirping crickets combined with the faint croaks of frogs by the river play like background music. Moonlight fills in the shadows around me, casting soft silver-gold beams across the room.

I've placed my desk directly in front of the window. It's a simple writer's desk. One with whitewashed wood, a sage green inlay, and a drawer that sticks—a graduation gift from my grandfather, who was an avid woodsmith in his day. On top sits my trusty MacBook, a little milk glass desk lamp, an Iowa State coffee mug filled with pens in every color, and a framed photo of Atticus at age two at the state fair, grinning like a champion after winning a stuffed cow at the midway.

Outside, the trees sway lazily, and the gravel drive is empty.

But my thoughts aren't.

I keep seeing *him*—the man at the meat counter earlier today.

Defined jaw.

Rough hands.

Sweeping broad shoulders.

Close-shaved beard.

Hair the color of dark chocolate.

The tiniest hint of salt-and-pepper at his temples.

Gorgeous bright blue eyes that played off his suntanned complexion.

I couldn't stop staring no matter how hard I tried . . . and believe me, I *tried.*

There was something about the way he stood. Like he didn't want to be noticed but knew he would be. And the way he didn't flirt back with the butcher? She was cute and funny—and the way her face lit when she was practically throwing herself at him was painfully obvious. But Hunter couldn't have cared less about the whole thing. If anything, it seemed to annoy him.

He seemed guarded.

Private.

Aloof yet silently observant at the same time.

Which is why it caught me by surprise when he called me out on the grass-fed beef thing. I couldn't tell if he was trying to flirt, be helpful, or if he was just being a jerk. It all happened so fast and then it was over. By the time I got checked out and to the car, he was long gone.

I imagine I'll see him around town again.

And I hope I do.

Before I realize it, my pen is between my teeth. My fingers twitch for something—anything—to capture the mood wrapping itself around me like smoke. It's the kind of moment most writers dream of—an idea burning inside you so hot and fast you have to seize it immediately or it'll be gone forever.

I reach for the little sunflower-covered notebook I bought a year ago and haven't touched since. My grandma Betty always used to call me her "little sunflower." She said sunflowers are resilient and stubborn, they bloom under harsh conditions, and they're always reaching for the sun.

The pages are blank, but not for much longer.

Turns out I didn't need sunflowers to inspire me . . . I needed *him.*

I flip to the first page, draw a breath, and begin to write.

Hunter—

I wasn't going to write you.

I don't even know you.

But you've been haunting my thoughts for hours now, like a song stuck in my head, and I'm finding myself deeply intrigued with the idea of you.

The way you stood there with your back straight, jaw tight, pretending not to notice me standing behind you, yet somehow I felt the intensity of your attention anyway . . . I don't think I've ever felt more seen in complete silence.

Yet we're complete strangers, and perhaps we always will be.

You're not exactly warm and friendly. But if this town is my blank page, maybe you're the margin. You intrigue me.

And you look like a story that demands to be told.

There's something about you that makes me want to fill in all the blanks.

Anyway, I suppose it doesn't matter because you're never going to read this. All that matters is I'm writing again because of you. Maybe it's not a novel, but it's a start.

And honestly, I think I'm going to make a book out of you.

—Wren

5

Hunter

The soft whine of the planter mixes with the hum of the tractor Saturday morning as I crawl across the northern field, seeds sinking into warm spring soil like a promise. Sky's holding steady—clouds thin and high. If the wind doesn't kick up, I'll make good time today.

I lean back in the cab, one hand on the wheel, the other on the armrest like usual, when my phone buzzes in the cup holder.

I check the screen, half expecting it to be Glenda, my part-time bookkeeper. It's tax season, and she's always got random questions for me as she prepares our files for the accountant.

Only it's Rich Sanders.

About damn time.

Exhaling through my nose, I swipe to answer. "Rich."

"McCrae." His voice crackles through the headset like old vinyl. "Sorry. I'm down in Key Largo this week visiting an old Army buddy, but I got your message. You were wantin' to know about some blond girl at my property?"

The question lands heavy despite his casual tone.

I grip the wheel a little tighter. "Saw her around yesterday. Figured maybe she was a niece or long-lost daughter or something."

I try to keep it light, though I'm feeling heavier than a combine stuck in mud.

Rich chuffs. "Me? Nah. Never been married. Never had kids. You know that. Just a couple of knuckleheaded nephews out in California. That blonde's the daughter of some guy I used to work with at the John Deere plant way back in the day. He said she wanted to move back home to do some writing, and I've been wanting to relocate down south, so I sold her the place."

For a second, I say nothing. I just stare ahead at a horizon that blurs from sky blue to dirt brown. This must be the author the ladies at the coffee shop were talking about.

"You sold it," I finally speak.

He pauses. "I did."

My vision flashes red for a second, but I keep my voice steady.

How did I miss him moving out?

"We had an agreement, Rich." My voice is flat, steeped in irritability. It's early, my coffee's yet to kick in, and I don't have the energy to hide my extreme displeasure at this revelation.

"I know, McCrae. I know. But she came in with *city* money. Fancy author or something. Paid me twice what you would've."

"I would've paid more if you'd have given me the chance."

"She was ready. Quick close. No inspections. Sight unseen. Cash." He exhales. "We both know you're a hell of a negotiator. This was an easy sell. Easier than what you'd have put me through. You're a businessman. Surely you get it. Hell, you'd have done the same in my shoes. I know it."

While negotiating is an art I've managed to master after two decades of buying land, I wanted that parcel enough that I'd have swallowed my pride and done what I needed to do to close the deal.

I'm not sure what pisses me off more—Rich ripping off some unsuspecting woman or the fact that I've lost out on the last parcel of riverside farmland in all of Colton Valley, a parcel of land tied to a promise I'll never be able to fulfill now thanks to this greedy jackass.

"You've got ten thousand acres, McCrae," Rich says after a bout of silence, sighing at me like I'm some sore Monopoly loser. "What's forty more to you?"

"It's not about the number." I don't elaborate. He's been around here long enough. He knows exactly what it's about.

He clears his throat. "Look, I get it. I do. But you would've torn the house down. That place? My grandfather built it with his bare hands. I couldn't stomach seeing it flattened and turned into soybeans."

If it were any other piece of property, he'd be right.

I would've leveled it.

Same as I've done with every farm I've ever bought.

Land's more valuable when it works.

An empty house taking up fertile soil isn't just an eyesore, it's a liability, an expense.

But this is different.

The house would've stayed, just like I promised someone years ago.

"You should meet her," he says. "Seems nice. Polite. Said she grew up around here. Can't remember her name now. But her stepdad's Will Cunningham. You know him?"

I don't dignify his stupid question with a response.

Everyone knows Will.

You can't be living in Colton Valley and not know Will Cunningham.

He's done some trucking for me during harvest when I've been short on help. I knew he had children and he'd mention them from time to time, but I never paid much attention to the details as it was irrelevant to me. He'd ramble on about something, and I'd always change the subject back to work because time is money and he was on the clock. *My* clock.

"You seen her yet? Heard she's quite the looker," Rich adds, chuckling. "Won't be long before someone swoops in and snatches that one right up."

I grimace.

Never understood guys like Rich when it comes to women. The way they talk like women are game to be caught. Display pieces. Prey.

Trophies. It's dehumanizing, and it makes us seem like brain-dead Neanderthals with one thing on our mind.

Sure, beauty catches the eye.

But it also makes idiotic men do idiotic things.

That's all it's good for.

"You should introduce yourself," Rich pushes once more, as if he's hoping to bandage the damage by playing matchmaker, "now that you're neighbors."

"Gotta get back to work," I tell him, steering the tractor toward the next row.

"All right, all right. I know you're upset with me, McCrae, but it'll all be fine. You take care now."

I end what's likely our final call ever without saying goodbye.

The weight of this news settles around me like a suffocating second skin.

The last forty acres of farmable riverfront land in the county.

A neighbor I didn't want.

A promise I'll never get to keep.

No peace. No privacy.

Just me and some city blonde for miles and miles.

6

Wren

It's been two days since I saw Hunter last.

Two days—and I can't stop thinking about that handsome blue-eyed killjoy from the grocery store. Nor can I stop picturing him in those faded, dirt-covered jeans, dusty work boots, and holey gray sweatshirt that hugged his broad shoulders like it was its sole purpose in life. He might as well have been strutting the aisles in Italian couture, because those clothes were made for his physique.

And his hands.

My god, those hands . . .

They were generous and slightly weathered in the kind of way that tells you he can fix things. They didn't appear soft, like those of a man who spends his days pushing paper. They seemed capable, competent, steady. And the small traces of earth beneath his fingernails only added to their appeal.

I spent the weekend running errands, hoping maybe I'd run into him again, though in a town of two thousand, there weren't many errands to run and it took less than two hours to knock out my list.

It's quiet today. Almost unnervingly so. Atticus started his new day camp, though he seemed reluctant to leave this morning. He's turning into a wildling already—spending every minute he can outside, hair full of grass, jeans streaked with mud and bug juice, the happiest I've seen him in a year. The boy who used to plead for extra iPad time now begs for me to "check the fences" with him. Yesterday we caught a frog and started building a fort with sticks and rope and boundless imagination.

This place is already working its magic on him.

And in between all that magic, I've been teaching him to read. If I play my cards right, he'll be a little bookworm like me in no time *and* have an affinity for embracing life's adventures, big and small.

Later this afternoon, I'm going to look at that pony. A little palomino Shetland named Sugarplum my mom's neighbors are interested in rehoming. She's slow, gentle, practically a four-legged lawn ornament, but she's perfect. A starter horse, they called her. Amazing with kids. Atticus doesn't know yet, and I can't wait to see his face if I decide to bite the bullet and bring her home.

But for now, I'm alone. Free. Resting in a rare, delicious pocket of stillness and fatigue. Tired but wired with a mind that won't shut off.

A quick craving for coffee hits my tongue. That, and I could use an excuse to run into town again. While I love the peace and quiet out here, I'm still adjusting to the lack of people. Grabbing my phone and keys, I lock up the house—though I probably don't need to—and head out.

***

The Bean and Biscuit coffee shop is half-full when I walk in, all exposed brick and reclaimed wood and the faint scent of espresso mingling with cinnamon while Ella Fitzgerald croons from overhead speakers. My hair's still damp from the shower, tucked into a lazy braid. I order something with lavender syrup and oat milk, because a little part of me still misses the city. It might not be home anymore, but it was my home for almost two decades. The young barista informs me they don't have either of those ingredients, so I order a vanilla cappuccino instead, carry my drink to a corner table near the window, and sip slowly, scrolling through listings of used saddles on my phone.

I don't know the first thing about tack. I'm basically just googling "saddle that doesn't kill me financially" and hoping for the best.

That's when I feel it.

A shift.

The undeniable, invisible awareness of someone stepping into my orbit before I even see them.

The bell over the door jingles—and in walks Hunter.

Same beat-up jeans. Same dirt-brown boots. Same hard jaw, unreadable expression, and sun-kissed skin. Same dark hair tucked under a sun-faded burnt orange ball cap. Olive green Henley that clings to his wide shoulders like fabric draped over cut stone.

He struts with that same unbothered confidence, the kind I imagine only comes with men who don't feel the need to explain themselves to anyone.

I try to swallow but can't because I'm pretty sure my heart is beating in my throat. My ears burn cherry hot. I take a deep breath and try not to make it obvious I'm losing my cool over here.

He doesn't see me.

Or if he does, he's pretending not to.

He heads straight to the counter and orders a large black coffee. The barista behind the counter—nervously twirling her strawberry blond curls—leans a little too far over the register when she talks to him. Her emerald green doe eyes all but shimmer, and she hasn't stopped fighting a grin since he walked in.

Hunter's unfazed by any of it.

"You sure you don't want to try one of our muffins?" she asks, smiling too big. "They're cranberry orange today. Your favorite. Baked fresh so they're still warm."

"No thank you," he says, voice low and even as he digs into his wallet for a five-dollar bill.

"You know . . . you could try a latte sometime," she pushes, glancing at his hands like she wants him to pick her up along with his drink. She's a tiny thing. I bet he could easily hoist her up with one arm and throw her over his shoulder like a bag of seed. The thought of it sends a quick sear of hot jealousy through me, so I shove it out of my mind as quickly as possible. "Change it up a little?"

Hunter shrugs, nonchalant. "I'm good."

Behind the safety of my coffee cup, I continue to observe their exchange.

"Two dollars and forty-five cents," she tells him, her smile absent now.

He hands her the five and tells her to keep the change.

A minute later, she slides him his drink. He turns, scanning the quaint little café once—eyes gliding past the pastry case, the tables, the windows—and landing on me.

But only for a second.

He doesn't smile. He doesn't nod. He doesn't do anything that could remotely count as a greeting—not that he owes me one. But there's a flicker of recognition, a shift in his jaw—causing my stomach to somersault. And then it's gone, leaving me to wonder if I imagined it.

He struts past me and takes a seat near the door, back to the wall, out of my line of sight, but I feel him there, his presence like gravity pulling at the edges of my space.

I tap the side of my cup, heart suddenly louder in my chest than it was two minutes ago.

Maybe it's the caffeine buzzing through me like a live wire.

Or maybe it's him.

God, he'd make the best romance lead. Mysterious and aloof. Gruff and unapologetically handsome. The kind of man who'd soften for a woman he never saw coming.

I'm suddenly feeling . . . inspired . . . again.

My fingers ache for a pen that isn't there, for my sunflower notebook. I need to start bringing it with me.

I reach for my phone, opening the Notes app, and I'm well on my way to becoming lost in thought when the door jingles again and an elderly woman shuffles in, moving slow but steady with a floral canvas tote slung over one arm and a cardigan draped over the other. She reminds me of someone who smells like powder and peppermint, the kind of woman who bakes the best banana bread in town and never misses a church bulletin.

She passes by Hunter's table, gives him a little wave and a friendly smile. "Good morning, Hunter."

He offers a respectful nod, lifting his ball cap. "Morning, Mrs. Harrison."

She continues toward the counter, orders something in a paper cup, then turns to scan for a place to sit, eyeing an empty table in the middle of the shop. Except on her way to take a seat, her tote catches the edge of a nearby booth, and the coffee sloshes violently before the lid pops clean off, splattering across the floor in a hot arc. It lands with a series of wet, soft plops against the tile, a few brown droplets kissing the hem of her olive green polyester pants.

"Oh, my . . . clumsy old me," she says with an embarrassed chuckle, her hand clenching at her blouse as every eye in the place homes in on her.

Hunter's already moving.

Not a word. Just stands, grabs a stack of napkins from the condiment bar, and kneels beside her with the practiced quiet of someone who doesn't hesitate to do what needs to be done regardless of the task.

"Now quit that." She crouches down and swats at his hand. "I made the mess. I'll clean it up."

"You'll burn your fingers," he says with a practiced sort of calm confidence, like a man who doesn't take no for an answer.

She sighs and lets him take over, stepping aside while he dabs the worst of the spill, then sets the ruined cup on the edge of a table.

"I'll get you a new one," he says before walking back to the counter.

A minute later, Hunter brings the fresh cup back, places it in front of Mrs. Harrison, who meets him with an appreciative smile as she pats his arm like he's just changed her whole day.

"You're too good to me," she says, eyes twinkling. "Thank you."

He returns to his table in silence, refusing to make a big deal out of her praise, and retrieves his coffee cup, tipping it back to swallow the last drops before tossing it in the trash. A glance toward the door, and he's heading out—the bell over the entrance barely jingling as it swings shut behind him.

My mouth opens with a half-formed thought, question, greeting—but he's already outside. I was hoping he'd stay, that I could say hello, maybe introduce myself and ask him more about that grass-fed beef thing—any excuse to get him talking.

I turn in my chair just in time to catch sight of a big white truck backing out of a spot and easing down the street, Hunter behind the wheel.

No music.

No fanfare.

Just diesel and distance.

"Excuse me, ma'am," I say to the elderly woman. "Do you know that guy? The one who cleaned up your coffee?"

"Oh." She perks up, batting her mascara-caked lashes. "That's Hunter McCrae. Lovely man. I just adore him," Mrs. Harrison says, her dainty palm pressed against her chest. "When my Orville had open heart surgery a few years back, Hunter planted over two hundred acres for us. Saved our farm. Wouldn't accept a dollar for it either. But that's the kind of man he is. I knew his parents when they were still alive. He's a good one, that Hunter. They don't make 'em like him anymore."

A good man who wants nothing to do with anyone?

A good man who walks around like he's pissed off at the world?

Questions dance on the tip of my tongue—questions I have no right to ask.

"And what's your name, miss? I don't think I've seen you around here before," Mrs. Harrison says.

"Wren Jensen," I tell her. "I actually grew up here . . . just moved back with my son. We bought a little place by the river."

Her thin gray brows knit. "By the river, you say? Hunter owns all the riverfront property in town. Well, except Rich Sanders's place. You didn't buy Rich's place, did you?"

My throat tightens, though I don't know why. It's the way she says it, maybe. Like I did something bad.

"Actually yes, that's the place," I say.

Her face hardens into a wince for a moment, her lips pressing flat like she's biting her tongue. Without saying a word, she's got me under the impression I've done something bad, that I've committed some kind of Colton Valley faux pas.

"Well, I'm sure you'll be seeing a lot more of Hunter," she says with a forced smile that doesn't reach her eyes. "He's your neighbor."

I think of the white truck at the top of my driveway the other day, how he sped off before I could make it outside.

"You said he owns *all* the riverfront property around here?" I ask.

She nods. "In all of Jasperville County. I always thought he was going to buy Rich's place . . . it's quite odd that he didn't."

"What do you mean?" I can't help but ask. The Sanders property is small. Only forty little acres, five of which aren't even farmable. If Hunter owns that much land, surely he wouldn't care about my little place?

The bells chime on the door once more, stealing Mrs. Harrison's attention, and she waves to a trio of brightly dressed, silver-haired women who light up when they see her.

"I'm so sorry, but I'm meeting some friends for book club. It was lovely meeting you, Wren. And welcome back." She leaves me and heads toward her friends.

I turn back to my cooling coffee, her words swimming in my head yet not clicking into place. This man is nothing but walking contradictions. I think of how standoffish he was to the butcher and barista, how cold he was to me, and how he watched me from the top of my driveway but drove off before I could introduce myself . . . but he saved this woman's farm? Cleaned up her spilled coffee and got her another one?

If Hunter's my neighbor, then I at least owe him a proper introduction—and maybe even an apology for accidentally buying that land out from underneath him.

We don't have to be best friends, but if it's just the two of us (and Atticus) for miles and miles, it'd be nice to get acquainted.

Especially since I'm finally home.

And I don't plan on leaving ever again.

I'm halfway home when my phone chimes with a text. My stomach plummets when I see who it's from.

NICK: Wren . . . call me when you get a chance please. I know you probably hate me but it's important.

With my heart in my chest, I pull over and catch my breath. I hadn't heard from Nick since he left me the day of the wedding. He wouldn't even come get his things—he sent his parents, who are easily some of the kindest people I've ever met, to do his bidding. His mother sobbed while she boxed up his clothes, and his father's face was laced in unspoken apologies—not that he owed me any. They were wonderful people, and I miss them more than I miss Nick.

But Nick can wait a lifetime for all I care.

I won't be calling him.

Not now, not ever.

7

Hunter

The house is quiet.

Same as it always is.

Just as I like it.

Late lunch today—if you can even call it that. Standing over the sink, I down two bologna-and-white-bread sandwiches, then wash them down with a cold glass of milk. I've been in the field since just after six this morning, trying to get ahead of a storm system that might roll in tomorrow. Only took a break because I've got a seed sensor that's been blinking red all morning and I need a part from town.

I wipe my hands on a dish towel and grab the mail from the entry table—mostly junk, a flyer for a bull auction, and an open house invite from some new co-op. I'm sorting through the rest of it when I hear the distinct crunch of tires on gravel.

I don't get visitors.

Not up here, on top of the hill.

Not unless they're lost or trying to sell me something.

I walk to the front window, pull the curtain back, and see *her*.

Blondie: the land thief.

Maybe it's not fair to call her that. I can't imagine Rich told her he already had an arrangement with me. He was probably too busy salivating at all the cash he was going to walk away with. But still.

It isn't *her* . . . it's everything she represents.

Her glossy black SUV is idling in my driveway, and she's halfway up the walk, holding a clear container wrapped in twine. A pale-yellow sundress flutters around her knees, and she's got a messy knot of hair piled on top of her head like she wrestled with it and lost.

I stay frozen a second too long, wondering if I should pretend I'm not home, but she's already on the porch and my truck is parked out front.

She knocks three times, and I watch from my side of the window as she fusses with her skirt and brushes a loose strand of hair off her forehead. This woman looks too pretty for her own good, too dolled up for a weekday afternoon, that's for sure. If she's here to hit on me, she's wasting her time.

Pushing a breath through flared nostrils, I open the door.

"Hi," she says with a cautious smile, lifting the container. "I'm Wren—your new neighbor. I think we've seen each other around a couple of times, so I wanted to introduce myself."

I blink. Slow.

"I brought cookies," she adds with a disarming yet nervous smile before gazing up at me with her big doe eyes. God, she's adorable. And it catches me off guard for a second. But I snap out of it. She's just attractive, is all. Doesn't mean I need to go full idiot every time I see her.

She offers me the container, which smells faintly of oatmeal and peanut butter.

"You made these?" I ask, taking the warm dish in my palms. Traditionally I believe I'm the one supposed to bring a welcoming gift to a new neighbor. "For me?"

"Sure did." She places a hand on her hip and cocks her head to the side, yet another adorable move that makes me swallow hard. "Fair warning—I'm a terrible cook. Like burn-boiling-water bad. But I'm a *really* good baker."

I nod once, not sure what to do with her or this situation. No one's ever brought me cookies in my life, except for Mrs. Harrison after her husband had heart surgery and I planted their crop that spring. They're hardworking, honest people who don't have a lot. I refused to accept a dollar from them, so she baked me a dozen homemade chocolate chip cookies every week for a month until I firmly but politely asked her to stop.

She glances beyond my shoulders, into the house.

My jaw ticks. "I'd ask you to come inside, but the place is a bit of a mess right now. It's planting season."

Not that she looks like she'd know what that entails, but essentially all things get neglected until we get that last seed in the ground.

"I've got a four-year-old. You think I care about a little mess?" she teases, and for a moment, it feels like I've known her for years. Some people are like that, though—personable. That's all this is. She's like this with everyone, I'm sure.

I begin to say something, to protest this entire exchange by telling her I have to get to the parts store before they close, but the truth is they'll still be open another several hours and I'm kind of enjoying looking at her right now—as much as I hate to admit it.

Blondie flashes a megawatt grin that almost makes me forget about the whole land thing.

Almost.

"All right, then." I take a step back, and against my better judgment, I motion for her to come inside. "I've got a few minutes before I have to get going, but come on in."

I've never played with fire before, but I imagine it feels something like this—getting close enough to the heat to imagine the burn while knowing you're full well in control and can step away at any moment.

Her eyes light as she steps inside and slides her wedge shoes off her feet. I can't imagine she got all dolled up just to see me, but there's no denying she's looking like a ray of warm sunshine on a cool spring day. "Quite the place you've got here."

My home is moody and dramatic. All dark wood, exposed beams, big stone fireplace that extends twenty feet up. Taxidermy on the walls, antlers above the mantel. Lodge-style, rugged, quiet—like I like it. Not exactly magazine-worthy, but it's mine. Built it with my own hands. It's mine and mine alone, just the way I intended.

She takes a few steps inside, turning in a slow circle, lips parted, taking it all in.

"It's very . . ." she trails off, looking at a massive buck head mounted above the entry. I don't hunt, but my grandfather did. I don't get anything from looking at a dead-eyed animal, but I like having a little piece of him in here. "Rustic," she finishes diplomatically.

"Sorry, what was your name again?" I ask, setting the cookies on the counter and leaning against the kitchen island. I've always been terrible with names, dates, and generally most things outside my farming empire.

"Wren," she says. "Wren Jensen."

I commit her name to memory, silently repeating it a few times and hoping it sticks, but odds are it won't.

"Hunter McCrae," I say.

Her lips twist at one side and her eyes flash. "I know."

I run my palm along my beard, squinting. "You know . . . how?"

"I saw you at the coffee shop. That woman spilled her coffee, and you cleaned it up and got her a new one. She mentioned your name."

Ah, yes. Mrs. Harrison adores me to a concerning degree and rarely misses an opportunity to sing my praises.

"What do you do that you've got time to bake cookies for people you don't know?" I pretend I don't know she's the new author in town everyone's been yapping about.

"I write books."

"What kind of books?"

She tilts her head, hesitating, her expression reading like she's got some secret to tell. Meanwhile, she's standing in my dark kitchen looking like a full-on sunbeam. The whole thing is distracting and surreal.

I hate it.

Or at least I want to hate it.

"Romance." She fights a sly smile, her cheeks turning a deeper shade of pink.

I don't grill her on her genre of choice as I know nothing about it. Never read a romance book in my life and sure as hell don't intend to start. Last thing I want is for her to start leaving signed paperbacks at my doorstep like homework I don't have time for.

"So *you're* the one everyone's been talking about lately," I say.

She lifts her brows. "What do you mean?"

"Been a lot of buzz around town about some famous author from here moving back."

Chuckling, she tucks a strand of hair behind one ear and takes the smallest step closer. "I wouldn't call myself famous, but I guess it makes the gossip juicier, doesn't it?"

"Why'd you move back?"

"Story for another day." She flattens her full lips, effectively sealing them.

"Ever owned an acreage before?"

She fights a smile. "Nope. I'm an acreage-owning virgin."

I chuff at the image of this five-foot-nothing blonde driving a mowing tractor. It's even funnier picturing her attaching a snow blade to the front of it to plow herself out in the wintertime. And I bet she's never had to set a mousetrap or deal with a corn snake a day in her life.

"Why'd you come back?" I ask.

"You already asked that."

"I know. But maybe I don't want to wait for another day to hear the story." I want to know if there's a chance this was some decision made on a whim. If it was, she might be willing to sell the place to me at some point.

"Wanted to be closer to family," she says, "and needed a change of scenery. It's been a rough year, and it's been hard to write."

"So buying a farm seemed like the logical solution to that?"

She chuckles, her nose crinkling and her cheeks turning pink. "Yes, Hunter. It did seem like the logical solution to that. And I hope it is. I've only been here since Friday, and I'm already feeling . . . inspired."

Her gaze drips up and down the length of me, though I'm unsure if she realizes she's doing it. Our eyes lock. A stretch of silence rests between us. If I didn't know any better, I'd say she's stuck in a daydream right here, right now . . . about me.

I clear my throat and force myself to break both the silence and the eye contact. "Well, if you decide country living's not what you thought it'd be, let me know. I'd be happy to take that place off your hands. Just name your price."

"I appreciate the offer, but we're not going anywhere." The charm in her voice is now replaced with a polite amount of grit that somehow infuriates me and turns me on.

"Just saying, if your circumstances change, you've got a buyer."

"They won't," she says with an impressive amount of self-assuredness. "I've had wings for the last twenty years. This time I'm planting roots." Her eyes soften, but there's a hardness in her voice that piques my curiosity more than I'd like, and her lips flutter as if she's got something else on her mind but hasn't mussed up the courage to say it. "Anyway, I just wanted to introduce myself since we're neighbors. You keep looking at the clock, so I'm sure you have somewhere to be."

I hadn't realized I'd looked at the clock once since she got here. If I did, I've no recollection of doing so. I've been too busy staring at her, which ironically seemed to make time stand still.

I adjust my hat and massage the back of my neck. "Yeah, I've got a part to pick up before I head back out to the field. Appreciate the cookies. You didn't have to do that."

Her shoulders relax ever so slightly, and she peers up at me in a way that makes me temporarily weak in the knees.

For the love of god, *what is going on with me?*

"So you live alone up here? On this big hill? In this massive house?" She scans the surroundings of my lodge-style house one more time, taking in the sweeping ceilings, twenty-foot windows, and abundance of stone and rough-hewn beams.

"I do."

"Do you ever get lonely? All this space and no one to share it with?"

"Never," I answer without hesitation, though for some unknown reason my answer somehow feels like a lie. "Too busy working to be lonely."

She scrutinizes me with a tiny smirk on her pink lips. "If you say so."

There's something about her energy—soft but not fragile. Warm but not desperate. Friendly but not imposing. I'm drawn to her in a way I've not been drawn to anyone in a long time. I'm sure the feeling will pass as these things do.

Lust is one hell of a drug.

"Your kid adjusting okay to the move?" I ask as I walk her to the door. I don't know why I'm asking. It's none of my business and I definitely shouldn't care. But picturing a little boy living in that house brings me back . . .

She nods, slipping back into her fancy shoes. "Better than I expected. I think this place is exactly what he needed. So much for him to do. I can hardly keep up with him half the time . . ."

"Just be careful with that river," I say. "The current's stronger than it looks sometimes."

"Atticus and I have discussed water safety several times," she says sweetly. "But thank you. I appreciate the reminder."

"And what about you?" I ask. "How're you adjusting?"

She glances up at me again with those dark blues. We're so close now I can see the little white starbursts in her irises. They're so hypnotic, I almost have to remind myself to blink.

"Better than I expected," she says with an exhale that borders on dreamy. She blinks, unhurried through a thick fringe of lashes. Does she do this with everyone?

There's a tightness in my chest that crawls to my throat, and my feet are anchored in place. I need to go, but I'm not ready to watch her leave just yet. The way she fills my entry with literal sunshine, cookies, and an intoxicatingly sweet scent, the way she half smiles and gives me those playful eyes but isn't overtly throwing herself at me like everyone else tends to do—I have to admit, she's nothing short of captivating.

I gesture toward the cookies. "So is this some kind of research for your next book?"

She rolls her eyes. "What are you talking about?"

"You moved back to your hometown. Bought a farmhouse. Now you're baking cookies for the bachelor farmer next door . . ."

"Okay, yeah," she laughs. "Fair point when you put it that way. But in my defense, everything about you is literally a character out of a romance novel."

Out of all the things women have said to me in my forty-two years—that's not been one of them.

I smirk before I can stop myself.

She watches me, half amused. "Well, look at that. You *do* smile."

I fix my face. "Not if I can help it."

"If we were in one of my books right now, this would be the scene where I decide to make it my mission to make you smile again."

"Please don't."

"Why? Do you hate smiling or something?" Her eyes sparkle under the daylight that filters in around us.

She's flirting.

She's definitely flirting.

But I shut it down.

"Don't romanticize the country too much," I say, reaching for the doorknob, though what I really want to tell her is not to romanticize me. "It's not all fireflies and harvest moons and wraparound porches."

She steps outside and turns back. "I'm a romance writer. I can romanticize anything."

"Sounds like a good way to get your heart trampled on." I lean against the doorframe, taking her in like it's the last time I'm going to see her but knowing damn well it won't be since we're neighbors now.

"See you around, Hunter." There's a wistfulness in her voice that wasn't there before. As she turns to leave, the wind catches her hair.

I stare at the cookies.

Then back at the door.

Then down at my chest, where something unfamiliar has started to stir—something I haven't felt in a long, long time.

I'm stuck in a daydream of my own when she's suddenly traipsing back to the front door. She came back . . . but why?

"I'm sorry," she says, half breathless with an apologetic smile on her lips. "I have to be honest about something. I didn't just come here to bring you cookies and introduce myself."

The moonshine cocktail of emotions I was starting to feel a second ago turns me stone-cold sober. Only thing worse than a liar is someone with an ulterior motive.

I hook my fingers in my belt loops and cock my head. "I'm listening."

"At the coffee shop the other day, Mrs. Harrison made a face when I told her I bought the Sanders place." She bites her lip. "It made me feel like I did something wrong. And then she told me you'd always planned on buying it. Is that true?"

I press my lips flat and exhale through my nose. "Yeah. It is."

The gorgeous land thief's eyes soften. "I had no idea."

"You paid twice what that property's worth. I bet you didn't know that either."

Her mouth opens for a second but nothing comes out. Maybe I shouldn't have said anything but a part of me is still bitter about the whole thing. Doesn't help she said she didn't intend on ever selling either.

"Like I said," I add, "I'd be happy to take it off your hands anytime."

Squinting, she angles her face to the side, studying me. "Why do you want that property so bad? What's so special about it?"

"Story for another day." I use her words.

"Maybe I don't want to wait for another day to hear the story." She uses mine.

"Sorry, honey." I step out on the front porch and shut the door behind me. I've got things to do, and this day's not getting any younger. "But you're gonna have to."

8

Wren

I hear the trailer before I see it—the low rumble of my stepdad's Ram truck, then soon after the soft clink of a halter buckle. I step onto the porch, the sight waiting for me so wholesome it could be a scene straight out of a Hallmark movie.

"You didn't . . ." I clamp a hand over my mouth.

I'd gone to look at Sugarplum Monday afternoon, but I'd yet to commit to buying her. I wanted to do some research first. Plus Atticus turns five in two weeks, and I was hoping Sugarplum could be his big gift. Apparently my parents took my visit to meet Sugarplum as a sign that I was ready to bite the bullet—er, bite the *bit* in this case.

"Surprise!" Mom calls from the passenger seat, her arm waving out the window like she's a homecoming queen in a parade.

Will wastes no time hopping out and unhooking the latch on the back of the trailer.

"Tell me that's not the cutest thing you've ever seen," Mom says, already tearing up at the sight of the stocky, shaggy little pony with a forelock that looks like she walked through a wind tunnel. "I can't wait to see the look on Atti's face when he sees her."

Atticus is going to lose his ever-loving mind.

"He home yet?" Will asks.

"Just got off the day camp bus a few minutes ago. He ran inside to change into play clothes," I say.

"Well then," Will says, grinning, "go tell the kid he's got a four-legged responsibility waiting for him."

I head back inside, where Atticus is mid-sock-change, and try to play it cool.

"Hey, bud? Can you help me outside for a sec?" I ask.

He frowns. "Do I have to carry groceries?"

"No groceries," I promise.

He follows me out the front door—reluctantly, at first—and freezes the second he sees the trailer. The pony is halfway down the ramp, and Will's holding the lead rope like he's presenting royalty.

Atticus sucks in a long gasp.

And then, silence.

He doesn't scream or jump up and down or burst into tears like I expect.

Instead, he tiptoes forward like he's afraid it isn't real.

"Is that . . . is he mine?"

I crouch beside him. "She's yours. Her name is Sugarplum. She's very old, very gentle, and very much needs a little boy to love her."

Atticus throws his arms around my neck and squeezes hard.

"This is the best day of my life," he whispers.

I blink fast, fighting the lump in my throat as I remember the last day he said those exact words, almost exactly six months ago, the morning of the wedding that never happened. He's only four so I don't expect he remembers saying it, but I'll never forget—because what happened after he said them changed *everything* for us.

***

Later, after the excitement wears off and Sugarplum is tucked into the little corral beside the barn with a flake of hay and a full water bucket, we sit on the porch with iced tea while Atticus runs around the yard in his boots, playing some imaginary game where he's somehow both the sheriff and the outlaw.

"He's going to sleep hard tonight," Mom says, rocking gently beside me.

"He's already asking if Sugarplum can sleep in his room." I roll my eyes.

Will chuckles. "You might wanna draw a firm line there or you're gonna have hoofprints on your hardwood."

I glance toward the tree line, the late afternoon light glowing gold behind the oaks. Beyond that, and on the top of the hill, is Hunter's lodge.

Nothing about him makes sense.

The man is an even bigger enigma than I originally thought.

"Thank you guys for delivering the pony. Seriously," I say. "You didn't have to do that."

Mom pats my leg. "Of course we did."

"What, you were going to hook a trailer up to that hybrid thingy of yours?" Will teases.

Mom rolls her eyes at him, swatting his leg. "I know we said this already, but it's really nice having you close again. We're here for you and Atticus. Anything you need, never hesitate to ask."

After a quiet beat, I ask, "Hey, what do you guys know about Hunter McCrae?"

Will tilts his head, considering. "Good guy. Hard worker. Local farmer. Been around forever. I've done some trucking for him, but he keeps to himself, mostly."

"Oh, that's right. You two are neighbors now," Mom says. "He lives in that big house on top of the hill. He built that not too long ago, you know." She leans in closer to me, like she's about to divulge some top secret. "I heard he never invites anyone over."

Fitting . . .

"I brought him cookies today. Thought I'd properly introduce myself. I don't think he knew what to make of me," I say.

Will smiles. "He's not the most talkative guy, but you'll never hear a bad word about him. People around here respect him. You're fortunate to have him for a neighbor. Honestly, it makes me feel better knowing he's here if you ever need anything."

I snicker myself. I don't imagine I'll ever ask him for a thing. I can't even imagine asking him for a cup of sugar.

"Why do you think he keeps to himself?" I ask.

Will purses his lips and shrugs, but I know my stepdad. The expression on his face tells me he knows more than he's letting on. "Some men just prefer quiet. Life's easier that way."

I don't buy it.

There has to be more to the story.

There always is.

I glance down the road again, where the edge of his property kisses the edge of mine.

So close . . . yet so far away.

***

At night, after Atticus is asleep and the house is still, I light a candle in my office and sit down at my desk.

The moon is full, casting a soft, pale glow across the room. Outside, the frogs and crickets have begun their nightly chorus, and I can spot the outline of Sugarplum bathing in the moonlight near the barn.

Reaching for my sunflower notebook, I flip to a fresh page.

The words come easier tonight

Hunter—

Today you opened your front door and let me in.

You didn't have to. I could tell you didn't want to. But you did anyway.

I brought you cookies, but I think I really just wanted a reason to be near you again. And when I walked into that house of yours—all stone and wood and silence—it felt like stepping into another world.

You live alone.

But the kind of alone you carry isn't just about space.

It's about walls.

And I can't help but wonder what it would feel like to be the one to tear them down.

I don't want to fix you.

But I do want to know you.

And maybe that's worse.

You're like a book with no cover, no title, no description. Nothing to go on but gut instinct and blind faith. And something in my gut says you could easily be a page turner, something I could devour in one sitting, if you let me.

I don't think you will. But my god . . . imagine if you did?

—Wren

9

Hunter

Today's bologna is past its prime, but I'm starving so I don't care.

I slap a slice between two pieces of white bread, squirt some mustard over it, and call it lunch. No plate. Just me, the sandwich, and the view from my kitchen window—four hundred acres of rolling pasture, trees, and sky.

And now . . . a pony?

I narrow my eyes.

Sure enough, right at the edge of Wren's little barn, there's a shaggy pony with a frizzy blond mane, a marshmallow body, and legs like pretzel sticks, meandering in a small paddock.

"Well, I'll be damned." I take a bite of my sandwich and chew slowly, watching.

The city girl has a pony now.

Of course she does.

First she takes my land, now she's buying livestock?

If this woman builds a chicken coop next, I just might lose it.

She's out there in a pair of jeans and some kind of jacket that looks better suited for sipping sangria on a trendy rooftop bar than shoveling manure. I chuckle at the sight of her holding a yellow five-gallon bucket, trying to coax the pony toward her. It just stands there, blinking like it's forgotten what a human is. Or maybe the poor thing is old, deaf, and blind, and Wren's making a fool of herself for no good reason.

If that thing gets out and causes damage on my side, she's liable. Willing to bet that's yet another thing she's not prepared for.

Typical city folk.

They think buying a few acres and a house with a wraparound porch makes them farmers. Next thing you know, they're calling the co-op, asking where to buy goat milk for their yard birds.

Still, I'm compelled to keep watching because I've been staring at nothing but dirt fields upon dirt fields for days and this is mildly entertaining.

I've only been around her a few times now, but each time I find it harder to look away than the time before. Lately my mind's been wandering her way, wondering what she's up to, thinking about how she looked in that sundress yesterday, remembering how sweet she smelled at the grocery store and the way she lit up my entryway with nothing but her presence and a smile.

I'm being honest, this whole thing is frustrating the hell out of me.

I've been around plenty of beautiful women in my time. Some were a fun time. Some were bad news. Some were disasters drenched in cheap perfume. Wren should be no different—I'm just struggling to figure out how to categorize her just yet.

I mean, the woman stole my land—even if it wasn't intentional. I'm going to be reminded of it every time I see that pretty face, and I don't need to go layering on any unwelcome emotions on top of it. Life's already complicated. No need to make it worse.

I grab two of her oatmeal peanut butter cookies—which are easily the best cookies I've had in my life, chewy and moist—and wash them down with a glass of milk before returning my attention to the window, watching Wren muddy up her city boots, trying to coax that pony like it's some friendly golden retriever and not some ancient four-hundred-pound beast.

I take another bite, a half-cocked grin forming on my lips when I chew.

Damn it.

She's got me smiling again.

10

Wren

I'm leaving to pick up Atticus when the sky turns the color of a two-day-old bruise, the heavens crack open, and a downpour of biblical proportions is unleashed above me. I grip the wheel of my Audi with white knuckles as I crawl down the washed-out gravel road that leads away from the house, windshield wipers working overtime with nothing to show for it.

The tires slide once. Twice.

The third time, they don't catch.

I wouldn't be out in this had Atticus not missed his day camp bus. I'm not sure how that happened, but my heart about leaped into my throat when I saw the facility was calling me. The front desk assured me he was fine, but I was in panic mode, grabbing my shoes and car keys and flying out the door. I hadn't even thought to check the weather. All I was focused on was getting to the other side of town.

"Come on . . ." I whisper, easing off the gas and gently trying again. Nothing. Just a slow, sickening sink as the back end drifts sideways into the soft shoulder.

I hit the brake, but I'm already stuck.

Thunder rolls overhead like it's laughing at me.

I try calling my mom.

No answer.

Will.

Voicemail.

Perfect.

Rain hammers the roof of the car, coming down harder by the second, and I sit there for a moment, unsure what to do. I'm supposed to be picking up Atticus, and now I'm marooned on a back road that looks more like a winding river.

I shove my door open and step out—and immediately regret it. Mud squelches over my ankle, filling my sneakers, and the cold rain hits me like a slap, soaking my T-shirt and jeans all the way through in seconds.

I pop the hatch and start rummaging for anything—rope, gravel, a miracle—but all I've got is an old reusable grocery bag and a box of juice pouches.

Just when I'm about to cry, scream, or both—I hear it.

The low, steady rumble of a truck engine.

A flash of white through the blur of rain.

He pulls up beside me, engine idling, and rolls down his window like this is the most normal thing in the world. Raindrops pelt his face, but like with everything else, it doesn't faze him.

"You always go off-roading in a luxury import during flood season?" Hunter asks, one brow lifted.

I exhale, rain streaming off my nose. "I'm trying out for the next *Fast & Furious*. Country edition."

He doesn't smile, but something flickers at the corner of his mouth. Amusement?

"Just get in," he tells me, rolling up his window before I can protest—not that I would.

Next thing I know, I'm opening the door and climbing up into the cab. The black leather is warm and uncracked, the cab smells like leather, dirt, diesel fuel, and something distinctly *him*.

He reaches behind the seat and tosses me a tan Carhartt jacket, stiff, oil-stained, and twice my size.

I shrug into it without a word. It swallows me whole and feels like a dry hug that's oddly comforting—until my teeth begin to chatter. I hadn't realized how cold it was with that downpour. The wet clothes don't help.

Without saying a word, he reaches over and flicks on my seat warmer, then cranks the heat to the maximum setting.

"You're a saint," I mutter, pulling the collar up around my chin. I resist the urge to tell him this, too, could be a scene from a romance novel. He seems like he might be in a mood today . . . then again, that's not much different from any other day. Still, I'm not about to give him any crap, because he's helping me out and he doesn't have to.

He shifts into drive, silent, determined.

"Where are we going?" I ask.

"My shop. Gotta get a tow strap."

"Oh," I say. "You don't just carry one around with you?"

"Usually do. Haven't needed to use it lately," he says, turning to me, "until now."

The rain drums against his windshield. Outside, the trees bow under the wind, and the gravel road disappears in spots beneath a sheen of water. His truck sits high, imposing almost, giving a sense of refuge from the storm.

Safety.

"This keeps happening," he says under his breath. "Road was supposed to be reinforced years ago. County keeps dragging their feet. Seems like they only want to spend money on football stadiums, not maintaining gravel roads."

"How long do you think it'll take to fix?"

"Don't hold your breath."

I exhale, watching the trees blur past. I check my phone again to see if my mom has responded to my text about Atticus. I need to pick him up, but I hate to ask Hunter to run me to town when he's already doing this. I shoot her another text, hoping to catch her attention, but she's notorious for misplacing her phone and there's no guarantee.

"You're going to need something with bigger tires if you're planning on living out here," he says.

"Why would I need that when I've got you for a neighbor?" My tone is serious but I'm teasing.

That earns me a small huff of air.

He pulls into a long gravel drive leading to a metal sided shop, big enough to house several pieces of machinery and a half dozen trucks. The rain thunders against the steel roof as we roll inside, the automatic doors sliding shut behind us.

He parks and climbs out.

I stay in the truck, watching him move—efficient, no-nonsense, hyperfocused, and in his element. He grabs a coiled strap from a wall hook and tosses it into the bed before getting back in.

"Five minutes, tops," he says.

"Thank you," I tell him, quieter now. I don't think he appreciates my sense of humor, at least not when he's in the middle of a rescue mission. "Seriously. Thank you."

He doesn't answer.

I study his profile—strong jaw, wet hair clinging to the nape of his neck, that same unreadable expression he always wears.

A couple of years ago, I got a flat on the interstate during rush hour in the midst of an eerily similar downpour. I called Nick several times, only he didn't answer. When I texted him that I was stranded, he replied almost immediately with, "Sorry. Just got to the gym, babe. You'll have to call AAA."

I didn't even have AAA.

In my moment of need today, Hunter was just . . . there.

He showed up. Didn't ask questions. Didn't make me feel burdensome. Just did what needed to be done like it was the most natural thing in the world. Didn't even expect a thank-you.

I write about men like Hunter all the time—I had no idea they actually existed.

11

Hunter

With the fields finally dried out, we've been back to planting. Going on four days now with little to no sleep. I'm barely functioning. The tractor drones beneath me like a metronome. Constant. Steady. Loud enough to rattle my bones but not loud enough to drown out the thoughts crawling around in my head. Normally I find the noise comforting, like the low rumble of a distant freight train.

Today it's obnoxious.

Doesn't help that I've been in this seat since before the sun even considered showing up. My coffee's cold. My back feels like it's been wrung out and hung to dry. And I've eaten nothing but a stale, mystery protein bar I found under the jump seat. Glenda would lose her shit on me if she knew I forgot to pack something to eat. Ever since my mother passed several years ago, Glenda's tried to carefully fill some of that void. Not that anyone could ever replace my mother. But Glenda's pretty much the next best thing.

At this point in the planting season, I'm so sleep deprived it's all I can do just to function most days. I'm in survival mode, which sometimes entails forgetting to pack lunch and being too stubborn to take a break, and I'm sure as hell not going to stop one of my farmhands to have them run me something. Glenda's busy with my tax season bookwork and her grandkids. It wouldn't be right bugging her either—plus any food she'd bring would come with a side of lecturing.

Sky's turning that familiar grayish tint on the western horizon, just like it did last week when we got that sudden downpour. Rain's coming. Again. And we're starting to push into May, which means if I don't get this stretch by the river done today, I'm screwed.

I lean forward and check the monitor. Another phantom sensor warning. Same one that's been blinking since this morning and magically disappears the second I stop to check it.

I swear this machine's got a sense of humor.

I scrub a hand down my face and glance out the window, just in time to catch a flash of movement along the river.

Tiny.

Fast.

Too close to the water.

I sit up straighter.

It's the neighbor's kid.

He's down near the bend where the bank gets steep and slick. There's a little wooden footbridge down there too, half-rotted and uneven. Rich was too lazy to ever tear it down. Kid's holding a stick and swinging it like a sword, shouting something I can't hear.

But that's not what makes my stomach twist.

It's how close he is to the edge. With all that rain we just had, the river's higher than usual, and there's a pretty strong current through this part. If he loses his footing . . .

I can almost see it happening before it does.

My stomach twists into the hardest knot.

Without another thought, I hit the brake.

The tractor lurches, jerking to a stop mid-row. I press my hand to the glass and squint as the kid hops down a muddy incline and disappears from view. It wasn't an intentional fall either, it was quick, like he dropped off the face of the earth.

I listen for a scream, a splash, anything, but it'd be impossible to hear any of that over the engine noise.

Suddenly, I'm not in the cab anymore. I'm in another memory. One with a similar scream and that same riverbank and cold water.

My vision goes dark for half a second—a flashback I haven't watched in ages.

Then I snap out of it.

Door flies open before I even register reaching for it. Boots hit the dirt hard. I'm sprinting. Lungs on fire. Heart pounding. My hat flies off somewhere behind me.

By the time I get to the river, the kid's grasping at a broken tree branch, struggling to pull himself out—sputtering, soaked, water rushing over his head every couple seconds. By the time he hooks his arms around it, it breaks off, leaving him flailing for something else to grab onto.

"Jesus Christ," I mutter under my breath before jumping into the chest-high icy water and yanking him the rest of the way up by the armpits. By the time we're back on dry land, we're both heaving, shivering, and gasping for air. "What the hell were you doing out here?"

His teeth chatter. "I—I slipped."

"Yeah, I can see that," I snap. "Damn near gave me a heart attack."

He blinks up at me with wide, scared eyes. He's not hurt. Just cold and muddy. But still. He could've . . .

No.

I refuse to finish that thought.

Behind me, a slamming screen door cuts through the static in my head.

"Atticus?! Oh my god—what happened?!" Wren races toward us.

I wait, hands on my hips, jaw tight, pulse still hammering, chest on fire.

She's barefoot and wild-eyed, her long braid half unraveled.

"He fell in the damn river," I say. "I warned you about that current. What the hell was he doing down here alone?"

Normally I wouldn't talk like this to a woman or in front of a kid. But I'm going off no sleep. My mental bandwidth is low. I'm running on fumes. Editing my words requires more energy than I can spare right now.

Her eyes cut to mine, sharp and instantly defensive. "He was playing in the backyard. I went inside for *two* minutes."

"Two minutes is all it takes. You live *on* the river. You don't let a four-year-old run off unsupervised."

"You think I meant for this to happen?" Her brows are furrowed and she's got one hand clamped over her heart. There's anger directed at me but a hint of disappointment in her eyes—almost like she let herself down too. "You think I don't already feel sick to my stomach right now?"

Same . . .

"You should keep a better eye on your kid." I tighten the distance between us, though not intentionally. Something about her draws me in every time.

She steps closer to me, matching my energy, I assume.

"I really don't appreciate your tone right now." She cocks an eyebrow, not backing down.

"My *tone*? I just saved your kid from drowning."

If she only knew . . .

"Have you seen that current? And all that rain we've been getting has the river higher than usual." I rub my dirt-stained hands along my brows. Is this conversation actually happening or am I imagining it? I'm so sleep deprived I could be hallucinating. "You sure you're cut out for country life?"

"I went inside for *two* minutes," she says again. "God forbid a single mother has to use the bathroom. Ugh, I knew I should've put that leash on him. What was I thinking?"

Now she's being sarcastic—which both infuriates me and turns me on in a way I wasn't expecting.

We're standing inches apart, close enough I can smell the stress and hand soap on her skin. Her chest rises and falls fast, eyes flashing like the lightning rolling in behind us. So much for getting these last riverside acres done tonight.

"Do *you* have kids?" she asks.

"You've been in my house. Does it look like I have kids?" I match her attitude.

"I'm just saying, you try being a single parent and juggling it all. This is truly my worst nightmare and while I appreciate your help, there's no need to make me feel worse than I already do."

Okay. Maybe that's fair.

"Look. I'm exhausted," I say, still clipped. "I've been in a tractor for fourteen hours a day for the last four days. Haven't eaten. Haven't slept. My nerves are shot. And seeing him fall in that water . . ."

Her expression softens, but her arms remain crossed and her posture is still rigid.

"You could've just said you were scared," she says. "Would've gone a lot further than trying to make me feel like a horrible mother."

I stare at her, jaw tightening as I'm unable to find the right words. She's not wrong. But damn if it doesn't piss me off to be told.

She gathers her soaking-wet kid in her arms and turns toward the house without another word. I hate that he saw that exchange. He's probably too young to understand we were both just worried about him.

Halfway between me and the back door, she tosses one more look my way, though I can't interpret it. I mistook this woman for being soft and helpless, but she's got some bite to her; a little kick.

I don't hate it either.

Sure wish I did.

"Thank you," she calls out, though the expression on her face reads pissed.

I stand there, soaked in sweat and river air and something else I can't name.

No one talks to me like that.

No one has *ever* talked to me like that.

And I should be mad.

I *want* to be mad.

But all I feel is this low, simmering heat in my chest—a sensation I don't know what to do with.

She's good with her words, with expressing how she feels.

Guess that's why she's the writer and I'm the dirt farmer.

Lightning cracks the sky open, followed by a rumble of thunder and the soft padding of raindrops that grow thicker by the second. I trudge back to my planter, contending with the fact that the rest of the night's a bust.

Rain cuts loose right above me.

I get the tractor out of the field before it gets stuck, and then I make my way to the shop to busy myself with work because there's always work to be done.

God knows I need the sleep, but something tells me even as exhausted as I am, I'd probably just lie in bed and think about . . . *her*.

And there's nothing productive about that.

12

Wren

Atticus is warm, clean, and finally not smelling like river sludge. His damp curls rest against the pillow, still carrying the faint scent of lavender shampoo. He's tucked under a sunflower quilt my grandma stitched before I was born, the corners fraying just enough to feel like home.

His breathing has slowed, one thumb tucked loosely under his chin. He fought sleep for a good twenty minutes, tossing and turning mostly—probably residual adrenaline. I don't blame him. That water was cold. Fast. Unforgiving.

And that whole scene scared the hell out of me.

He had to have seen the fear in my eyes and heard the terror in my voice.

I didn't even know he'd wandered that far until I heard Hunter yelling outside, loud and panicked, echoing through the trees like a warning bell.

I rub a hand across my face and exhale, guilt curling in my stomach. I should've kept a better eye on him. I know that. I also didn't deserve to be barked at or for someone who hardly knows me to assume I'd ever carelessly put my son in danger.

Still . . .

Hunter was the one who pulled Atticus out. He was the one who got there first. The one who noticed.

I shouldn't have snapped at him either.

The moment was too big. Too charged. Too close to the kind of thing that changes everything in an instant. And I think that scared both of us more than either of us could admit.

I press a kiss to Atticus's forehead and pull the quilt a little higher, my throat tightening as I whisper, "I love you so much, Atti."

He doesn't stir, just breathes slow and even. Peaceful. Whole. Safe.

On my way to the door, I notice his closet light is on. Reaching in to tug the string, I stop when I see some etchings in the wooden doorframe. I crouch closer, reading words carved in childlike handwriting.

BEN FARTED HERE 9-4-1993
NO GIRLS ALLOWED
ALIENS TOOK JIMMY
COWS ARE DUMB
HUNTER WAS HERE

They make me giggle, but the last one gives me pause. What are the odds Hunter wanted this property and his name is carved on the inside of what was clearly some little boy's closet? And who is Ben? These are questions I realize have a slim chance of ever being answered, so I tug the light string and save them for another day.

Leaving Atticus's door cracked like always, I head downstairs, flipping on the hobnail milk glass lamp in my office—a vintage piece gifted to me from the same grandmother who sewed a sunflower blanket for her "little sunflower." The light glows soft and golden through its papery white shade, casting shadows across my desk. The river's quiet again, less in a hurry than it was earlier. Nothing but the croak of frogs and the whisper of breeze through the trees. Despite the stillness, I replay tonight's events in my mind on a loop at least a dozen times.

Seeing my small son—my whole world—in Hunter's strong arms, the seriousness in his bright blue eyes contrasting against the panic chiseled into his face as he rushed Atticus over to me . . .

It was all the things, all at once. The sensations burn at the top of my skin, begging for a release. If I don't get these words on paper, it's going to be physically painful.

I settle into my chair and pull out the sunflower notebook. Flipping past the last entry, my fingers are already tingling.

I uncap my pen and take the deepest breath I can muster.

Hunter—

You saved my son today.

I would thank you but I don't think there are enough thank-yous in the world to show you how much that meant to me nor do I think you'd want to hear that.

You keep doing that. Saving me. Saving us. And the strangest part is I've never been someone who needs saving.

Despite writing dozens upon dozens of books that center around the classic fantasy of being rescued . . . I've always worn my hyperindependence like a badge of honor. Relying on someone felt like a detriment to my soul, an affront to everything I've ever built myself up to be. A terrifying reality I never wanted to know.

But then you show up—mud-covered, stormy-eyed, furious—and now I kind of want to be saved.

I don't even know from what.

Exhaustion? Uncertainty? Myself?

I hope I never need saving again, but if I do, I kind of hope you're the one who does it.

—Wren

I cap my pen and set it down, watching the ink dry. It feels good to write again. Not just pretend writing or word counts in a Word doc, but *this*. Raw. Unfiltered. Personal.

I push the chair back and stand, stretching my lower back side to side.

And then I remember something else.

Something small. Offhand. Something I almost missed.

He said he hadn't eaten.

He'd been in the tractor fourteen hours, four days in a row. No lunch. No dinner. Nothing but diesel fumes and dirt and whatever's left of that banged-up body of his. With those long legs, broad shoulders, and a mentally and physically demanding job, he needs to eat *something*.

I think of him alone up there in that big house on that big hill—and no one to come home to. No one waiting to greet him with a smile when he walks in at the end of the day in his ripped jeans and dirty boots. No one to pluck the cap off his head, ruffle the dust out of his hair, and throw their arms around him.

No one to make sure he's fed.

No one peering up at him through sleepy eyes, waiting to hear about his day.

No one to say you don't have to do this all by yourself.

I chew the inside of my cheek and glance toward the kitchen.

Tomorrow, I'll cook something—or I'll try, anyway.

I'll pack it up and bring it out to the field.

I'll say thank you with more than words.

He saved my son.

The least I can do is feed the man.

13

Hunter

The rain came hard last night and stuck around just long enough to turn most of my remaining unplanted acres into a damn sponge.

It's a tortuous thing, being forced to sit still. I'm used to the blur of planting season—work sunrise to midnight, eat when you remember, sleep when you can. But now I've got hours on my hands and nothing to throw them at. Nothing I want to throw them at anyway. I'd much rather be planting. This time of year, my chest is heavy with unease that only lifts once the final seed goes into the ground.

Heading to the shop, I sharpen every blade I own, reorganize the tool wall, change the oil in the grain truck, order a few parts, and clean out the back seat of my pickup just for the hell of it.

And when all that's done, I head to the house and heat up a can of chili, debating whether I should bother with a bowl or just eat it straight out of the tin.

I choose the latter. Less dishes to deal with, not that I don't have the time today.

I'm rinsing a spoon when I hear the crunch of tires.

I glance up.

Black SUV.

Wren.

She's walking up the front steps a second later, hands full, messy blond braid slung over one shoulder, cheeks pink from the cold wind this last system brought with it.

She's holding something—glass dish. Foil on top.

I dry my hands on a dish towel and open the door before she can knock.

"Hi," she says, a little breathless. I must've caught her off guard, but to be fair, she caught me off guard too. No one just shows up here. Not without calling first. Not even my hired men. "I brought you something. Just . . . as a thank-you. For yesterday."

I nod for her to come in, stepping aside.

She walks past me, leaving a trail of perfume behind her, something citrusy and warm, like summer snuck in early. She puts the dish on my kitchen island and peels back the foil.

"Chicken and rice casserole." She bites her lower lip, trying to fight a smile. "Or, it's supposed to be. I was going to bring it out to the field, but I didn't see any tractors. Figured you got rained out."

"Appreciate it."

"Also, I'm sorry for snapping at you last night." Her eyes flick to mine and her smile fades away. I find myself almost missing it the second it's gone.

"No need. Emotions were high."

She observes me for a second, like she's expecting me to elaborate, but that's all she's getting. I'm not the type to drag things out. A man does what needs doing, and if he's got anything left after that, he gets on with his day. No need to complicate things.

"It's lunchtime," I say, motioning toward the dish. "You hungry?"

Her face lights with a small, surprised smile. "Sure."

That canned chili sits heavy in my stomach, but I'm not in the business of being rude, so I grab two plates from the cabinet—real ones, not paper—and forks from the drawer. She helps dish it up. The sauce is thick and a little too wet, and something about the smell tells me she got generous with the seasoned salt.

We sit across from each other at my table—oak, heavy, hand built. It hasn't seen a meal with company in years. At least not a woman my age. Glenda, my sixty-year-old bookkeeper, doesn't count. She's more family than anything, and even she knows better than to bring me food.

I don't like being doted on, but more than that, I don't like the feeling of owing someone.

I take a bite.

It's . . . not great.

Oversalted. The rice is half mush, half crunch. The chicken's dry and chewy like it's been re-cooked three times or worse—from a can.

I keep chewing as Wren studies me.

I don't say a word.

She doesn't either, just picks at her plate and pretends not to notice how slow I'm eating.

"So." I clear my throat. "How'd you end up with Rich Sanders's place anyway?"

She stops pushing the food around with her fork and glances up with raised brows. "Rich knew my stepdad. They used to work together at the John Deere plant back in the day. My mom mentioned I was looking for a place—somewhere quiet with land. He said he'd been thinking of moving south. I saw the photos and it was perfect. I made him a cash offer—one he couldn't refuse—and now here we are."

I'd love to know what she paid, but it's none of my business, and it'll be on the assessor page soon enough.

"Did you even look at any other properties?" I ask.

"Didn't need to." She doesn't miss a beat.

"How do you know you paid a fair price?"

She lifts a shoulder. "Things are only worth whatever someone's willing to pay for it."

"Guess it must've been worth to you whatever you paid for it" is all I manage to say as I choke down another bite of casserole.

"You don't sound like you mean that."

How she picked up on the contempt in my voice is beyond me. I'm normally better than that at hiding my true feelings. I've never worn them on my sleeve, my face, or any place else they'd be exposed to the world. My father always said a man should never show his cards unless he wants to be taken advantage of.

"For the last eight years, Sanders has been promising he'd sell the place to me. Said it was mine when the time came. Would never put it in writing, but we shook on it. We had an understanding. At least, I thought we did."

Her mouth parts a little. "Oh."

I nod once, take another bite of the salt-bomb chicken.

"It's just forty acres and a little house." Her voice is soft, laced with an unspoken apology. "Was it really that important to you? Don't you have thousands of acres already?"

"Yes and yes. But it's not worth explaining. You bought the piece. It is what it is now, I suppose."

Her eyes flash. "Explain. I want to know."

There it is again—that spark. That low flame behind her words that tells me she's not the type to let things lie just because I say so.

I exhale, leaning back in my chair. "That parcel was the last piece of riverfront ground in the county. If I'd gotten it, I wouldn't have had another neighbor for five miles in any direction. That kind of space? That kind of quiet? That's peace to me. That's freedom."

It's not the whole story, but it's as much as I care to share right now.

There's a knowingness behind her sapphire eyes. Like she's watching me, seeing past every word. Like she knows there's more and she's just waiting me out.

This woman makes me feel like goddamned cellophane under a microscope. No one's ever made me feel that way before.

"So you enjoy being alone," she says.

I nod. "I do."

Her full lips press together then bunch at one side, like she's trying to decide whether she believes me. "No one actually likes being alone. Some people tell themselves they do. But we're not meant to be alone."

I don't respond. Because maybe she's right.

I once imagined a scenario in which I die alone and no one finds my body for weeks. The thought of it depressed me until I reminded myself that if I were dead, I wouldn't be around to care anyway.

"As a species, I mean," she explains. "By design, we're social. Being together, pairing up, it's a survival mechanism. Sure, the media and society romanticizes it, but having a partner serves many purposes."

I let her words marinate, though I'm not sure where she's going with this.

I scratch the side of my temple with my knuckle. "And you're a romance writer?"

She lets out a breathy laugh. "What's that supposed to mean?"

"Pretty sure the least romantic thing I've ever heard anyone say."

"Two things can be true, you know." She tilts her pretty face, staring me down like she's got some kind of agenda to peel back my layers one by one. "We can accept that being with someone can serve a functional purpose, and we can also accept that it's okay to desire things like love and romance and happy endings and companionship."

I take another bite. This one intentionally too big. I'd rather choke down this rubbery chicken mush than dignify that with a response—because she might be right, but it doesn't change how I feel.

It's easier to be alone.

She picks at her food a little longer before setting her fork down. "Where'd you grow up?"

I blink, surprised she's changing the subject. "Here."

"In Colton Valley?"

"About five miles east of town. Went to the Colombia-Newville high school, then went to Iowa State for ag business. My parents passed shortly after graduation. Took over their operation when I was twenty-four."

She rests her chin against her palm. "And you've just . . . stayed? Ever since?"

"Where else would I have gone?" I look around at the room, the furniture. "I find comfort in the familiar, in the things I know. So much of life is unpredictable and out of our control. You can leave home," I add, "but home can never leave you."

"That's kind of poetic." She flashes me a quick smile that makes my stomach do some stupid somersault thing.

I kick myself for saying the kind of thing I'd usually keep to myself. No one gives a shit about anyone's philosophical ramblings, especially not mine.

The clock on the wall ticks loud in the silence between us.

"I went to Iowa State too," she says. "How old are you? Maybe we were there at the same time."

"Forty-two." It's been a long time since anyone's asked me my age. Saying it out loud hits me like a quick shove to the chest—not because I care about my age, but because it's a reminder of how quickly the years pass when you're not paying them much attention.

"I'll be thirty-nine this summer." She sits straighter, a hint of excitement in her tone. "I bet we walked by each other on campus a hundred times and didn't even know it."

"You majored in ag studies too?" I tease. I push my chair back and grab our plates. "I should get back to the shop. Clean off some equipment before the next window opens."

She stands too. "Of course. I'll let you get back to work."

I walk her to the door. She lingers for half a second on the threshold, peering up at me through a fringe of curled lashes that make her look a hair younger than her thirty-nine years.

"Thanks for eating my cooking," she says. "Even if it was terrible."

"Best chicken rice casserole I've ever had in my life."

"You're a terrible liar." She lifts a brow and we exchange a look that, for a sliver of a moment, makes me feel like I've known her for years, not weeks. "In case you didn't know that."

I smirk, sniffing a laugh before I can stop myself. It doesn't feel bad. Smiling. Honestly can't recall the last time I did before she came around. I'd almost forgotten what it felt like.

With that, Wren turns and struts back to her SUV, hair lifting in the breeze, the hem of her sundress catching around her legs with each step, braid bouncing against her back.

And I stand, idling a minute longer than I should, watching her go.

There's something different about this woman.

She pushes against me. Doesn't just accept the scraps I offer. Doesn't seem scared of me either. Most people find me intimidating. They respect me, but they never test my limits—personally, professionally, or otherwise.

And I don't know yet if that's going to be a good thing . . .

Or the worst thing that's ever happened to me.

14

Wren

It's a quarter past ten when the power goes out.

One minute I'm rinsing a coffee mug and watching lightning thread across the far side of the river—and the next, the whole house sighs into silence. No refrigerator hum, no fan in the hallway, just the distant rumble of thunder and the rustling of early spring leaves through the open windows.

I pause for a moment, listening, taking it in as if it's the first time I've ever truly experienced a storm rolling through.

It's amazing what you can see and hear without the sound and light pollution of the city.

Atticus is out cold upstairs. He had a busy day of playing at his grandparents' and was halfway to dreamland before his head even hit the pillow. And with the windows open and the air still mild, I'm not worried about him waking up sweaty or uncomfortable.

Despite the beauty and stillness of the moment, the silence of being out here in the country feels more profound in the dark.

I could easily turn on the TV and distract myself, but tonight I choose to embrace it by grabbing a book and my little clip-on reading light, and heading out to the porch. The swing creaks softly under my weight, and the cushion still holds the sun-warmed memory of the day.

The storm's moving east, but the air still smells like rain and electricity and the damp earth beneath it all. Sweet petrichor.

I don't get five pages in before I hear the faint growl of a diesel engine in the distance.

Headlights round the bend that leads into my driveway and sweep across the trees like a determined spotlight before coming to a hard stop. I squint into the beams, shielding my eyes with my hand until my vision settles on a big white truck.

Hunter.

Of course.

He climbs out, messing with some electrical box near the road, before returning to the cab of his truck and idling down my driveway like this is just another Tuesday night.

I stay seated, book in my lap, reading light clipped to the edge of the cover and cutting unapologetically bright through the night darkness.

He's holding something. A portable generator, maybe? I think I've seen one of those in my stepdad's garage before.

"What are you doing?" I ask, half laughing because this is absurd.

"I had to disconnect the power at the road so when the power comes on it doesn't fry this generator." He nods toward the sizable object in his hand. "You lost power, yeah?"

"Yeah," I say slowly as I watch him get to work. Who *is* this man? "Just a little while ago."

"Me too. Transformer's out at the corner," he says. "Happens every time there's a storm. Power company's notorious for being slow to fix it this far out. Thought I'd save you a long night."

"So you just . . . you just . . . *brought* me a generator?" I ask, sitting up a little, lashes batting like they've got a mind of their own.

"Don't go getting any ideas, honey," he says, stepping onto the porch. "Just because I did this doesn't mean you need to go making me another casserole."

He holds up my empty baking dish in his other hand. I hadn't noticed it until now.

"Looks kinda expensive," he says. "Thought you might want it back."

I grin. "It was an engagement gift."

He arches a brow but asks no questions. Maybe he's afraid to ask, just like I was afraid to ask about the carvings in the closet when I took him lunch. The question was on the tip of my tongue the whole time, but I couldn't bring myself to say the words. Call it a hunch maybe, but I can't help but feel his attachment to that place has more to do with this "Ben" person and less to do with all that talk about privacy.

"For a wedding that never happened," I add.

"Smart man." His expression is unreadable, but somehow I know he's teasing.

I grab the dish from him, our fingers brushing in the exchange. "Just for that, I'm definitely making you another casserole. Something with eggplant. Extra soggy."

He exhales, half amused, half exasperated. "Just . . . practice on someone else next time. Maybe that poor old mare you've got in the barn."

"Nope. You're officially my test subject now."

He heads to the side of the house, near the garage, and hooks up the generator like he's done it a thousand times before. Efficient. Quiet. Focused. I lean against the front porch rails, watching his broad shoulders flex beneath his gray T-shirt. As he works, I take him all in, paying close attention to the way his sleeves cling to his biceps just enough to be distracting, how his jeans are worn in a way that looks effortless, not trendy. The way his hands are rough, steady, calloused, and capable.

God help me, this man could ruin me and never even know it.

When he finishes, he wipes his hands on a shop rag he pulls from his back pocket. He doesn't look at me at first, just scans the dark horizon like he's already mentally gone and onto the next thing. I can't help but wonder if this man ever stays still long enough to just . . . be.

Doubtful.

"You always show up like this? All heroic?" I ask. "Ready to save the day at a moment's notice?"

He glances over, frowning. "I'm not heroic."

"You say that. But you keep saving me anyway. That's what heroes do."

He doesn't answer, just turns back to finishing the task at hand.

"I appreciate it," I say. "And I don't know how to show you that other than subjecting you to my really awful cooking. Maybe if you told me something more about yourself, I could, I don't know—"

He cuts me off. "I don't need you to get me anything or return the favor. It's not about that."

"What's it about, then?"

He seems annoyed, exhaling hard through his nose, but I'm still going to press. I have a feeling he rarely gets pressed, but I think it could be good for him.

"Why does it have to be about something? You're a single mom with a small child, living alone in the country. I'm your closest neighbor. You got your car stuck. You lost power. Your kid almost . . ." He doesn't finish the sentence. "What kind of man would I be if I watched you struggle and did nothing to help?"

My mind immediately goes to my ex-fiancé and a half dozen scenarios where he feigned incompetence to get out of actually having to help me with something. I've always had an independent streak a mile wide, and I never expected him to do everything for me, but too many times I made excuses for him.

Nick was good with Atticus, he helped with half the expenses even though I outearned him by a landslide, and he was funny. I'd focused so much on what I liked about him that I was willfully ignorant to all the reasons he wasn't the ideal match for me.

"Well maybe one of these days *you'll* need *me*," I kid. "And I'll get to rescue you."

He snickers, peering over his shoulder and tossing me a half smile that lights up his face and takes away all the intimidation that tends to live there when he's looking all serious.

"Rescue me from what exactly?" he counters.

"I dunno." I lift a shoulder to my ear, lips cocked. "Maybe from yourself?"

Something flickers across his handsome face—just a flash of something sad or scared, or maybe he's just tired and I'm making it into something it's not. He rakes a hand along his beard, appearing lost in thought for a moment. The curiosity that was already simmering inside me roars to life.

"I don't need to be saved from myself," he says. "Last I checked, I'm getting along just fine."

"Okay. Then maybe," I say gently, "you just need to be needed."

He doesn't speak.

Just stands there, staring at the trees like they might have the answers.

"You're describing a hero complex," he finally speaks. "I don't have that."

"If you say so." I return to the porch swing and put my book aside, patting the spot next to me. "Come. Sit down. Stay awhile. It's so quiet out here. I'm still getting used to the lack of . . . people. I could use some company."

He hesitates, his dirty boots planted firm in the wet grass.

I nod toward the far end of the swing. "Don't make me beg."

He shakes his head, lips parting like he's about to mutter some kind of flimsy excuse, but then to my surprise, he trudges over, climbs the creaky, broken front steps, and lowers himself onto the swing. He's careful not to crowd me, leaving plenty of space between us.

"Don't go anywhere." I get up, disappear inside for a moment, and come back with a bottle of red wine from some local vineyard and two stemless glasses. This time, I sit closer to him. Maybe a good nine inches is all that separates us, but it might as well be a country mile. His walls are up, but I'm determined to take them down even if I have to knock them over with a little help from my friend Cabernet Sauvignon.

"You don't strike me as a wine guy," I say, "but it's all I've got."

He takes the glass I hand him. Doesn't complain.

I curl my legs against my chest, breathing deeply while Hunter sits rigid against the opposite armrest, the wind stirring the trees and the generator humming low in the background.

"You always drink on your porch with strange men in the dark?" he asks.

"Only the ones who bring me backup power."

He huffs out something close to a laugh.

I sip my wine. "We're not really strangers anymore, though. You told me where you grew up and where you went to school. I can see your house from here. I've been in your kitchen and in your truck. We ate lunch together. I know how old you are. We went to the same college. I've seen you around town. Only thing I don't know about you is your Social Security number and your mother's maiden name."

He chuffs, peering my way through his dark lashes.

It's been a long time since I was able to crack a dumb joke or come up with something witty on the fly. The longer I'm back in Colton Valley, the more it feels like my old self is coming back to me in pieces. That, and despite Hunter's guardedness, I can't help but feel unguarded in his presence.

It's a kind of safety I've never felt with anyone else before, one I can't quite pinpoint but also couldn't deny if I tried.

"Were you close to your parents?" I ask.

He takes a long drink. "When they were still around, yes."

"You ever been married?" I ask.

He turns his head, brow lifting. "Are you launching some kind of FBI investigation? What's with all the questions?"

"Oh, I'm sorry." I press my palm against my chest, feigning shock. "Did you think we were just going to awkwardly drink wine in silence and watch the storm roll out?"

"Yeah." He turns to me, his eyes drinking me in. "That's exactly what I thought we were doing."

I gently nudge my elbow against his bicep. "Something you should know about me is I'm very curious and I ask a lot of questions, and if that's going to be a problem for you, then maybe you should stop rescuing me and we should go back to being strangers."

The tiniest glimmer resides in his eyes. I see it, even in the dark, under the faint glow of my book light sitting off to the side. Amusement, maybe? Mutual curiosity? He easily could've turned down the wine and gone home. Lord knows it's late.

But he didn't.

He stayed.

I top off his glass and clear my throat. "Okay, where were we? Oh, right. Have you ever been married?"

He hesitates, though I think it's for dramatic effect. "Who wants to know?"

"Don't deflect. Just answer the question, Hunter."

"Never. You?" His gaze diverts my way.

"Never."

"Why not?"

I feign shock again. "Whoa, whoa, whoa. I'm the one asking the questions here. You'll get your turn."

He rolls his eyes and takes a sip, hiding a smile that's creeping across his lips. I don't know what this man has against smiling, but I wish he'd let it go. He's a gorgeous specimen of rugged man, but he's *beautiful* when he smiles. And I bet he has no idea.

I refill my glass. The bottle's getting lower by the minute, and we're only getting started. It's late. Atticus will be up early. But I don't want this night to end.

"I was engaged," I say. "To the wrong guy. He called it off the day of our wedding. The end."

It's all I want to say about it for now. I hold my breath, waiting for an onslaught of questions I don't feel like answering because Nick is irrelevant.

"I thought you were a storyteller," he says. "That's a horrible story."

"Not every story is worth telling."

"Well, it's his loss," Hunter says, taking a slow drink. "Because look who got to keep that casserole dish."

I snort mid-sip, wine almost shooting out my nose.

He *does* have a sense of humor.

"What's your story?" I redirect the conversation back to him, where it belongs. "How does an attractive, successful, confident, capable man like yourself end up single at forty-two? Why hasn't anyone snatched you up yet?"

"The ass-kissing is not necessary. It's actually insulting."

"What? How?"

"You think a little flattery's going to get me to open up to you about my personal life?"

"No, not at all . . ." I frown. "I was just describing you the way I see you."

His lips press flat and the slightest wince paints his face, as if I've struck a sore spot.

A rumble of thunder is followed by an endless bout of silence.

After a bit more consideration, he shrugs. "Just never met the right one, I guess."

I drag in a lungful of petrichor, trying my hardest to read between those lines. I bet there's a whole novel there. Pages upon pages of memories. Of near misses. Of broken hearts. A man doesn't run a massive farming empire only to live in a huge house on top of a hill, miles from the nearest neighbor . . . only to spend his life alone.

"Have you had girlfriends?" I ask.

He rolls his eyes. "Yes, I've had girlfriends."

"And?"

His dark brows lift. "And what?"

"And what happened?"

He takes a swig of wine. "Nothing. Which is why I never married any of them."

"They couldn't have all been that bad."

He draws in a breath. "You're right. There was one *almost*."

My heart catches in my throat. I love that he's sharing this, but I also hate it at the same time because now whenever I look at him, I'm going to see a man pining after the one who got away and not the stubborn, hyperindependent curmudgeon waiting for the right one to come along.

"She cheated with a buddy of mine," he adds, zero emotion in his voice. "And as you so eloquently stated about your situation . . . *the end*."

I exhale and pray he doesn't see the relief wafting off me in real time. As a romance author, I romanticize almost everything. It's part of the job, it's second nature. Safe to say Hunter's not pining over this woman.

"When you're young," he continues, miraculously without any prodding, "you always think you have all the time in the world."

"Right? It's like you blink and a year goes by. You blink again, then five years go by."

"You focus on work, you keep thinking it'll happen when it's meant to happen." He rubs the pad of his thumb against his glass, leaving a smudge in its place that he studies. "Soon all your friends start pairing off. You get older. The dating pool gets thinner. Pretty soon the pool is so thin it's not even worth taking a dip."

"Do you ever date?" I ask. "Now, I mean?"

He chuffs. "Dating market's pretty bleak here. Even if it wasn't . . . I don't know. Seems like all the good ones are taken."

"Hold on. I've seen the way women look at you in public," I say. "You're probably Colton Valley's most eligible bachelor. You could have anyone you want. You can't *not* know that."

He chuckles. Actually fully chuckles. And drags his hand along his beard, giving it a good scratch. "You're blowing smoke."

"Don't bullshit me, Hunter. You can't be this good looking and this humble *and* have a hero complex. What's really going on?" My skin is flushed warm from the wine, and my entire body is electric. I angle closer to him, resting my elbow on the back of the swing and cocking my cheek against my hand as I give him my full attention. "What's the real story, huh?"

"There is no real story."

"There's always a real story." With that, I rise. "Don't go anywhere. I'm getting more wine. You're not allowed to leave until you give me the unabridged version."

"You realize some of us have to work tomorrow, right?" he calls after me as I head inside.

I pretend not to hear him.

When I return, freshly uncorked wine bottle in hand, he's standing by the broken porch steps, hands shoved in his pockets. "Generator should keep you good 'til morning. I'll come back for it once the power's restored."

He watches as the excitement that resided on my face mere moments ago fades.

His eyes hold mine. Something shifts between us.

"Really?" I ask. "You're just going to . . . leave? We were just about to do a deep dive into your dating life."

"I told you there's no story," he says. "And I don't want to waste any more of your time."

My jaw turns slack, then I purse my lips. I thought we were connecting. He was opening up. Laughing. Cracking jokes. I know it's late, but it's not *that* late. It's going to be too wet to plant tomorrow, so he shouldn't have to get up before sunrise.

He holds my gaze for a second that lingers a little longer than it should. I say nothing in hopes that he'll fill the silence with the words it looks like he wants to say.

"Night, Wren." He trots down the steps, his boots heavy on the cracked wood as he disappears into the muggy darkness.

No fanfare.

No promises.

Just diesel and distance and that damn ache that settles in deeper the longer he stays just out of reach.

15

Hunter

It's been decades since I sat on that porch swing. I almost couldn't bring myself to do it either. But somewhere between my hesitation and her insistence, it felt like something I had to do. And by the time she poured me a glass of wine and looked at me like I was the only man in the world—or at least in her world—I wasn't thinking about that porch, that swing, that house, or that land.

Just . . . her.

Gravel crunches beneath my tires as I ease the truck into gear and head back up the hill. Wine's still ambling through my veins, but it's not the reason my hands feel so restless on the wheel.

I shouldn't have left.

I should've stayed on that swing, let the silence stretch between us a little longer, maybe even said what was really on my mind for once.

Or hell—kissed her. Lord knows every part of me wanted to.

It's been a while since I felt soft lips like those on mine, and I could easily imagine the way her fingertips would feel stroking through my beard, grazing the side of my face.

That look in her eyes, the way she tilted her chin and leaned a little closer—she would've let me kiss her. I'm certain of that.

But I didn't.

Because it's easier to leave than to stay. Easier to pretend I didn't feel what I felt the second she smiled at me with that glass of wine in her hand and the night breeze lifting her hair like something out of a dream I've never let myself have.

I park outside my house on the hilltop, kill the engine, and sit for a minute. Just breathing. Alone with my thoughts—thoughts that are louder tonight than they've ever been.

She's too much.

Too soft.

Too pretty.

Too close to the parts of me I can't remember the last time I let anyone see.

Every part of me wants her like I haven't wanted anything in a long, long time.

But the truth is, I like control.

I *need* it.

Hell, I don't know who I am without it.

I can control the type of seeds and chemicals I use. I can manage my weather expectations, employee output, finances, and acreage bids. I can plan and prepare. I can always fix what breaks. These are things I know . . . things I do and do well—better than most, if I'm being honest.

But I can't control the way my chest tightens every time Wren looks at me like I'm someone worth knowing.

I can't control the way it feels to hear my name on her lips or how it knocks the air out of me to watch her walk away.

My heart? That's the one thing I can't control.

And that's the one thing that scares me most.

Because I know what happens when you hand it over. I've watched love disappoint. Watched it walk away. Watched it die. Everything I've ever loved, I've lost.

Everything but land.

But hearts? They do their own thing regardless of what you want them to do, and it's human nature to avoid pain and suffering. I might be good at managing an operation, but in pouring my focus into my farm, I've become good at avoiding emotional anguish too.

I stare out the windshield at the dark stretch of river valley below, the clouds slowly thinning in the distance, outlined by the glow of a full moon. Half a mile away, Wren's little porch light glows soft at the edge of her tree line, a tiny beacon that shouldn't matter but does.

I imagine she'll sit there for a while longer. Maybe finish that wine since she already opened it. Maybe think about me the way I'm thinking about her.

Or maybe not.

Maybe I'm just a man with a broken compass, too set in his ways to find his true north.

I scrub a hand down my face, exhale hard, and climb out of the truck, the taste of red wine still on my tongue and the heat of her body still warm on my shoulder.

Heading in for the night, I fall asleep with one thought on my mind and one thought only: *I should've kissed her.*

16

Wren

The porch creaks softly as I rise from the swing, wineglass still warm from where my fingers wrapped it too tightly.

I watched the taillights of his truck disappear over the hill a few minutes ago, swallowed by the trees, leaving me in silence. A breeze lifts the loose tendrils of hair around my face, cool against the alcohol-and-embarrassment-induced flush still clinging to my cheeks. The bottle I'd opened is still full and untouched, the air still charged like it was when he was sitting next to me.

And yet he left.

Just like that.

I linger for a minute longer, telling myself it was fine. It *is* fine. *I'm* fine.

Not ready to head in yet, I sink back into the swing, legs tucked beneath me as the last bit of moonlight fades behind the night clouds. I hate that I feel like this. Hollow and a little bit foolish. Like I've built up something in my head that didn't really exist.

Maybe it was the wine and the fact that he showed up with a generator when I didn't even ask, when I was perfectly content to use candles and shower in cold water in the morning and wait patiently for the power company to do their thing.

It felt more meaningful than I suppose it was.

And then he stayed. Had wine. Answered my questions. Let his eyes linger on my lips. His face softened from time to time. I had him smiling.

I could've sworn that when he left, there was almost a heaviness in the way he told me good night, like it pained him to say it, like something in him *wanted* to stay.

But he didn't.

And I should be used to that by now.

I've never been the girl someone chooses—not really.

Not when it counts.

Not the boy in high school, who asked out my best friend instead.

Not my college boyfriend, who ghosted me the second I started talking about long-term plans.

Not Atticus's biological father, who swore up and down he'd always be there for us, then changed his number when the pressure got too real.

Not even the fiancé who promised me and my son forever then left me standing in a white dress with a sinking heart and a four-year-old who didn't understand why his mommy cried for days.

You'd think after all that I'd be jaded.

Sometimes I wish I was.

But I'm not.

I'm a hopeless romantic in the most tragic sense of the word; a woman who's made a living writing about love and devotion and men who move mountains to be with the women they adore—and I've never had any of that for myself. Not once. Not even close.

And somehow, I've always been okay with it. I've always made peace with the idea that maybe I was meant to write the stories, not live them. That the fantasy was always better than the reality anyway. The men I write about in my books are fictional for a reason. They don't exist in the real world.

But then came Hunter.

Rugged, broody, and heroic, driving up in a big white pickup instead of riding up on a big white horse, though it's all the same.

At first glance, he seems impossible to read. He's not warm or flirty. He doesn't make big declarations or play games or give false hope—at least not on purpose. But every once in a while, he looks at me like he wants to rewrite every rule he's ever lived by.

God, I can only imagine how it must feel to be chosen by this man . . .

I exhale and rise to my feet, heading inside, flicking off porch lights one by one until the house is cloaked in warm darkness and filled with the distant rumble of the generator outside.

On my way upstairs, I peek my head into my son's room. Atticus is fast asleep upstairs, sprawled diagonally across his little bed, dreams probably filled with ponies and tire swings and frogs caught in mason jars.

I should be exhausted, but for some reason I'm not. My mind is whirring, replaying tonight's exchange again and again, wondering if I misread any signs or if there's more I could've read between the lines of our conversation.

I tiptoe downstairs and make my way to my office, that little sanctuary where the words are starting to come easier now thanks to the man who somehow feels the need to both rescue me and keep me at an arm's length.

Scanning my desk for my sunflower notebook, I don't see it where I left it. I check under stacks of papers, a pen-filled mug, and various framed photos. It's nowhere to be found.

Panic sears through me, hot and forceful.

I toss a throw blanket off the chair.

Not there either.

My heart climbs into my throat. I *always* leave it right here—in the center of my writing desk, where I can't miss it, where it sits out in the open, silently reminding me there are always words needing to be written.

Just when I'm about to tear the place apart, I spot the white-and-yellow edge peeking out from beneath a pile of mail on the bookshelf.

I don't remember putting it there . . .

Sometimes Atticus plays in here, so there's a chance he moved some things around, but panic lingers inside me like a warning bell regardless.

If I lost this thing, it'd be akin to losing a diary. A writer's personal words are more precious than gold. They come from a different part of them altogether. A deeply personal place that can't always be easily accessed. The idea of losing this and someone finding it and reading all the things I never meant to share—especially if it's one person in particular . . .

I can't finish the thought.

I center myself with a deep breath and reach for a pen before taking a seat. Cracking the notebook open, I flip past the last letter and find a fresh page.

Emotions swirl with feelings, both in and under my skin, scorching and pressing, full of hope, doubt, disappointment, and determination as I write yet another letter to a man who'll never read it. But the sooner I get these words on paper, the sooner I'll get them out of my head, and that's the only way I'm going to get any real sleep tonight.

> Hunter—
>
> You could've stayed.
>
> I would've let you.
>
> We could've sat on the porch until the moon traded places with the sun. I'd have poured you more wine, even if you didn't want it. I'd have asked more questions and you would've pretended to be annoyed but you'd have answered them anyway. During bouts of silence, we would've listened to the frogs by the river as the space between us kept getting smaller.
>
> And eventually—if we were both brave enough—we would've closed that space altogether.

You could've kissed me.

And I would've kissed you back.

Soft. Slow. Like the world was holding its breath just for us.

We could've let our guards down for once. Yours built of silence and solitude, mine built of stories and curiosity.

Instead, you left.

And I told myself it didn't hurt.

I told myself I didn't care.

But I'm writing this, aren't I?

Which means I must.

So maybe this is just my way of creating the moment I didn't get to have.

The moment that might've been.

The moment I hope, someday, finds its way back to me. If not with you, then with someone who chooses me. I want to be chosen.

God, I want to be chosen.

I've never said that out loud before. Or written it on paper. And as a highly accomplished and independent woman, it feels jarring to admit . . . but just once I'd like to be chased, desired, and desperately wanted. I'd like to be with a man who doesn't make me earn my place in his life. Who doesn't require performance, only authenticity and presence. A man who tells me I'm enough, just as I am. A man who makes it clear he's been waiting his whole life . . . for me.

That's the whole point, isn't it?

That's why I write love stories and that's why people read them.

The fantasy of being someone's special person. Their one and only.

I'm realizing now that I've always been the chaser, the performer, the one who diminishes her needs in an attempt to be easier to love . . . and where has that gotten me? Pregnant. Alone. Jilted. Confused.

You piqued my curiosity with your enigmatic ways, Hunter. You got me to pick up the pen again. But I don't think this is healthy for me anymore, fantasizing about you and imagining in my head that you're so much more than you really are, that there's any chance we could be something.

That's just limerence in disguise.

Limerence isn't romantic.

Real love is.

You're just a fantasy.

And I've accepted now that it's all you'll ever be.

—Wren

17

Hunter

Rain's still clinging to the air like a stubborn houseguest that doesn't know when to leave. Makes the shop smell like damp concrete and oil spills. Familiar. Steady. Nostalgic. Everything I've ever known.

Cal's ass is parked on a stack of five-gallon buckets, work boots propped on the axle of a stripped-down cultivator. Truitt leans against the workbench, fiddling with the same damn pocketknife he's been pretending to need for the past ten minutes. I'm perched on the edge of my rolling stool, oil-stained hands wrapped around a thermos of black coffee that tastes more like burnt toast than caffeine, but it does the job.

Too wet to plant. Too early to call it a day.

We've already greased tractors and planters, fueled equipment, and replaced bearings. We're always grateful for a little forced respite during planting season, but now we're just three bored men who don't know what to do with themselves when they're not busy being busy.

It's a dangerous combination.

"You know what I hate?" Cal says, squinting at the ceiling like he's searching for divine support. "Spring forecasts. They tease you into thinking you've got a good run coming, and then they shit all over your schedule like a lactose-intolerant toddler on a dairy binge."

Truitt snorts, his smile stretching as wide as his face and his eyes crinkling in the corners. "Damn, man. Too vivid."

Cal smirks, satisfied to get a rise out of his easier-going colleague.

Cal's got this cocky swagger to him—wiry, sharp-eyed, and always two steps ahead of everyone in the room. Mouthier than a jackrabbit on espresso, but there isn't a single piece of equipment he can't fix. Saved me more times than I can count. I hired him straight out of high school, and he showed up the next day like he'd been born with a wrench in one hand and a chip on his shoulder.

"Should be back in the field by tomorrow, I'd think?" Truitt says, wiping his palms down the front of his dusty jeans like he's hoping to wring the rain out of the air. He's the quieter of the two. Slightly softer around the edges. Loyal to a fault. I've never seen anyone work harder or care more. It's like he owes the ground something and he's determined to pay it back in sweat.

"If we're lucky. Ground's holding water like a damn sponge," I tell him. "We'll know more in a couple days."

Truitt nods and goes back to pretending that stupid pocketknife is going to solve all our problems.

Silence stretches between the sounds of a fly buzzing near the window and the distant rumble of a semi down on 49.

"You've been off your game lately, boss," Cal says, leveling me with that look of his—the one that's half amusement, half challenge. "Distracted. You're missing stuff. Like yesterday? You called me 'Truitt.' Twice."

Truitt chuckles. "Yeah. I wasn't gonna say anything, but I was starting to wonder if we should both just answer to my name now."

"Hell, why not?" Cal shrugs. "I mean, he's the nice one. I'm the pretty one. We're both damn good at our jobs. Between us, you've got a full-functioning adult male."

"Go sweep the shop." I ignore their banter, sipping my coffee.

Cal chuffs, elbowing Truitt before leaning close. "He's not denying it, though."

Truitt leans forward, expression more somber now. "Seriously. You all right, boss? You're probably just antsy not being in the field. We all are."

That'd be the easy answer, but it's not the truth.

Because the truth is . . . I'm antsy because *she's* in my head.

Every damn second of the day, Wren Jensen invades my every thought.

That knowing half smile.

The stubborn tilt of her chin when she's challenging me.

The intoxicating scent of her hair when she sat too close last night, pouring me that second glass of wine on her porch.

While I've been planting corn and beans, she's planted herself inside me and started taking root without permission—like a weed I can't control.

Only she's not a weed.

She's more like a pretty flower—the ones that grow like weeds. I think of the sunflowers my mother used to love. She had a whole garden of 'em when I was a kid. They made her happy, the way they always tilted toward the light and grew in any kind of condition.

My mind wanders to the way Wren looked when I pulled up, all curled up in that swing with a book in her lap, her bare feet tucked under her like she's always belonged here.

It's distracting as hell, knowing she's half a mile away from me every night.

"Maybe he's got a woman." Cal lifts his brows like he's about to make a joke out of it, and I suppose it would be funny as hell to them, seeing me focused on anything other than my operation. "I mean, that'd explain everything. Grumpier than usual. Little bags under the eyes. Walking around like he hasn't slept in a week. Women will do that to ya if you're not careful."

I shoot him a look. "Don't you have a boom to work on or something?"

Cal throws up his hands. "Just saying. You've got that dazed look about you. Like a man who's either falling for someone or trying like hell not to."

I don't answer.

I just know that the second I saw her hauling that glass dish up my porch steps, I forgot how to breathe. She's got this way about her—soft edges, sharp tongue, eyes that see more than they should. She doesn't just walk into a room, she settles into it. Fills it. Makes it warmer. Turns heads and probably doesn't even realize it. There's an aura around her, something I've never noticed in anyone else.

That said, I never wanted company up on that hill. Didn't want a neighbor. Sure as hell didn't want a woman complicating my simple little life. And yet now, when things go quiet, when the machines shut down and the world pauses for a beat—she's the only thing I can think about.

Wren Jensen.

Her name's like a song stuck on repeat, one I can't get out of my head no matter how hard I try.

18

Wren

The generator clatters harder than it should when I set it down on the concrete floor of his shop.

"Here," I say, wiping my hands on my jeans without looking at him. "It's all yours. Thanks again."

Hunter doesn't move. Just watches me from across the space, arms crossed, shirt clinging to his chest from the heat of the day, jaw tight like he's grinding back something he can't say.

Typical.

I take a step toward the open garage door, late day sun streaking in sideways. After Atticus came home from day camp, he requested to go to my mom's for tater tot casserole—my least favorite meal of all time because we ate it at least once a week growing up. I told my parents I had some errands to run and I'd be back to get him after a while, then my mom insisted on having Atticus stay the night.

"Wren," Hunter says.

I pause, hand hovering in midair like I might wave goodbye.

"Yes?" I don't look at him. I can't. I don't want to get my hopes up again, and that tends to happen every time we lock eyes.

"You mad?"

I slowly turn to face him, arms folded tight across my chest, heart pounding but gaze averted. "Why would I be mad?"

There's a heavy pause, then he shifts his weight like he wants to move but doesn't.

"I don't know," he says. I feel him studying me. "You seem . . . different."

The way I see it, I can play dumb, brush it off, and get out of here—or I can tell him how it made me feel when he left so abruptly after we were having what I thought was a nice conversation.

Option one feels safest. Option two makes me look like a fool for thinking he was remotely interested in me.

"You got somewhere to be?" he rubs the back of his neck, still watching me. "I've got some beer in the fridge. Was just about to have one."

"I always have somewhere to be."

He snickers, like he finds my defensiveness amusing, and then he struts over to an old fridge in the corner, retrieving two Busch Lights and handing me one.

I hate beer.

And I don't love emotionally unavailable men.

I should be halfway to my car by now, but the soles of my sneakers might as well be glued to this concrete floor. Something in me won't let me leave.

He cracks his beer. I don't.

"I'm not sure what you're trying to do here, but I don't do the hot-and-cold thing. I've got a kid and a career and too much dignity to sit around, begging some broody guy to toss me a crumb of warmth."

Silence follows, then I make the mistake of meeting his heavy gaze.

My lungs burn with the breath I'm holding in too tight.

This feels like a tipping point, one that could go in the worst direction if I let it. This is not the kind of man to put an ounce of hopes or dreams on. Carelessly fantasizing about him is playing with fire. Getting attached? That could be the death of me.

"I have to go," I force myself to say before turning for the door.

Only without warning or hesitation, Hunter crosses the floor in four long strides, grips my waist, and hauls me into him. Before I can protest, his mouth crashes onto mine—hot, rough, hungry.

I whimper against his lips, hands fisting the front of his shirt, and he growls low in his throat like he can't stand another second of distance between us.

"I should've kissed you the first time I had the chance." His voice is low and gravelly, colored with want. "I'm not making that mistake again."

He lifts me by the thighs, and I instinctively wrap my legs around his waist. With his mouth still on mine, he carries me effortlessly across the shop and sets me down on the tailgate of his truck. My body feels safe and tiny in his massive arms. By the time we come up for air, his hands are already under my shirt, pushing it up over my head and tossing it somewhere behind us. His lips trail kisses down my neck before reaching my chest, where he sucks one nipple into his mouth while palming the other, fingers squeezing just shy of too hard.

"Oh god," I gasp, head falling back. I can't remember the last time I was touched with hands and lips as greedy as his.

His fingers slide between my legs.

"Jesus, Wren," he mutters. "You're soaked."

That's all it takes.

I melt against him.

My defenses are weak, my resolve disarmed.

I want him to want me—and I want him in the worst way.

Physically.

I don't want messy. I don't want emotions. I don't want to get my heart broken again because that's exactly what would happen with someone like this. But if he can make me feel *this* desired? *This* consumed? He can have my body . . . just this once.

Hunter flips me fast, bends me over the tailgate, my warm cheek pressed to the cold, dirty metal. He yanks my jeans down to my knees next, taking my underwear with them, and then I hear the unmistakable sound of his zipper followed by the soft drag of denim.

"Goddamn," he whispers, gripping my hips before lining himself up behind me. "You're gonna ruin me, honey."

With one brutal, perfect thrust, he's inside me.

I gasp, mouth open, eyes wide, muscles clenching around him.

He just *takes*.

And I let him.

Because I need this. I need to be taken like I'm the only thing in the world he can think about—even if it's just this once. Even if it never happens again.

I need this release.

He grabs a fist of my hair and yanks gently, just enough to force me to arch my back, to bare my throat.

"You feel that?" he growls, hips snapping against my ass. "That's what you do to me."

Each thrust is deep, punishing, perfect.

"You drive me fucking wild," he says. "I can't get you out of my head. I can't stop thinking about you . . ."

I steady myself against the tailgate, knuckles white, body bracing as he pounds into me.

As his grip tightens on my hair, I instinctively moan—loud, needy, desperate. The sounds coming from my mouth are carnal and primitive, and I don't know that I've ever made them until now.

"That's it. You're doing so good for me." His tone unexpectedly encouraging and dominant at the same time. "God, you feel . . ."

His words disappear into heavy sighs as he slides one hand around to my front, his fingers finding my clit like he's memorized it, before rubbing tight, perfect circles. My mind goes blank as the world around me dissolves. I'm simply a body on the verge of losing complete control.

I'm close . . . so close I'm shaking.

Every unremitting thrust brings me closer to the edge.

"Come for me, Wren." His breath is hot against my ear. "You need this. I know you do. You need it just as bad as I do."

He's not wrong.

But I don't want this to end.

Not yet.

"You're taking me so well," he says with a groan, feeding me every inch. "It's like you were made for me."

Without warning, the release I was holding on to for dear life begins to overtake me. I can't fight it any longer. My legs go light, jerking and trembling as he pins me with each thrust. As sounds escaping my lips grow louder, he cups a hand over my mouth—which makes me orgasm almost instantly.

As soon as my body stops convulsing, he curses through gritted teeth, slamming into me a final time before pulling out completely and spilling his seed down my left ass cheek, hot, wet, and dripping.

We stay like that—bent, panting, spent.

His hands slide off my hips.

I grab a nearby shop rag, wipe him off me, and pull my jeans up, slowly swallowing the ache in my throat as I struggle to keep my balance. My body vibrates with little aftershocks, numb and electric at the same time.

Neither of us says a word.

But maybe there's nothing to be said.

We both got what we needed.

End of story.

I find my shirt and pull it on without meeting his gaze.

"I have to go pick up Atticus," I lie, brushing my hair into place.

Hunter zips his jeans, still breathless. "I should run into town. Parts store."

It's after six. I doubt the parts store is even open.

I nod once, back already turned, keys in hand.

We don't say goodbye.

We don't make plans to see each other again.

We don't ask what this was.

We both just walk away like what just happened was the most natural thing in the world.

On the drive home—and for the rest of the night—I convince myself it meant nothing, and I promise myself it'll never happen again.

While I've been the recipient of a million broken promises in my thirty-nine years, I've never broken one to myself—and I don't intend to start now.

19

Hunter

I catch my reflection in the rearview on my way to the shop the next morning. No denying I look like hell. Didn't sleep more than a handful of hours and not for lack of trying either. My mind ran laps all night—around the shop, around the mess we made, around the way her mouth made the sexiest sounds I've ever heard as her body surrendered and all but conformed to mine.

Didn't plan for it to happen like that. Hell, I didn't plan for it to happen at all. But the second she walked into that shop—avoiding my gaze like she was allergic to me—I swear something overtook me. I needed to see her smile again. I wanted to see those sparkly indigo eyes. Some part of me craved her warmth and softness, the things she gave to me so freely before I left her on her front porch that night.

Can't blame her for being cold to me yesterday. I imagine I made her feel foolish, rejected. But in my desperation, I created a whole new set of feelings—feelings I'm still attempting to untangle.

My mind wanders to the first time I saw her and our brief conversation at the meat counter. Then I think about how I pretended not to notice her at the coffee shop despite feeling the weight of her stare the entire time. Then there was the batch of cookies she brought me. Getting her unstuck in the rain as she sat shivering in my old Carhartt jacket in my truck. Eating that god-awful casserole together. Sipping wine with her as she razzed me while wearing the cutest smirk on her pretty little face . . .

Goddamn it, I want this woman—and I've wanted her since the moment I first laid eyes on her.

I'm not a word guy. Never have been. I don't sit around journaling my feelings or talking them out like Cal after three beers. I fix things. I act. If I care about something, I *do* something about it. That's why I pulled her car out of the ditch. Why I brought her the generator. It's why I let her in at all.

Hell. I don't just want her . . . I *need* her.

And it terrifies the shit out of me because it's the one thing that's beyond my control. I spent years convincing myself I didn't need anyone—and then she comes into my life like a hailstorm in mid-July, bowling over everything I've worked for without warning.

"Jesus," Cal mutters as he walks into the shop. Truitt's two steps behind him, two tumblers in hand. "Someone drag you behind the 7600 last night or something?"

No, but it sure feels that way.

"I was gonna say maybe he fell in the bin and got churned up a bit," Truitt adds, smirking as he passes me a coffee I didn't ask for.

I grunt a quick thank-you anyway.

"You sick?" Cal asks, voice quieter now.

"No," I shoot back.

"You, uh, hittin' the sauce, boss?" Truitt narrows his eyes like he's about to stage an intervention.

"No," I clip.

They exchange a glance.

"Is the farm in trouble?" Cal asks.

"*No*," I say again. Firmer this time.

They're quiet for a beat, like they're waiting for something else. A crack in the armor. Some sign of weakness. Elaboration of any kind.

I give them nothing.

"Big day today. Believe it or not, fields dried out overnight," I say, already walking to the door. "Get moving, boys."

I head to my truck, pop the door, and linger for a second. The sun's barely over the trees, light stretching across the fields in long, gold fingers. Dew's still clinging to the grass.

And all I can think about is her.

I look toward the house.

Her curtains are closed. No sign of movement. Not that I'd know what to do if there was.

We left things awkward last night. Rushed and breathless and tangled and unfinished. I didn't say much after—not because I didn't want to. Because I didn't know what to say or how to say what I really wanted to say.

Looking back, that was disrespectful of me.

She deserves more than that. She deserves better than that.

I just don't know how to give it to her.

But I will. I'll learn.

Even if I have to figure it out the hard way.

Because she's already mine—she just doesn't know it yet.

20

Wren

The town square looks different in the morning. Quieter. Softer around the edges. The shops are just starting to open, and there's a hush over everything, like the town hasn't had its first cup of coffee yet.

I park in front of Iris & Ivy, Natalie Dinsmore's boutique, and take a second before I get out. Atticus is at day camp until four, which means I have seven hours of me-time and zero excuses to avoid being social.

I'm also in desperate need of a distraction because I've spent the past sixteen hours doing my best not to think about what happened in the shop with Hunter McCrae last night.

I failed, miserably.

Because it's all I've been thinking about.

The way he looked at me—like I was something he hadn't let himself want in a long time. The way he touched me—like it wasn't about sex: it was about need. The way he plunged himself deep inside me, urgent and punitive—like he was almost upset with himself for wanting me the way that he did. Of course, I don't know that any of this is true . . . I'm an author. I make up stories for a living. But last night could've easily been a scene from one of my books, and if he were the hero in my book, that's what he'd have been thinking.

I drag in a long, slow breath and let it go.

It was a release. That's all.

Nothing more.

I remind myself of that again as I walk through the glass door of Natalie's shop.

A little bell tinkles above me. The air inside smells like eucalyptus and vanilla, and Natalie herself is behind the counter, adjusting a mannequin in a gauzy linen romper.

She glances up, eyes lighting as a mile-wide grin captures her face. "Wren. Jensen. Shut. *Up.*"

"Hey, stranger." I stride her way, laughing. "It's been a minute."

"A minute? More like fifteen years," she says, breezing around the counter to give me a hug that smells like expensive shampoo and argan oil lotion. "God, you look amazing. You're even prettier than you were in your twenties, and I didn't think that was possible."

I smile. "Oh, stop. You're too sweet. And you? This place is adorable."

She waves a hand like she's swatting away a compliment but beams anyway. "Thanks. I've been open about two years now. I'm trying to keep it small and curated—you know, little capsule pieces, indie brands. Colton Valley doesn't always know what to do with me, but they're coming around. I like to treat every customer like they're my only customer. Everyone who walks in here gets the full Natalie treatment. Speaking of, could I interest you in some sparkling mineral water? Maybe some oolong jasmine tea?"

"I love that," I say, running my fingers along a display of straw hats and linen scarves. "And I'd love some tea. I might be here a while . . . you've got quite the place here and I haven't really shopped for myself in ages."

The last thing I bought was a seersucker dress I intended to wear on my honeymoon with Nick. After everything went down, buying myself things I didn't need suddenly didn't feel like a priority.

"I miss when you used to style me back in high school," I say, gently inspecting a rack of blouses. "I never had to think about what to wear. You'd come over on Sundays and put together all my outfits for the week."

Natalie laughs. "Styling people is still my favorite thing to do. Twenty years later, nothing's changed. I still drive a Honda Pilot. Newer model, of course. I still know every Alanis Morissette song by heart. And I still have terrible taste in men."

We chat for a few minutes—easy conversation about old classmates, local school board drama, the retired couple who just opened a smoothie place down the street. Nat's still single, which doesn't surprise me. She always had a rotation of admirers. Pretty, chatty, magnetic, she could sell ice to a polar bear.

"Where are you living now?" she asks, looping a necklace onto a bust near the register.

"Down on Riverstone. That white farmhouse near the river."

Natalie's head pops up. "Oh, I know exactly where that is."

"Of course you do," I say, chuckling. Natalie was also our prom queen and class president. I don't blame her for never leaving a town that's only ever been good to her. I try on a handful of outfits before checking out with three new tops, a peplum skirt, and a pair of denim shorts. "I'd stick around and shop more, but I've got a million things on my to-do list today. You free tonight? Atticus goes to bed early—usually around seven thirty. If you wanted to stop by . . . maybe bring a bottle and catch up? I feel like we've barely scratched the surface."

Her grin widens. "I'd love that."

Spending the evening doing mom things and playing outside with Atticus followed by catching up with Natalie means I'll be too busy to stare at Hunter's farmhouse. A little wine and some good conversation might keep me from thinking too hard about that moment in the shop that keeps looping in my brain like a scene from a movie I shouldn't have watched.

It didn't mean anything.

It was a thing that happened.

That doesn't mean it has to change anything.

And it won't.

21

Hunter

She's had company all night.

Some dark SUV pulled up outside her place just after dinner, windows tinted, undistinguishable silhouette behind the wheel. I told myself it was none of my business. Told myself to stop glancing toward her porch like some restless fool pacing inside his own skin.

But it didn't work.

Now it's been there for hours. At least three, by my count.

Her lights are on. Porch lights too. I can almost hear the sweet sound of her voice floating across the yard. Light, laughing, soft in that way it gets when she's had a glass or two.

I think of her ex, the one who left her on their wedding day. It's an unforgivable act in my book, but the thought of him chasing after her, trying to convince her he made a mistake, invades my thoughts tonight.

My insides burn, but it's not jealousy—it's something worse: the sick, sinking feeling of a missed opportunity.

All day, I've been thinking about what I should've said to her . . .

And I was going to head over tonight, but by the time I got home from the field, that SUV was already there.

It's almost eleven o'clock before the car finally pulls away. Taillights fade down the gravel road, and the quiet settles like dust after a storm. I didn't see Wren walk her visitor out, somehow I missed that. But after they're gone, she doesn't go inside.

She takes a seat on the swing, one leg curled beneath her, elbow on the armrest. She's nursing what looks like the last of a wineglass, the breeze playing with her hair. Her face is tilted up toward the sky, like she's watching stars only she can see—or lost in thought.

I should leave it.

It's late.

But I don't.

Without wasting another second, I snatch my truck keys. Two minutes later, I'm pulling into her driveway. She sits straighter when she sees me. I climb out, boots crunching on gravel, hands shoved in my back pockets because I don't trust them not to do something stupid—like reach for her without asking again.

She doesn't react when I step onto her porch. Just keeps swinging as she stares up at me with those sparkling, curious blues.

"I know it's late," I begin. My heart's pounding so hard, I feel it in my ears.

Wren turns her head, eyes a little glassy, lips curved into something that's almost a smile but not quite. "If this is about last night, you don't have to explain anything."

Her voice is calm. Measured. Almost too casual.

Maybe I had my chance and blew it.

Or maybe she thinks I'm just like every other guy who's disappointed her, so she's keeping me at an arm's length now.

Her gaze drops to her wineglass before she tips the rest into her mouth. One long sip. Then she sets the glass down on the little table beside her.

"What happened," I say anyway, ignoring the way her shoulders tense just slightly. "That wasn't my intention. Something came over me when I saw you and . . ."

She shakes her head. "Hunter, don't. Please. Don't make this weird. Don't make it a thing. It's—"

"No, I owe you an apology."

"You don't owe me *anything*," she says. Her voice is gentle but firm. "We barely know each other. We had sex. That's all. I'm not asking for a postmortem."

Her tone is breezy, but her eyes don't match it. There's something wistful in them.

"Here's the thing," she adds quietly, tucking her hair behind her ear. "You . . . you seem like the kind of person who could really hurt me. And maybe that's a strange thing to say because I hardly know you. But I know myself, and I know how you make me feel, and I just moved here and we're neighbors and I've had one hell of a year and I don't have the bandwidth for . . . whatever this is—or isn't."

I exhale through my nose, jaw tight. "I would never hurt you."

She gives me a sympathetic look before cocking her head. "You can't promise things like that. You barely know me."

She stands then, slowly, wrapping her arms around her middle as she leans against one of the porch posts.

"My friend tonight?" she adds. "She grew up here. She knows you. Says you've got a bit of a reputation."

I raise a brow. "Oh, yeah?"

"Yeah. Breaking hearts. Leaving before things get too serious. Or just never getting serious at all."

I almost laugh, and I don't waste my breath asking who it was either. "A lot of people here think they know me, Wren. Doesn't mean they do."

She shrugs. "Fair enough. But I'm not really in the market to be another name on some list. Yours or anyone else's."

Her words hit harder than I expect.

I try to imagine how she sees me. The grumpy neighbor. The rough-around-the-edges guy who can't get his act together long enough to want something real. The kind of guy who ignores her at a coffee shop, cuts our late-night conversation short, then takes her over the back of his tailgate like he's starving for air and she's his own personal oxygen supply.

I'm sure there's some truth mixed into some of the things she's heard about me, but it's different with her already. I can tell. I've never been this consumed by anyone—or anything. Except maybe land. And right now, I want her more than I've ever wanted an acre of land in my life.

"Regardless of anything you've heard," I say. "The whole casual thing? It's not me. I don't let a lot of people in. I'm picky with who I spend time with. If it's not working, I cut them loose. I don't want to waste anyone's time."

Her eyes flick up to mine, searching, contemplating.

"I can't get you out of my head," I tell her, voice lower now. "And I didn't know it was possible to feel something this intense over someone I hardly know. That's got to mean something, don't you think? You feel something too. I know you do. You wouldn't fight it so hard if you didn't."

A breath catches in her throat, and she looks away.

"I'm just as confused about this whole thing as you are," I admit, dragging a hand through my hair.

She huffs a quiet laugh. "Yeah. Well. I'm not confused. And I'll make it uncomplicated for you."

My chest tightens.

"I don't want anything from you," she says, firm and unwavering. "What happened was fun, but it can never happen again."

I stare at her. This conversation went a whole lot differently in my head when I planned it out a hundred times today.

"I should head inside," she whispers. "It's late."

"Yeah." I've never been good with words, and once again she has me at a loss for them.

She brushes past me, and I breathe her in—warm skin, wine, something soft and citrusy.

Her hand is on the door when she turns back just long enough to say, "Good night, Hunter. I appreciate you stopping by."

And then she's gone.

22

Wren

Colton Valley Tractor Supply on a Saturday morning smells like hay dust and motor oil and the ghost of something grilled last week out back.

Atticus is bouncing beside the cart like he's mainlining pure excitement—as he has been since his birthday the other day. He's wearing his "pony whisperer" T-shirt my parents got him, a faded green number with a crooked iron-on of a horse that he insists gives him special powers. We're here for grain and a few treats for Sugarplum—who he insists is part pony, part unicorn, part dog . . . however that works.

He's in that sweet spot where the novelty of our new, country-fied lifestyle is still fresh, and I imagine this trip to the farm store is basically rural Disney World with fluorescent lighting.

"I think she'd like the apple oat better than the alfalfa ones," he announces, holding up two bags of treats, one in each hand.

"You sure? Last week she spit out the apple oat ones."

"That's because I fed them to her *after* she'd already eaten carrots. Her palate was probably tired."

I try not to laugh. He's serious. So serious I can't even correct his use of the word "palate."

We're halfway down the aisle when Atticus suddenly freezes, eyes locked on something—or someone—behind me.

Then he's off like a shot. "Hey! You're the guy from the river!"

I turn just as Atticus barrels into Hunter McCrae, grinning like he just found out Santa is real *and* lives next door.

I haven't seen him for almost a week now. Not since he showed up at my place late that night, after Natalie left. But I'd be lying if I said I hadn't thought of him every hour of every day that's passed since then.

Hunter's holding a bag of fencing staples and looking mildly stunned, though not annoyed. If anything, he seems . . . charmed.

"Oh, hey, buddy," he says, offering a small smile. "You doing okay? Staying away from that river?"

Atticus nods fast. "Yeah! My mom says I was being reckless, but I didn't know it was gonna be deep there. You saved me. That was so cool. You're like a cowboy or a hero or something."

I catch up, heart suddenly in my throat. "Atticus . . ."

Hunter glances at me, then back at my son. "You got a pony, right? What's her name again?"

"Sugarplum." Atticus beams. "She's light tan with a white stripe on her nose and I brush her every day, and I'm trying to teach her to bow when I say 'majesty.'"

Hunter lets out a small chuckle, then squats to Atticus's level.

"You ever ride her?" he asks.

Atticus shakes his head. "Not yet. Mom says I'm not ready."

Hunter lifts a brow and glances at me, like he's waiting for confirmation. I give a tiny shrug.

"We don't have tack yet," I say. "And I have no clue what I'm doing."

"She's kinda short," Atticus adds. "I think I could just climb on the fence then jump on her back, but Mom says it's not safe without a saddle and stuff."

"She's not wrong," Hunter says, eyeing me for approval. "If you want, I could show you how to saddle her up sometime. I've got an old kid-size one in the barn. Might even still fit."

Atticus gasps like Hunter just offered him a ticket to the moon. "Really?!"

Hunter stands, eyes shifting to mine. "If it's okay with your mother, that is."

I hesitate.

Every instinct in me screams to say no, to keep a clean line between what's safe and what could potentially wreck our hearts all over again. But Atticus is looking at me like this is the best thing that's happened to him all week. And truth be told, I could use the help with the damn pony because I have no idea what I'm doing.

But still . . . I know how this goes. It starts with a few lessons and ends with Atticus crying into his pillow because someone else left, because someone else promised things they didn't mean to.

Atticus clasps his little hands together and gives me a pleading look.

"Sure," I give in. "That'd be . . . nice."

Atticus explodes into chatter, asking Hunter about sugar cubes and hoof oil and whether Sugarplum can be trained to pull a cart. He's clearly been watching too many YouTube videos, and that's on me.

I let him drift toward the feed bins, distracted by the rows of colorful bags, before I turn to Hunter.

"What are you doing?" I keep my voice low.

His brow furrows. "What do you mean?"

"With Atticus."

His mouth tightens. "I don't understand what you're implying. He came up to me. I wasn't going to ignore him."

"You're charming him," I say. "You're using him to get to me."

Hunter blinks like I just slapped him. "What?"

I fold my arms. "Don't pretend like you don't know how this works. You're good with him. He likes you. You're trying to use the horse thing to be around me more. You know exactly what you're doing."

His expression shifts—something raw and frustrated flashing across it.

"I'm not that guy," he says quietly. "I don't use people. Especially not kids."

He looks down the aisle toward Atticus, then back at me. "You really think I'd do that?"

"I've seen it before. More than once."

He exhales hard through his nose, like he's trying to keep something in. He almost looks physically wounded, making me second-guess my harsh accusation. I'm on the verge of apologizing, my mind dancing between justifying my protectiveness versus being open to the idea of Hunter just trying to be a good neighbor.

But before I can make up my mind, he's striding off, ruffling Atticus's hair as he walks by. He mentions something about how he'll show him how to tack up a saddle next week if the weather holds. And then he's gone—heading to the checkout, leaving me standing in the aisle like *I'm* the one who just crossed a line.

Maybe I did.

But I've got a son to protect.

If not from Hunter, then from me—from my history of choosing the wrong man every time.

23

Hunter

The helmet's a little big, but I manage to rig it so it holds tight. He's got it strapped on like a soldier going into battle, his little chest puffed out and eyes wild with excitement. He's grinning so wide I half expect it to split his face clean in two.

"Like this?" he asks, gripping the reins like he's seen in a movie.

"Just like that," I say, tightening the girth strap and double-checking the stirrups. "You're a natural."

"Sugarplum likes me," he declares, patting her neck. "She only makes that snorty sound when she's happy."

I bite the inside of my cheek to keep from smiling. Kid's got theories for everything. He reminds me a bit of myself at that age, talking to anyone who'd listen. Over the years, I traded my yapping for quietude, but I was quite the social butterfly back in my day.

Behind us, Wren leans against the gate, arms crossed, a lazy breeze tugging strands of hair loose around her face. She's in cutoff jean shorts and a boxy white tee, but there's something about the way she stands—effortless, strong, all eyes and fire and quiet grace—that makes it hard to look away. I've stolen as many glances as I can from my periphery, but I imagine she'll notice, if I don't stop being greedy about it.

Atticus trots a few paces in the dusty corral, wobbly but determined.

And all I can think about is the irony of it all: same corral where I learned to ride, same posts, same fence lines. I must've been about Atticus's age when my old man tossed me up on a mare named Jenny and told me not to fall off unless I wanted to eat dirt.

Back then, I used to picture raising my own kids here someday.

A wife. Maybe two or three little ones, tagging along behind me in overalls and muddy boots. I used to think it was a guarantee—just a matter of time.

But life had other plans.

And then two decades later, Wren shows up—bright and bold and warm and also infuriatingly stubborn—and somehow makes this place feel like it could still be home for someone other than the ghosts of my past.

"He's doing great," she says, pushing off the gate as I come to stand beside her.

"He's got good instincts," I say. "Braver than most grown men I know."

"He gets that from me," she says, smirking.

I nod slowly. "Explains a lot."

She side-eyes me, mock offense dancing in her expression.

"He likes you," she adds after a beat. "Probably more than I want him to."

I glance at her, sensing the shift in her voice.

"If you hurt me," she says, quiet now. "That's one thing." She looks at me then—really looks at me. "But don't hurt my son."

There's nothing flirtatious in her tone. No teasing. Just the raw, protective edge of a mother who's seen what happens when people walk away.

I nod once, serious. "I won't."

She watches me a moment longer before the tension softens slightly.

God, she's good. Good in the way that gets under your skin and makes a home there before you realize what's happening. Good in the way she mothers that boy, the way she watches him like he's her whole world.

It's sexy as hell, but I keep that to myself—for now.

"I need to start dinner soon," she says, glancing toward the house. "I'd ask you to stay but, you know. You made it pretty clear you don't like my cooking."

"That's not true," I say. "I never said I didn't like it."

"Oh?" she challenges, brow lifting.

"I said I'd choke it down," I add, mouth tugging into a grin. "If it means I get to see you a little longer."

She laughs—really laughs—and the sound does something to my insides I can't explain.

"Laying it on thick tonight, aren't we?" She cocks her head to one side. "A little overkill, don't you think?"

Maybe.

But I don't care.

I've never had a woman stuck in my head like this before. Never found myself rerouting my entire day just to steal a few minutes in her orbit.

And the more she resists me, the more bound and determined I am to make her mine.

She has no idea how good her life is about to get.

24

WREN

The house is quiet after dinner. Atticus is tucked in, freshly bathed and sun-drunk from his long afternoon with Hunter and Sugarplum. He must've ridden for hours. Tonight he fell asleep mid-sentence, something about building her a stable out of sticks and duct tape. I pressed a kiss to his forehead, pulled the covers to his chin, and stood in the doorway for longer than necessary, just watching him breathe.

I'm making my way back downstairs when I hear water running and dishes clinking. Stopping at the bottom step, I peek into the kitchen.

Hunter McCrae is washing my dishes.

He's got his sleeves rolled up, his stance relaxed, like this is just something he does.

Like it's normal. Like *we're* normal.

I fold my arms and lean against the doorframe.

"You're still here," I finally say.

He glances over his shoulder. "What, like I had somewhere else to be?"

When he turns back to rinse a plate, I swear I see the faintest smile playing on his lips.

We finish the rest together—quietly, efficiently, without any of the weird tension I expected. It's a kind of silence that's easy, not empty. Natural, almost.

When the last dish is in the rack, I reach for a towel and dry my hands.

"I feel like I need to pay you for your services today," I say. "What do I owe you?"

Hunter tosses the damp dish rag on the counter. "Come outside and talk to me and I'll consider it even."

I squint before pressing the back of my hand to his forehead. "You feeling okay?"

He captures my wrist, eyes locked on mine. "Haven't felt okay since the day you walked into my world and turned it upside down, honey."

My stomach flips.

"You're romanticizing me." I pull my hand back with a smirk. "I'll talk to you outside, but don't kiss me."

He drags his finger across his chest, marking an X. "I promise I won't kiss you."

We step out onto the porch, the night wrapping around us like a worn quilt. No wine. No beer. Just the creak of the swing and a million stars overhead. The seat shifts beneath us as we settle in, and Hunter leans back, arm stretched along the backrest, close but not quite touching me.

"So tell me about that idiot who left you at the altar," he says out of nowhere, like it's a question he's been waiting forever to ask.

"That's . . . random."

"Not at all." His brows lift as he stares straight ahead, confident. "I want to know how he fumbled you so I don't make the same mistake."

I fight a laugh and shoot him a look. "You won't make the same mistake."

"How do you know?"

"Because you won't have the opportunity," I cut back. "Nice try, though. That was a good line. I should use that in a book."

"Fine. I'll give you exclusive rights to use that line in a book—but only if you tell me what happened."

I wait a beat, exhale, then say, "The day of our wedding, his high school girlfriend messaged him on Facebook."

"Why was he checking Facebook on his wedding day? Shouldn't he have been . . . I don't know, doing more important things?"

"That's a great question, and I don't particularly need to know the answer anymore."

"Did he get back with her?"

"Don't know, don't care," I say, leaving out any mention of Nick texting me the other week. I didn't respond, and he hasn't reached out since. There's nothing he could possibly say to change how I feel about him and what went down. As callous as it may sound, Nick is dead to me. "And he didn't technically leave me at the altar. I was in the parking lot outside the church. With my dad. Minutes from being walked down the aisle."

A quiet beat rests between us.

"I'd written him this beautiful love letter for that morning. Had my maid of honor, Reese, deliver it to his hotel suite along with these platinum cuff links I had custom made with his monogram. Anyway, that letter . . . poured my heart and soul into it. It was more personal than anything I'd ever written—I mean, I thought I was writing to the man I was going to spend the rest of my life with." I suck in my cheeks, the phantom sting of foolishness sending a flash of heat to them. "When I spotted him in the church parking lot before our ceremony, I thought it was odd he wasn't inside, waiting for me at the altar. He wasn't smiling. Didn't seem happy to see me. His expression alone was a punch to the gut. Before he said a word . . . I knew. And then he handed me a folded-up piece of paper, a letter written on hotel stationery. Told me he was sorry. Got into his car and drove away."

"Jesus." Hunter massages the back of his neck before blowing a breath between his lips. I wait for him to ask what the letter said, but he doesn't, and I'm grateful for that because I don't even remember. It was some hastily scribbled half-assed apology about how he realized he's still in love with his ex and marrying me wouldn't be right.

"Cliché, right?" I shake my head. "Thing is, it hurt. It was humiliating. But the worst part was what it did to my son. Atti thought Nick was going to be his dad." I stare down at my hands, wringing them. "I'll never let anyone do that to him again."

Hunter's quiet for a while. "I don't blame you. Anyone with half a brain would feel the same."

I glance at him. "You said once that why you're single was a story for another day. And, well, it's another day and I want the story."

He exhales slowly, eyes still on the stars.

"We've had a pretty good night, don't you think?" he asks. "Let's not go ruining it."

That just makes me more curious.

He must see it on my face, because he smirks and adds, "Let's talk about you instead. I kinda like talking about you. You're a helluva lot more interesting than me."

I roll my eyes at his compliment before adding, "You're deflecting."

"Maybe a little." He pauses. "It's just that I had you pegged wrong from the start."

"How so?"

"I thought you were this stuck-up city transplant with too much attitude and no sense of grit. Someone who'd flake the second it got hard. But you're not. You're tough as hell and you're soft where it matters. You're sunshine and a rainstorm at the same time. And the way you love that boy. You're—" He stops, like he's editing himself. "You're magnetic."

I swallow hard.

"No one's ever gotten in my head the way you have," he says. "I'm still trying to make sense of it." A moment passes, then he adds, "And after the other week, I got one taste of you and now I can't stop thinking about it."

I give him a look. "You were probably just horny. You don't date, remember? I bet you haven't gotten laid in a while."

He rolls his eyes, brushing my theory off. "If you knew how obsessed I'm becoming with you, you'd think I had a real problem."

I snort. "Okay, *Romeo*. I'm also stealing *that* line for a book. It's too good not to use."

He groans, tipping his head back. "Wren."

"I'm serious. You have a way with words," I say, nudging his knee. "I'm using the shop scene too."

He gives me a side-eye, not amused. Panicked, almost. Heavy on the silence, like the thought of it sucked all the air from his lungs.

"I'm kidding," I add quickly. "You're just . . . giving me the kind of inspiration I haven't had in a long time. Seems wrong to waste it. The stuff I write about in books is the very same stuff you've been saying and doing. You're a real-life romance hero, and I don't think you even realize it. That's the crazy part. Sometimes I feel like I wrote you into existence."

His eyes soften at that, and he reaches for my hand but doesn't take it, just rests his fingers nearby.

The air is dense with unspoken things, but neither of us moves to fill it.

Eventually, he checks his watch and stands.

"I should head home. Have to run my truck to the mechanic early in the morning. Bad DEF sensor," he says. This time it doesn't feel like a made-up excuse, and I don't even know what DEF is. "Thanks for dinner. Best spaghetti and meatballs I've ever had."

Boxed Barilla pasta. Jarred Prego sauce. Frozen store-brand meatballs.

"You're welcome, bad liar." I rise, too, shoving my hands in my back pockets.

I walk him to the edge of the driveway, a few feet from his parked truck. We don't hug. We don't kiss. But the energy between us is loud and undeniable.

Once I'm inside and the door closes behind me, I head straight for my notebook.

And I write another letter.

Again the words come easily—easier than ever. Maybe it's because they're from the heart. I'd always thought fiction was easier to write. It was less personal. Now I'm not so sure. I'm hoping it won't be long before I'm back to writing romance books, but until then . . . this feels like bridging the gap—in the best way.

> Hunter—
>
> I told myself I wasn't going to write to you or about you, that I was done fantasizing about some idealized version I crafted in my head. But here I am once again holding onto hope I've got no business gripping this tight.
>
> What is this?
>
> What are we doing?
>
> I keep thinking about the way you looked tonight, casually standing at my sink, sleeves rolled up, hands in my dishwater like it was the most normal thing in the world.
>
> I also keep thinking about how you watched Atticus ride that pony like it mattered, making sure his helmet was tight, that he knew all the commands. Teaching him what to do if he ever got bucked off. You genuinely cared about my son's safety.
>
> Additionally, I can't stop thinking about how easy it is to talk to you when I'm not trying hard not to. How you can come across so cold and aloof to everyone else yet let me peek behind the curtain of your world is . . . fascinating.
>
> I'm dying to know what it means.
>
> I want to stop writing about you, but every time I stop, I find myself right back here, a blue-inked pen pressed hard against these lined pages, my handwriting

barely able to keep up with my mind because it's moving so fast.

Tonight you said you pegged me all wrong.

I'm beginning to wonder, though, if it's the other way around.

And I'm not sure if that excites me . . . or scares me.

—Wren

25

Hunter

"Chapter fifty-two. Charlie." A woman's voice plays over my AirPods.

Earlier this morning, I got a wild hair to listen to one of Wren's romance books on audio. I'm in this damned tractor all day, every day, so I've got plenty of time.

The narrator's reading from *The Summer She Forgot*, some big-city tale with a prickly heroine and a broken billionaire hero with secrets that are yet to be revealed. I downloaded it this morning out of morbid curiosity, figuring I'd get bored after five minutes and switch back to my usual lineup of ag podcasts and classic rock. Instead, I'm fifty-two chapters deep and fighting the urge to slow my planting pace just so the story doesn't end before I'm ready.

The narrator's voice is smooth and warm, like early coffee or fresh linen on sun-baked skin. She paces the narration like she's lived every syllable, coaxing each emotion to the surface and dragging me along for the ride.

"He kissed her like he was sorry. Like he'd waited his whole life to be that close to someone, and he was terrified of getting it wrong."

My grip on the throttle tightens.

Jesus.

How is that sexy and sad at the same time? It stirs something in me, like Wren wrote that line just for me, though I know she didn't.

I've got one mile left of this field before I have to move equipment. Hopefully another week or so of planting after that. No more long days living in these machines. No more excuses to keep my distance. And maybe that's a good thing.

Or maybe it's the worst damn idea I've had in years.

Because I'm already too fixated on Wren.

And she's the kind of woman you don't let yourself want if you plan on keeping your life uncomplicated.

But I do want her.

More than I want to admit.

Hell, I've been half-crazed since she showed up on my porch in that yellow sundress with those delicious cookies, big doe eyes, and that hopeful smile. She called herself my "new neighbor," like that was supposed to soften the fact that she bought the one piece of land I spent years trying to acquire. But the moment she handed me that warm Tupperware, I almost forgot all about it. Forgot about planting. Forgot about Rich. Forgot about how I don't trust most people on principle.

And Atticus?

That kid's a trip. Funny little dude with a big personality and a heart the size of Nebraska. We planted some wildflower seeds together last weekend while Wren was doing some more unpacking. Said he wanted to "help the bees." I don't know a single five-year-old who gives a shit about pollinators, but there he was—tiny cowboy boots, dirt under his nails, yelling at a bumblebee like it was late to work.

I like the kid.

He makes me feel . . . lighter.

You can't fake that kind of joy.

He reminds me not to take life so seriously.

If I didn't already know better, I'd say he's getting to me, which means I need to be careful. Wren's been through enough. She doesn't need some lonely farmer playing hero just because he's bored and emotionally constipated.

"She didn't trust anyone, and yet she let him touch her like she was already broken. Like maybe if he held her tight enough, the pieces would fit together again."

I shift in my seat, running a hand across my mouth.

Damn.

She's good.

Too good.

I try to picture Wren at her desk, cross-legged in front of some open window, pen between her teeth and laptop glowing, highlighting all those pretty features I've studied more times than I care to admit. I bet she writes barefoot and in pajamas. I bet she hums to herself when she gets stuck. I bet she laughs at her own jokes.

And I bet no one's told her lately just how talented she is.

How magnetic.

How real.

I don't even have her number—not that I'd know what to say if I did. I'd probably come off gruff and awkward. "Hey, I liked your cookies. And I like your voice. And your kid. And the way you wear your hair like it's no big deal but it is."

No.

Better to play it cool. Maybe find an excuse to drop by. See if she needs help fixing her garden fence or hanging a screen door. Something neighborly. Something safe.

"You can't love someone into healing. But maybe, if you're lucky, you can make them feel less alone while they figure it out."

I kill the engine and lean forward, elbows on my knees.

The woman's voice trails off as the chapter ends, leaving a quiet ache in its place.

I'm screwed.

Fully, completely, royally screwed.

26

Wren

Friday night consists of me, Atticus, and a bowl of half-stale popcorn.

We're curled up on the worn leather couch in the living room, a stack of mismatched blankets piled over our laps, watching *Cars 2* for what has to be the hundredth time. I'm pretty sure I could recite the script by memory at this point, which probably isn't the flex I think it is.

He's snuggled against my side, warm and squishy, the faint smell of his lavender shampoo still clinging to his hair. He doesn't even like cars, not really. He just likes watching Mater be a "dumbo" and Lightning McQueen be a "show-off." His words, not mine.

Halfway through the movie, he shifts under the blanket and looks up at me with those sleepy, clear-blue eyes of his. "Mom?"

"Hmm?"

"When can I see Hunter again?" he asks.

The question hits like a flick to the temple—sharp and unexpected.

I pull my attention from the screen, my heart doing that annoying little stutter thing it does whenever his name comes up. "Hunter?"

"Yeah. He's funny," he says. "And he knows everything about farms. Like, everything. I miss him."

"We just met him, buddy," I say. "He's our neighbor."

Atticus squints, his nose scrunching like I just told him two plus two equals seven. "I know, but . . . is he ever coming over again?"

I smooth a hand over his still-damp curls, trying to keep my face neutral. "He's pretty busy running his farm, but I'm sure we'll see him around."

Atticus turns his attention back to the movie, but the way he asked stays lodged in my chest like a splinter I can't dig out.

There was no weight to his question, no hidden desire for a dad or some father figure. Just innocent curiosity. A kid asking when he's going to see the cool guy who knows about tractors and wildflowers.

I've been so busy putting up walls around us, labeling Hunter as nothing more than "the neighbor," that it never occurred to me maybe . . . just maybe . . . I'm being too protective. Not that I'm looking to pawn my son off on some man—not after everything we've been through.

But still.

Atticus deserves more than a helicopter mom with a keyboard for a best friend.

He deserves someone to show him how to bait a hook, fix a busted fence, and teach him the names of trees just by the shape of their leaves.

Hunter's that kind of man. The kind who knows things. The kind who does things. And despite his tendency to brood and scowl, he likes my kid. I saw it in the way he humored Atticus's never-ending questions, how he knelt in the dirt to plant wildflower seeds with him like it wasn't a waste of time.

No man's ever done that for my son before. Not even Nick. Especially not Nick. Nick only ever took him to do the things he wanted to do—hockey games, golf outings, live music festivals. Atticus wasn't into any of that, but he was always tickled to be his sidekick.

By the time the credits roll and Atticus is fast asleep on my shoulder, I've decided I'm possibly overthinking this, overcompensating for all the things that went wrong before. Maybe it isn't fair to hold Hunter accountable for the so-called crimes of the men who came before him.

I carry my son upstairs and tuck him into bed, brushing a stray lock of hair from his forehead before I head back down.

Tonight, the house is the kind of quiet that's heavy and drags your thoughts to places they don't need to go. I need some fresh air, so I make my way to the porch, flipping on the switch to the old carriage light next to the front door. The bulb buzzes faintly, casting a warm halo over the steps.

Last time I sat out here with this light on, Hunter showed up out of nowhere. For all I know, that thing might be some kind of Bat-Signal for grumpy blue-eyed farmers.

More than likely it isn't, but I sit down on the porch swing, curling my knees to my chest, my gaze flicking to the ribbon of gravel road just past the trees. The moon's thin and crooked tonight, hanging low in the sky like it's watching and waiting too.

I don't know what I'm waiting for.

Maybe nothing.

Maybe everything.

Either way, the light stays on.

Just in case.

27

Hunter

I wake up in the cab of my tractor with a crick in my neck and my mouth tasting like morning breath and regret.

6:04 a.m.

I must've dozed off sometime around three, after wrapping up the south field. I told myself I'd rest my eyes for just a minute, let the engine idle while I mustered up the energy to climb out and drive home, but that was three hours ago, and the only thing that cooled was my body to the point I can't feel my damn fingers.

I rub my eyes, kick the engine back to life, use the wipers to scrape the dew off the glass, and ease the planter into position for the last twenty-acre stretch. If the rain holds off, I'll be done by noon. Should've been done two weeks ago. Late is better than never.

The cab still smells like coffee, sweat, and the apple-scented air freshener Truitt stuck in here last month. Said the place "smelled like dead animals and armpits," and he wasn't wrong.

I pull up my audiobook app and cue another Wren book. I finished the last one yesterday, and now the only thing I want are her words in my head. They're soothing. Calming. They make me think. Make me feel a lot of things I haven't felt in ages. This one's called *One Last First Kiss.*

I started it last night when I was half-delirious from the dark, the solitude, and the sound of my own head echoing too loud. Thought I'd listen to a chapter, maybe two, and then switch to music when I got bored—but five chapters in, I couldn't turn it off.

The woman writes like she sees things nobody else does. The way people work. The way they want. She's clever about it, sharp in her observations, but not in a way that feels smug or showy. She's soft and strong in equal measure. Even in the words she writes, there's this push-pull, like she wants to carry the whole damn world on her back but is quietly waiting for someone to offer to carry her for once.

I get that.

I've been the same way my whole life. Never needed anyone. Told myself I was better for it. Stronger. Smarter. Wore it like a badge of honor. But lately I'm starting to think that's just something lonely people say to make themselves feel better about being alone.

I'd never admit it out loud, but I'm starting to think it'd be nice to be needed . . .

. . . by her.

And not for fence repairs or tractor rides. Not for country life lessons or heavy lifting. But for her. The real her. The messy, complicated, contradicting, maddeningly beautiful woman behind those sparkly indigo eyes, her contagious grin, and that stubborn pride. The woman who writes love stories for a living but pretends like she's not looking for love herself.

Sometimes I think we're two sides of the same coin.

I click the play button, the narrator's voice coming through my AirPods, filling my head and wrapping around me like morning fog.

Wish I could bottle every last one of her words and carry them with me everywhere I go.

If I can't have her—yet—this is almost the next best thing.

28

Wren

By the time Natalie and I squeeze into a table at the Tipsy Turtle, my senses are already overloaded and the bottom of my heels stick like Velcro against the floor.

The place is packed and smells vaguely like fryer grease, spilled beer, and men whose deodorant clocked off the job hours ago. It's the only bar in town, so naturally every soul with a pulse has crammed themselves inside tonight. The walls are lined with neon beer signs and old taxidermy. A forgotten jukebox in the corner flashes like it's still 1995. The parking lot is filled with Polaris RANGERs in every size and color, and every third person is wearing camo like there's an open season on alcohol.

It's perfect.

And downtown Des Moines could never.

Natalie flags down the server and orders us a round of vodka sodas while I peel off my denim jacket, already regretting my choice of long sleeves. I dressed for the cooler weather that hits on these late spring nights, but in here, it might as well be subtropical.

"You're officially back." She grins. "You can't call yourself a Colton Valley girl again until you've sweated through your bra at the Tipsy Turtle at least once."

"Is that the town motto?" I tease.

"It should be."

We're mid-catch-up when two women approach our table—both blond, perky, and painted in enough self-tanner to survive a long winter underground. Natalie recognizes them immediately.

"Hey, girls," she says, gesturing to me. "This is Wren. She's the one I told you about. The one who charmed the uncharmable farmer."

Both their faces change, eyes wide, lips curving into the kind of knowing smirks that say they're very aware of who she means.

"No shit? You're the one who charmed Hunter McCrae?" one of them asks, not even trying to hide her intrigue. She leans against our table, resting her chin on the top of her hand. "Tell me all your secrets. Teach me your ways."

I try to wave it off. "We're just neighbors."

"Mm-hmm," the other one sings, shooting me a look like *Sure, Jan.*

They peel off before I can correct the record, and Natalie chuckles into her drink.

"You're kinda famous around here now and not because you write books," she says. "Better get used to being 'Hunter's neighbor' for the foreseeable future."

"We're not a thing," I clarify, because that feels important to say out loud, even though I'm the only one who needs convincing.

She arches a brow. "You know he's the most eligible, most grumpy, most off-limits man in this county, right?"

"Maybe I have a type."

"Apparently you do. But just so you know, you've got *another* admirer tonight."

I blink. "What?"

She tips her chin across the room, where an objectively attractive man has been posted up at the bar, gaze locked on me like he's already decided how the night's going to end. Tall, built, wavy dark blond hair, dimpled smile. He's dressed like half the other guys here—jeans, boots, some kind of farm cap—but he wears it with a little more swagger.

"That's Cole Benton," Natalie says, sitting straighter. "Runs a huge farm on the west side of the county. We went to school with his sister, Cara. I don't know if you remember her. She was always really quiet. Anyway, he's single, stupid rich, and allergic to long-term commitment. Just a heads-up on that."

I barely have time to register any of that before he pushes off his stool and saunters our way, beer in hand, confidence dripping off him like sweat.

"I hear you're the new author in town," he says, stopping just shy of my knee.

"That's what you're leading with?" I say, blinking up at him.

"I figured the stories were exaggerated, but . . ." His gaze slides down, then back up, and I fight the urge to cross my arms. "I don't think they did you justice."

He's charming—in a cringey way, I'll give him that. A Des Moines girl would eat him for breakfast. This sort of thing would never work there. But here? His smile is sharp and smooth, the kind that's probably gotten him out of speeding tickets and into an awful lot of beds.

"Can I buy you a drink?" he asks, voice slick.

"I'm good, thanks," I tell him, holding up my half-full glass.

He sits anyway, plopping onto the seat beside me, elbows on his knees like we're already mid-conversation. "You always this hard to impress?"

"Only when I'm not trying to be impressed."

Natalie lets out a low laugh beside me, covering her mouth.

"You write those . . . dirty books . . . don't you?" Cole asks, leaning in closer like we're sharing a secret.

"Contemporary romance novels," I say. "Not erotica, if that's what you're assuming. There's a difference. Not that there's anything wrong with writing erotica. Just setting the record straight."

Regardless, he gives me a look like he's just caught me red-handed stealing from the smut shelf at the library.

"Should've known a woman that sexy would be a writer," he says, practically drooling from the corner of his mouth. If I had to guess, Cole's about six beers in and the night is young. "Bet you've got quite the imagination."

I force a polite smile, already over it.

I don't want to smell his cheap cologne or catch another whiff of his stale beer breath.

"What do I gotta do to get you on my arm tonight?" he asks, flashing a grin like it's the most reasonable question in the world.

"I'm not looking for anything," I say, decisive.

"Oh come on. Doesn't have to be serious," he shoots back, his knee knocking into mine like it's intentional. "Just a little fun."

"I'm not into casual," I say.

His smile falters for half a second before he tries again, leaning closer. His breath smells like bourbon and bravado.

"Tell you what," he says, "I'll put you on my payroll. How's a hundred grand a year sound? You hang on my arm, smile pretty, let me show you off, keep my bed warm on those lonely nights. That's your only job."

I laugh, because I can't not. "You serious right now?"

He shrugs like it's nothing. "Easiest money you'll ever make."

I shake my head, an incredulous grin stretching despite myself. "It'd take a lot more than that to make me want to be with someone who thinks they can buy me."

His grin fades, and the cheap charm wafting off him a second ago vanishes like a snapped light switch.

"Please," he sneers, speaking between clenched teeth like I suddenly disgust him. "You're just a smut writer. *I'd* be doing *you* a favor."

I open my mouth, but Natalie's already shooting up, standing between us like she's about to throw hands in the middle of the Tipsy Turtle.

"Okay, time for you to get the fuck out of here, Cole," she says, jabbing a finger at his chest. "Go harass someone else."

Cole throws his hands up, muttering something under his breath before slinking off toward the bar like the coward he is.

I sit there, stunned, heart pounding.

Natalie sits beside me again, her mouth tight. "All men suck."

"Yeah," I whisper, but I'm only half listening because my mind's somewhere else.

On someone else.

Hunter.

He doesn't suck.

At least not yet.

Not so far.

He's rough, sure. Grumpy as hell. But he's never once treated me like I was less than. He's never once looked at me like I was a thing to win or buy or collect.

I stare down into my drink, swishing the ice.

I'm not ready for love. And I'm definitely not looking.

But if I ever gave someone a chance again . . . maybe it'd be him.

Not now.

Not yet.

But maybe someday.

Maybe.

29

Hunter

I catch a glimpse of them on my way to the shop Sunday night—Wren and Atticus in the yard, Sugarplum trotting slow circles around the front pasture while the boy bounces and beams like he's just won the damn lottery and a Disney cruise at the same time.

I ease my truck to the side of the gravel road and kill the engine, already halfway out the door before I realize I don't have a real reason to stop—not beyond the fact that I haven't seen her in days and I'm hankering for a Wren fix like an addict anxious for his next hit.

She waves when she sees me, and I wave back, trudging through the ditch and up the side of her drive. Today she's in cutoff jean shorts and a white Iowa State T-shirt, her hair in some messy braid that's all but coming undone. She looks like a warm evening. Soft. Uncomplicated. The kind of easy beauty you don't see coming.

"Hey there, neighbor," she says, warm and receptive.

I nod toward Atticus, who's trying to steer Sugarplum like she's a trick pony and not a sleepy lawn ornament. "Looks like the little man's living his best life."

"He's obsessed," she says, her eyes soft. "I'm thinking about finding him some leather chaps. He won't stop asking for them. I don't even know if they come in his size."

"He'll want a belt buckle the size of Texas next," I say. "This is only the beginning."

She chuckles, and I tuck my hands in my back pockets to keep from reaching for her. My palms itch and ache, longing to touch her soft skin and brush that wayward strand of hair off her brow.

When Atticus guides Sugarplum to the far side of the yard, I drop my voice. "How was your weekend?"

Wren shrugs, her smile fading. "Eventful."

"Yeah?"

"Had a girls' night out with one of my old high school friends."

"That explains it. You hungover?"

"Not exactly," she says, eyes glittering with something unspoken. "Do you know a guy named Cole Benton?"

Every muscle in my body tenses. "Too well and I wish I didn't. Why?"

She scratches the back of her neck, looking away for a second. "Ran into him at the Tipsy Turtle. He, uh, propositioned me, and then he insulted me."

I stare, waiting for the punch line. When it doesn't come, my fists clench tight at my sides. "Propositioned?"

"He offered to put me on his payroll for a hundred grand," she says with a half laugh, like she's still trying to believe it herself. "Said all I had to do was keep his bed warm and let him show me off. I told him to shove it. Well, my friend did. I was . . . too stunned to speak."

My vision blurs at the edges. I didn't think I had it in me to go full caveman over a woman, but I'm two seconds away from driving to his acreage on the west side of the county and introducing Cole's teeth to my knuckles. It wouldn't be the first time I've wanted to do that, but now I'd actually have good reason to.

I don't say anything, just breathe slow and stare past her shoulder, watching Atticus circle back around.

She steps closer, studying me. "Why are you looking like that? All pensive."

I shake my head, jaw tight. "Guy's a piece of shit, that's all."

She waves it off, like it's not a big deal. "It's fine. We scared him off. Sent him running back to his buddies with his tail tucked. It was actually pretty funny."

"It's not fine," I mutter, eyes locked on her. "Cole's got a reputation. Ruined more than a few marriages around here. Pays off his girlfriends to keep their mouths shut and look pretty until he's done using 'em. Guy like that gives men like me a bad name."

Her brows pull together. "Men like you?"

I don't answer because I'm not even sure what I mean by that. All I know is the thought of Cole Benton looking at her like she's a prize to buy makes me want to burn something down.

She senses the shift in me, because she changes the subject—asks about planting, about the weather coming in next week, about anything that isn't Cole Benton or what I'd do to him if he tried that shit again.

But even as I answer her, even as I watch Atticus giggle and shout from atop that lazy pony, my mind's already made up.

It's only a matter of time before I run into Cole again.

And when I do?

We're having words.

30

Wren

Atticus is starting to slump forward on Sugarplum, his little legs barely gripping the pony's sides, and I can tell by the way she keeps glancing back at him—disapproving and disinterested—that she's about done with her job for the day.

"Come on, bud," I call. "Time to wrap it up."

He groans but turns her around, guiding her back toward the barn with exaggerated sadness, like he's leading a dying soldier to her final resting place. I hide my smile. He's nothing if not dramatic, especially when he's tired.

Hunter watches the whole thing, quiet, observant, hands tucked in his back pockets like always. The sky behind him is peach and lavender, the sun dragging itself down past the hills, and for a minute I just stand there appreciating the view—the man, the sky, the whole moment.

I'm still thinking about his reaction to my Cole Benton story. It's as if it offended him on some personal level, like the proposition was an insult to *him*, not me—and that makes no sense.

Why would he care that much?

We're just neighbors.

Just two people who share a fence line and the occasional awkward conversation.

Still, I'm enjoying this. Hunter's presence alone has a weird way of softening the space around me, like the air stretches out just a little warmer when he's near, making it a little easier to breathe.

But the day's catching up to me, and Atticus is covered in dust, which means bath time and bedtime and the never-ending gauntlet of the nighttime routine is waiting.

I sigh. "I should probably get inside. Get Atticus fed and cleaned up."

Hunter nods, but there's a flicker of disappointment in his eyes. He doesn't say anything, though. Just rocks back on his heels like he's making himself leave when he'd rather not.

I walk him to his truck, the air getting cooler with every step, gravel crunching beneath our shuffling, dragging feet.

When we get to the driver's side, he stops, turning to face me. His eyes trail from mine to my mouth and back again, and for a second I forget how to stand still.

"Been meaning to ask . . . can I get your number?" His brows are lifted, his eyes hopeful. In this moment, he isn't intimidating or gruff for once. He's almost vulnerable.

I cock my head. "Hunter, I told you. I'm not looking for a relationship right now."

His lips twitch like he expected that answer. "That's not why I'm asking."

"No?"

He shakes his head, slow and sure.

"You've been gone a long time, which means you're practically new here. You don't know how things work yet. A lot of people are gonna try and take advantage of that." His gaze pins me in place, serious and certain. "I promise you, Wren, I'm not one of them. I just want you to have my number in case you guys ever need anything."

The way he says it, low and steady, like it's a vow, makes my stomach dip.

I give a small, almost reluctant nod. "Okay. Yeah. That'd be . . . smart. I should give you mine . . . just so you have it."

I rattle off my number, and he plugs it into his phone, his thumbs moving slower than necessary like he's buying himself a few more seconds before he has to leave.

When he's done, he slides his phone in his pocket, eyes meeting mine again. There's something in them I can't read. Something he's holding back. Or maybe I'm seeing what I want to see. I've done that in the past more times than I'd ever admit.

"Wait," I say, reaching for my own phone. "I should grab your number too."

He rattles it off before reaching for the driver's side handle.

"Good night, Wren," he says before shutting the door.

"Good night, Hunter."

I watch him climb inside, wait for the engine to roar to life, and stand there longer than I need to, longer than I should, until his taillights disappear down the road.

31

Hunter

It's Monday morning, and the shop smells like burnt coffee because Truitt got here first today.

I'm crouched next to one of the sprayers, covered in hydraulic fluid and trying to replace an O-ring, when Cal strolls in late, like he owns the place.

"You look like you're getting sleep for once," Cal says, grabbing a wrench off the wall. "What's her name?"

"Jesus," I mutter, twisting the valve harder than necessary.

"He does look well rested, doesn't he? He's got that look," Truitt adds. "You know. Distracted. Happy but irritated about it. Like a guy who doesn't want to admit he's catching feelings."

I wipe the sweat from my brow with my forearm. "Last I checked, I'm not paying you two to stand around and comment on my looks."

Truitt chuckles, turning to Cal. "There's a girl. There's definitely a girl."

Cal smirks. "Oh I already know that. I heard through the grapevine it's that new chick in town. And I heard *you've* been talking to her."

Of course word's gotten around. Wren's been spending time with an old friend, and if she's like anyone else in town, she's probably got a mouth on her. Not to mention this town can't keep a secret to save its life.

"She's just a neighbor," I say, getting back to the valve. "Single mom. I helped her out a couple times."

"That's what they're calling it these days," Cal says under his breath. "Helping out."

Truitt elbows him. "What's she do? What's her deal?"

"She's a writer," I say without thinking.

"Wait. Is that the same woman the whole town's talking about?" Truitt asks, a light in his eyes like it's all registering.

"No shit?" Cal whistles. "Doesn't she write smut or something?"

I stand up straight, the wrench heavy in my grip. "Don't call it that."

Cal throws his hands up. "Okay, okay. Just saying. Those books are spicy. She probably knows all kinds of things most women around here don't."

I glare at him, not liking the way his mind works. "She's not like that."

"Fine," he says, still grinning like an idiot. "But don't come crying to me when you end up in one of those books. Everyone knows you two are talking, which means everyone's gonna know the next one's based on you."

The thought freezes me mid-motion.

Wren's joked about it—said she'd use my lines or that stolen moment in the shop, but she backed down pretty quickly when she saw my reaction. I didn't think anything more of it at the time, but Cal's words plant something sharp in the back of my brain.

I've spent twenty years building a reputation here. I keep to myself. I keep my business private. The last thing I need is some book floating around with a broody farmer character that everyone in Jasperville County can trace back to me.

If she writes me into a damn novel, I'll never hear the end of it. I'll be a running joke, a laughingstock. It could compromise land deals and God only knows what else.

I should talk to her.

I need to make it clear that whatever inspiration she's getting from me stays between us and her damn imagination.

I'll inspire her all she wants—privately.

Then again, I don't want to go making assumptions, and I can't imagine she'd want me telling her how to do her job any more than I'd want her telling me how to plant corn.

I need to think on this because one wrong move, and I might lose her before she's even mine.

32

Wren

"I have to say, Wren, you sound lighter since the last time we talked," my editor, Laurel, says, her enthusiastic voice crackling through my AirPods as I move laundry from the washer to the dryer. "Happier."

I pluck a sock from the bottom of the basket. "Yeah? Maybe it's all the fresh air. Or the complete lack of traffic."

She chuckles. "Maybe. But I'm telling you, this move? Best thing you could've done."

"I'm definitely feeling inspired again," I admit, closing the dryer door with my hip. "It's like everything slowed down just enough for me to breathe. And the ideas just . . . show up now."

Laurel sighs dramatically. "God, I love that for you."

We've been on the phone for twenty minutes, catching up on deadlines, contract talks, and the possibility of reviving my dying backlist. But now we're veering into personal territory, which Laurel loves. She likes to say she can't *technically* be my therapist because of the ethics of it all, but that's never stopped her from trying.

"What's it like out there?" she asks. "Paint me a picture."

"It's peaceful," I tell her, settling onto the couch. "Green fields and gravel roads for miles. Morning light that looks like a painting. There's this wraparound porch with a swing, and some days it feels like I'm living in a Hallmark movie."

"Do you have a cute farmer neighbor?" she teases. "Please tell me you at least have a cute farmer neighbor."

I pause, biting my lip. "Actually . . . yeah."

"*Stop*," she gasps. "You're telling me you've got all the makings of a small-town romance and you're just . . . sitting on it?"

I laugh. "I'm not with him, Laurel. We're just neighbors. He helped me out a couple times."

"So you're telling me you're literally living in a romance novel and you're not writing it? *Wren*."

I roll my eyes, but she's not wrong. Hunter is basically a romance hero come to life—grumpy, rugged, stupidly attractive. Private but quietly thoughtful. The type of man who builds things with his hands and looks at you like he's already undressing your soul.

"I think you've got your next book," she says with the confidence of someone who's just cracked a long and difficult code. "My advice? Don't let this go to waste."

After we hang up, I sit at my desk and pull out my sunflower notebook. My pen glides across the page before I can second-guess myself.

> Hunter—
>
> You're inspiring me in ways I don't know how to explain.
>
> Every time I see you, I get inspired. Last time, you made me want to write a scene where the hero looks at the heroine like she might be worth the trouble. I imagine a female main character who feels like she's always been too much and not enough at the same time, and a hero who sets out to show her she's perfect . . . perfect for him.
>
> I wish I could thank you for giving me my spark back, but I worry you'd see that as an open invitation.

> My life's starting to feel a lot less complicated lately, and I'm not looking to change that.
>
> But dreaming about it? About you? It's enough—for now.
>
> —Wren

I set the notebook aside, open my laptop, and pull up a blank Word doc. The cursor blinks at me, a quiet dare. Within moments, a story begins to come together in my mind, bit by bit, scene by scene, piece by piece. A broody farmer. A romance writer with writer's block. She writes him letters he'll never read, and he affects her in ways he'll never know.

I title the document *Unsent Love Letters*.

And I write the first chapter.

33

Hunter

I wasn't planning to eat in town today.

Hell, I wasn't planning to eat at all.

But I've been running on caffeine and fumes since before dawn, and the thought of one more gas station breakfast sandwich makes me want to drive headfirst into a ditch.

The diner's half full when I walk in. Smells like bacon grease and eggs over easy—the kind of scent that sticks to your skin until the next shower. I nod to the hostess, who tells me to sit anywhere. I'm halfway to my usual booth when I see her.

Wren.

Sitting by the window, laptop open, fingers flying over the keys while a half-eaten BLT and some soggy fries rest on a plate beside her. She's in some kind of sundress and a denim jacket, hair piled on top of her head like she wrestled it into place and gave up halfway through.

I must've been staring too long, because it doesn't take long for her to glance up, catch me, and wave me over.

I tell myself I should grab my usual booth. Eat in peace. Stick to the plan. But I'm already moving toward her before the thought finishes.

"Fancy seeing you here," she says, her mouth curving into this soft little smile that makes me feel stupid for even hesitating. There's always something so inviting about her, and I'm not convinced she realizes that. She's got this aura, this orbit that pulls you in like gravity.

I slide into the seat across from her. "Didn't take you for a diner kind of girl."

"They've got the best BLTs I've ever had," she says, nudging the plate like evidence. "Five bucks. Can you believe that? Also, I needed a change of scenery."

"What are you working on?"

She hesitates, then tilts her screen so I can see the title: *Unsent Love Letters*.

I arch a brow. "That your next book?"

She nods, eyes lit like the Fourth of July and Christmas at the same time.

The waitress comes by, sets a coffee in front of me before I even ask—small-town perks—and takes my order for my usual double burger and fries. When she leaves, Wren closes her laptop and leans in, like she's settling in for something longer than small talk.

"What's on the docket for you today?" she asks.

We end up sitting there for two hours.

In that time, we talk about everything. Places she's traveled—Prague, Rome, some beach in Greece I can't pronounce. She lights up talking about it, her eyes flashing, hands moving like she's trying to physically paint the pictures for me.

I tell her I've never traveled much. Always figured I'd go someday, but never saw the point in going alone. I don't even like going to movies alone.

"Places like that . . ." I say, tracing the rim of my coffee mug, "seems like the kind of thing you share with someone."

She nods like she gets it, like she understands the quiet parts of me I don't say out loud.

"I've traveled alone and with friends and partners," she says. "People like to romanticize traveling solo, but it's so much better to share those experiences with someone. Makes them more meaningful, I think."

Our eyes hold for what feels like forever, as if we're having a secondary, silent conversation or secretly imagining a world in which we're traveling together.

I clear my throat and change the subject, steering the focus to Colton Valley and how much it's changed since we were kids. She changes the subject to my career, asking questions like she's doing research for her next book. There's no way she finds any of this compelling, but she sure seems convincing. I tell her the best part of farming for me is planting season—even though it's brutal. The hours, the risk, the weather never cooperating. But there's something about starting from nothing and watching it grow.

She compares it to writing a book—starting with a blank page and building something that lives and breathes and transforms into a final product to be consumed.

"You can't force it," she says. "You just keep showing up every day and trust that something will come of it."

I stare at her a second too long, watching the way her eyes crinkle when she talks, the way she presses her tongue to the inside of her cheek when she's thinking.

I didn't notice the time passing until she glances at her phone and says, "Oh my god. We've been sitting here two hours."

I've got a million other places to be, but I don't regret a damn second of this.

We argue over who gets the check—I win, then we say our goodbyes, and I head to the parts store for a belt I need for the 7600.

That's when I see him.

Cole Benton.

Standing by his truck in the parking lot behind the store, talking to some guy I don't recognize. His laugh is obnoxious as ever, some bullshit show of bravado.

My chest is tight and my shoulders are tense, nothing but hard knots as I debate my next move. A hundred words—none of them nice—rest on the tip of my tongue.

"Yeah, you see that new girl in town yet?" Cole asks his buddy. "The smut writer?"

He emphasizes the words like they're meant to be some kind of insult that puts her beneath him, when he's the lowest of the low.

In that moment, my mental debate is over.

All I see is red.

I don't think about it. Don't hesitate.

I storm toward him, yell out his name, short and clipped, and the second he turns around—I plant my balled fist square in his nose.

He goes down fast, hands covering his face, blood pouring between his fingers.

The man he was talking to stumbles off, afraid, taking cover behind the bed of Cole's bright red Ford.

Chickenshit.

"What the fuck, McCrae?" Cole shouts, groaning from the pavement.

I stand over him, breathing hard, hands still curled at my sides, fist numb and throbbing.

"What the hell was that for?" he asks.

Options flip through my head like cards.

"That's for her," I say.

He just stares up at me, bleeding, humiliated, pathetic.

I walk off without another word, climb in my truck, and head back to the farm.

34

Wren

The porch is dark except for the soft glow of my phone screen, casting cold light across my lap, and the porch light drawing in dozens of milky white moths by the minute.

Atticus went to bed an hour ago, but I'm too restless to follow. My phone keeps buzzing, screen lighting up with the same name, over and over.

Nick.

I haven't heard from him in weeks, not since the texts stopped and the silence stretched long enough for me to believe he'd finally taken the hint. But now, out of nowhere, he wants to talk. Wants to "catch up." Wants to "check on me." And tonight, he asked if he could talk to Atticus.

Like hell.

Atticus is too young to understand. Too innocent to grasp that Nick was only ever playing house with us until something shinier came along. I'm not about to let him crack that little heart of his wide open just to disappear again. No way. If I have any say in it, Nick will be a faded, half-formed memory to Atticus—an old face in forgotten photos, nothing more.

I'm so caught up in my thoughts I don't realize a truck has pulled up until the crunch of gravel snaps me out of it.

My heart jumps until I see Hunter stepping out, his silhouette familiar even in the dark.

"I was driving past," he calls. "Saw your porch light on. Figured I'd stop. Neighborly thing to do."

I fight a smile, thinking of my Bat-Signal theory, but it pushes through anyway. He's standing at the bottom of my steps like he's asking permission to come closer, and I have no idea why that makes my stomach flutter the way it does.

"Just sitting here, scrolling my phone," I say.

He climbs the steps and sits on the swing beside me, his body warm and solid. He smells faintly like motor oil and soap, like someone who worked a full day and cleaned up just enough to be respectable.

I shouldn't be this happy to see him.

But I am.

So far, he's proven himself a man of his word. Solid. Steady. He said I could call if I ever needed anything. Which I haven't. And yet he continues showing up anyway.

Still, I remind myself—people are always on their best behavior in the beginning, before they're comfortable enough to show you their true colors.

"You have a good day?" he asks, his gaze lazy, comfortable.

"Yeah. Actually. I wrote ten thousand words."

His brow rises. "Is that good?"

"That's *really* good. Best day I've had in over a year," I say. "I think I'm getting my spark back."

It's because of him, but I keep that part to myself.

I wrote a scene today—dirty, unhinged, the kind of stuff I'd never admit was inspired by the man sitting next to me. I even thought about writing the truck scene—but it felt wrong. Like I'd be using him. I've always avoided putting real people in my books out of respect, even partners. It's a boundary I've never wanted to cross, and his reaction when I joked about using that scene the other day only reaffirmed that rule of mine.

He glances sideways at me. "What're you smirking about?"

I blink, caught. "Was I smirking?"

"You were."

I shrug. "Just . . . thinking."

Hunter looks at me like he's seeing something rare, something precious. His gaze lingers, substantial and easy all at once, and I don't think he even realizes he's doing it. But I notice. I notice everything.

No one's ever looked at me the way he does.

My phone buzzes again in my lap.

"You need to get that?" He points.

"Ex-fiancé." I roll my eyes. "He's been texting all day."

Hunter's face darkens, his jaw tightening. "He bothering you?"

"He's just—persistent," I say. "I block him, and he creates new Apple IDs to text me. It's annoying but harmless."

"Tell him to call you," he says.

"What?"

"Right now. Tell him to call you."

I laugh, shaking my head. "No way. I don't want to talk to him."

"Wren." His voice is firm but not unkind. "Let him call. You won't be the one talking to him anyway."

Another text from Nick pops up—I just want to talk, Wren. Please.

I lock eyes with Hunter before firing back: Fine. Call me. Right now.

The phone rings two seconds later. My heart starts this stupid uneven gallop, but Hunter holds out his hand. I hesitate but place the phone in his palm.

Hunter answers. "Is this the pathetic dumbass who fumbled Wren?"

There's a beat of silence, then I faintly hear Nick's voice. "Who . . . who *is* this?"

Hunter leans forward, elbows on his knees, calm as ever. "Sorry, pal. She's moved on. She doesn't want to hear from you again, so stop contacting her or you'll have bigger problems to deal with than your fragile ego. Consider this your first and final warning."

Then he ends the call without waiting for a response.

I sit there, stunned. Blinking. My heart hammering in the best way.

"You didn't have to do that," I finally say.

"Yes, I did," he tells me, voice low and sure. "Guys like that? They don't respect women. But the ironic part is, they're spineless. He'd never act like that around another man."

He hands me back my phone. "He's going to leave you alone now."

I stare at him, my chest tight, my throat warmer than I'd like to admit, and my lips on fire because I could *kiss* this man.

No one's ever stood up for me like that. Not really. Not like that.

God help me. I'm starting to think Hunter McCrae might actually be exactly who he says he is.

35

Hunter

"There you go rescuing me again," she says, her voice soft and teasing.

I shake my head. "Ignoring him wasn't working."

She sighs. "You don't have to protect me, you know."

I turn to her, eyes catching hers under the dim porch light. "Of course I do."

There's something about her that silently beckons me to keep her safe, to shield her from all the shitty people in this world who want to use her and take advantage of her in all the ways.

The air thickens between us. She's watching me like she's waiting for something. I don't know if it's an explanation or an excuse, but I give her the truth instead.

"You know, I spent a lot of years convincing myself I didn't need anyone," I admit. "And then you rolled into town, all sunshine and big blue eyes, and for the first time, I'm questioning things I've never questioned before."

She tilts her head, that amused half smile playing on her lips. "Such as?"

"Everything."

She laughs, soft and breathy. "Can you be more specific?"

I rest my arm along the back of the swing, close enough to touch her but still keeping space between us because I don't trust myself not to cross it. "I'm thinking about the future differently now. Used to be laser focused on growing the farm. More acres, more staff, more everything. That was enough for me."

I glance at her, watching her watch me.

"But now? Now I get in bed at night, and instead of sleeping, I just lay there, thinking about how it doesn't have to be like this. I'm working myself to death and for what? I didn't think there was another option until you showed up."

She shifts, barely, but her eyes are still locked on mine.

"I know it's crazy," I add. "We've known each other what—less than a month? But already I know you're different. You're not like anyone around here."

The corner of her mouth lifts, like she's trying to fight a smile. And maybe it's the porch light or the distance between us, but she's got that glow about her again. Like she's the only damn thing lighting up this night.

"And for the record," I add, my voice lower, thicker, "it's really fucking hard to sit next to you and not kiss you."

Her cheeks flush instantly, and I get the sense she wants me to, but there's hesitation in her demeanor, a flicker of restraint she's clinging to like a lifeline.

"You don't have to," I tell her, quiet. "I just wanted you to know how I feel. I'm not good with words. I've said more to you these last few weeks than I've probably said to anyone all year."

She lights, her eyes dancing. "You sure about that? You were pretty vocal when we—"

I groan, feeling the heat rush to my face. "Don't remind me."

She laughs, clamping a hand over her mouth, and I can't help but laugh too.

"I had no idea where any of that came from," I admit, still slightly embarrassed at the words that left my mouth that day as I was buried deep inside her. "Took me by surprise too."

I look her over, the way she's sitting there in her not-quite-sheer pajama top and matching shorts, her bare legs crossed, her hair messy from the day.

"It was primal," I say, my voice dipping lower. "Taking you over the back of my tailgate like that. You're so independent and strong, but when I had your hips in my hands and you just . . . surrendered to me—I couldn't think of anything else but owning every inch of you."

That does it.

She's flushed now, visibly affected, her thighs pressing tighter together, her breath growing slightly uneven as she exhales.

"What's wrong?" I ask, but I know.

She shakes her head, insistent. "Nothing. Just thinking about that. It was really hot, but it happened so fast. Almost feels like a fever dream."

"Yeah." I drag my palm along my beard. "If we could do it all over again, I'd take my time."

She watches me, eyes glinting in the porch light, unreadable but wanting.

"What are you thinking about?" I ask, needing to know. I've never cared or put too much thought into what other people are thinking, but with her, I'd kill to know what's going through that pretty little head of hers, especially when she's looking at me like I'm the only man in the world.

"Things I have no business thinking about."

I smile. "Yeah? Like what?"

She bites her lip, just a little, and tilts her head. "You tell me first."

I don't hesitate. "I'm thinking about how good it would feel having you in my arms again."

It's a bold statement, but saying it now, when she's receptive and looking at me like she's seconds from pouncing, it feels safe to say.

Her eyes flick down to my mouth and back up, and then, without a word, she climbs into my lap. She's straddling me now, her knees on either side of my hips, her hands tentative on my shoulders.

"Don't make me regret this," she whispers.

"You won't."

She kisses me, hot and hungry, and I kiss her back twice as hard. My hands grip her waist, pulling her closer, her body pressing to mine in a way that makes my head spin. Her mouth is soft, eager, tasting like remnants of some sweet wine she must've drank earlier.

I slide my hands up her back, fingers tangling in her hair, tilting her head back to taste her neck, deeper, slower. She makes this small sound in her throat that damn near undoes me.

When I finally pull back, we're both breathless.

"Come inside," she whispers against my lips.

She doesn't need to tell me twice.

"But we have to be quiet. Atticus is sleeping," she adds.

I lift her, her legs hooking around my waist like she belongs there, her mouth never leaving mine. She tastes sweet, like the wine she was drinking earlier, like the kind of indulgence a man could get addicted to if he's not careful.

She's warm and soft against me, fingers twisting in the hair at the back of my neck, her breath shallow and hot.

I carry her through the front door, up the stairs, guided by muscle memory more than sight. The whole time, she kisses me like she's starving, like I'm the only thing that's ever made sense.

By the time we make it to her room, we're both breathing heavy. The bed's unmade, the window cracked open just enough to let in the night air. It's cool against my overheated skin.

I set her down gently, standing between her knees. She's looking up at me, her hair a mess, cheeks flushed, lips red and swollen from kissing.

I push her hair back from her face, my thumb tracing the curve of her jaw. She looks so fucking beautiful it guts me. And those eyes? The way she looks at me? Half drunk on wine and half drunk on me? I'm a goner.

"I still got time to back out?" I ask, voice low.

She shakes her head, eyes locked on mine. "Don't you dare."

I grin and lean down, kissing her slow. Taking my time. No rush. Not like before. I want to memorize this—her.

Her hands are on my chest, pulling at my shirt, fingertips grazing my stomach, and I let her tug it off me. She sits up just enough to press her mouth to my chest, kissing a line down the center, her tongue flicking out just barely. It's enough to make my pulse spike, my body aching for more.

I let her explore, but not for long.

I slide my hands under her tank top, fingertips brushing her sides, her waist, her ribs, until she shivers beneath my touch.

"Off." I tug at the flimsy fabric.

She raises her arms, and I drag it over her head, tossing it somewhere behind me. She's not wearing a bra, and the sight of her bare like this, flushed and eager, makes my throat go dry.

I bend down and kiss her again, this time moving to her neck, her collarbone, down to her chest. She gasps when my mouth closes around her nipple, my tongue flicking, teeth grazing just enough to make her hips buck.

"Hunter," she breathes, her fingers threading through my hair, holding me there.

I take my time, tasting her, touching her, feeling every shiver, every hitch of her breath. I want to ruin her for anyone else. I want to make sure she never forgets what this feels like—what *I* feel like.

Her shorts come off next, dragged down her legs slow and deliberate. She watches me with slitted eyes, her chest rising and falling, her thighs pressing together like she's trying to hold herself together.

I kiss the inside of her knee, then her thigh, working my way up until I'm pressed between her legs, tasting her, teasing her, making her squirm.

She bites her lip to stay quiet, but I hear the way her breath catches, the muffled moans she's trying to swallow down.

When she's trembling, when her hands are fisting the sheets, I pull back and crawl up her body, kissing her stomach, her ribs, her neck, until we're face-to-face again.

"Condom?" I ask, my voice rough, barely holding it together. Last time happened so fast, that thought didn't cross my mind. I had to take her, then and there. This time? I want her to feel respected, wanted in a different way. Tonight I'm taking my time.

She nods, reaching to her nightstand, pulling one from the drawer.

I tear it open, roll it on, and then I'm settling between her legs, her body warm and inviting, her eyes locked on mine.

I push into her slow, deep, savoring every inch, every gasp, every dig of her nails in my back.

"Fuck," I mutter, my forehead resting against hers. "You feel . . . fuck, Wren. It's impossible to describe. It's just . . . incredible."

She bites her lip, eyes fluttering shut, her hands sliding down my back, her legs wrapping tighter around me like she wants to keep me there forever.

I move slow, deep, each thrust deliberate, wanting her to feel every second of this. I watch her face, the way her mouth parts, the little sounds she makes when she forgets to hold back.

When she starts getting louder, I press my hand over her mouth, eyes locked on hers.

"*Shh.*" I whisper in her ear, "Atticus is sleeping."

Her eyes go wide, dark and blown, and she nods beneath my hand, her breathing ragged, desperate.

I kiss her, hand still over her mouth, and she kisses me back just as fiercely, her hips meeting mine, her body clenching around me like she's about to fall apart.

"Goddamn, Wren," I say against her mouth. "You're gonna be my ruin, the way you keep doing this to me."

She digs her heels into my back, her body tensing, trembling, her hands gripping me like she's afraid I'll disappear. I feel her come apart beneath me, feel the way she tightens around me, her muffled moans like music in my ear.

I'm not far behind. I bury my face in her neck, breathing her in, moving faster now, chasing that edge until I finally let go, my body shuddering, falling apart with her.

I collapse onto her, careful not to crush her, my face still in her neck, my arms wrapped around her like I'm afraid to let go.

We're both breathing hard, the room quiet except for the sound of our hearts pounding, the faint buzz of crickets outside.

I kiss her neck, soft, lingering. She runs her fingers through my hair, gentle, slow.

I don't want to move. Don't want to leave the warmth of her body, the quiet of this moment.

Eventually, I pull back just enough to look at her, her hair a mess, her cheeks flushed, her lips swollen.

"You okay?" I ask.

She smiles, lazy and soft. "Better than."

I grin, kiss her forehead, and lie back beside her, pulling her into my arms, her head on my chest.

And for the first time in what feels like forever, I'm not thinking about work, or the farm, or the weather, or today's grain prices, or even what comes next.

I'm only thinking about *her*.

36

Wren

I sit up and reach for my clothes, scattered across the floor like evidence, but his hand catches my wrist.

"Don't," Hunter says, his voice low and lazy, like it costs him nothing to ask.

I glance over my shoulder. The room is bathed in moonlight, the soft silver glow spilling across the bed, catching the bare skin of my back, the curve of my hip. I should cover up. I should move.

But I don't.

I stay, perched on the edge of the bed, my hair a mess, my skin still flushed and warm from what we just did.

"Don't," he commands as his eyes trail down my body, stopping to linger where it curves and bends. "I'm not done looking at you yet."

I swallow, cheeks heating. No one's ever looked at me like that before. Like I'm a work of art or something worth memorizing.

It was different with Hunter tonight. Not rushed or reckless. Not primal—though the intensity was still there. But this time it was slow. Intentional. Like he was savoring every second. Like he didn't want to miss a thing.

I think about his hand over my mouth so we wouldn't wake Atticus, the soft taste of salt from his palm as I came.

The way his body moved with mine and his eyes never closed, not once.

He was careful. Attentive. Present.

I lie back, letting the cool sheets kiss my skin. He pulls me into his arms, warm and solid, his hand splayed across my stomach like he's claiming me.

"You don't have to do that," I tell him, trying to keep my voice light. "This whole thing, it's just physical."

He doesn't flinch.

Instead, he presses his lips to my temple, his voice deep and close to my ear. "Shh. Just relax. Be still for a minute."

I want to argue. To remind him that this is supposed to be nothing. Just two adults scratching an itch. But I don't.

Instead, I let him hold me.

He strokes my hair, fingers combing through the mess of it, slow and rhythmic. His breath is warm against my neck, his touch gentle, like he's not just touching me but *studying* me.

He looks at me like I'm a dream he's afraid to wake from.

And I hate that it feels so good.

Because I know better.

I've seen that look before—the *look of love*. Ex-boyfriends, flings, almost-relationships. They all had it at first. All dreamy smiles and glassy eyes like they're seeing their future in my eyes. But it never lasts. Science even backs it up—men fall faster. Harder. They're biologically wired to get hooked on the visual. On the newness. The lust.

But it fades.

It always does.

Once the glow wears off, once the novelty is gone, they all see me for what I really am: too complicated. Too messy. Too much.

Hunter will be just like the rest of them . . . which is why I *have* to keep this strictly physical—even if he's making it impossible to believe that right now.

He takes my hand, kisses the back of it, then trails his fingers down my arm, my ribs, the dip of my waist, slow and deliberate, like he's etching every inch of me into memory.

I close my eyes for a beat, swallowing the ache that rises in my throat.

I wish this was real.

I imagine this is exactly what it feels like to be seen, held, and cherished. To be treated like someone worth keeping and loving.

For a fleeting moment, wrapped in his arms under the glow of moonlight, I let myself pretend this is real . . . for research purposes, of course.

37

Hunter

Glenda's already at the lodge when I get back from checking the north field, her tiny silver SUV parked haphazardly next to the barn like she skidded in sideways. She's sitting at my kitchen table, glasses perched on the end of her nose, receipts and ledgers spread out like she's about to audit the entire county.

"Morning, sunshine," she says without looking up, pen scribbling away.

"Morning." I pour us coffees. "You're early."

"You're late," she shoots back with a grin. "But I'll let it slide since you look . . . lighter."

I raise a brow. "Lighter?"

"Like someone who got laid recently," she adds, eyes twinkling over her glasses.

I nearly choke on my coffee. Glenda has never been one to mince words, but this is the first time those words have been . . . like this.

"Relax, I'm just saying there's something different about you. Your eyes are shinier. You're cracking jokes. I heard you even smiled in public the other day."

I shake my head, chuckling as I sit across from her. "Don't start."

She points her pen at me. "People are talking, you know."

"What else is new?" I roll my eyes.

"Yeah, but this time they're saying you've got yourself a girlfriend."

I snort. "Definitely don't have one of those. Not yet."

Her brows lift at that. "Not yet, huh? What's her name?"

"Wren."

"I knew it!" She pauses, trying to place it. "Wren what?"

"She's an author. Grew up here. Moved back recently. Will Cunningham's stepdaughter."

That does it—her eyes widen in recognition. "Will Cunningham? Haven't heard that name in a while."

"Yeah."

Glenda sets her pen down, folding her hands. "When do I get to meet her?"

I shrug. "Not sure if that's on the table. She doesn't seem to want much to do with me. I'm working on changing her mind."

Glenda chuckles. "Well, sounds like you've got your work cut out for you. You know you've got a reputation around here, don't you?"

I glance at her, sighing. "Yeah. Heartbreaker. I've heard."

"Bothers you."

"Of course it does," I admit. "Makes me sound heartless. Like I get off on wasting people's time. Like I catch and release for sport."

She waits, knowing there's more.

"I've never done that," I tell her. "I just know what I want and what I don't. If I'm not feeling it, I'd rather cut it off than keep someone around for convenience. Felt like the noble thing, not leading anyone on. Guess that doesn't play well in a town like this."

Glenda smiles softly, that knowing mother-hen expression she reserves just for me. "You're the most eligible bachelor in Jasperville County. All the girls want to be with you. It's not the worst thing in the world, you know. In fact, that alone means you're allowed to be picky."

"Yeah, well," I grunt. "Don't think it's helping. Wren probably thinks I'm some antisocial, coldhearted perpetual bachelor."

Glenda shrugs. "So what? Keep trying. That's all you can do. With enough time, she'll see you for who you really are."

I nod, because she's right. "That's the plan."

38

Wren

I'm already five chapters into *Unsent Love Letters*, and I still can't decide if it's brilliant or way too on the nose.

It's a book about a romance writer with writer's block who moves back to her hometown to start fresh, and wouldn't you know it—she's got a grumpy farmer neighbor. She writes him love letters she'll never send, just to get her spark back.

It's suspiciously familiar, but no one needs to know that besides me and my editor.

Hunter, if he ever found out, would probably have a fit about me putting personal details in my books. But I won't. Maybe a cute line or two, sure—but the things we do together, especially in the bedroom? That's ours. Just ours. I'd never put that in print, no matter how much the world might eat it up.

I finish polishing chapter five and email the first batch of chapters to Laurel before my stomach grumbles loud enough to startle me. Closing my laptop, I stretch before heading to the kitchen to fix myself a sandwich.

Out the window, I spot Hunter's truck rumbling past, headed toward his shop up the hill, a trail of gravel dust in its wake.

And just like that, my plans change.

I throw together a couple of ham sandwiches, toss in some chips, and grab two bottled waters. At the last second, I slip into a pair of cutoff jean shorts, a white tank—no bra because why bother—and slide on some leather thong sandals.

Ten minutes later, I'm pushing open the door to his shop. The space is massive, all high ceilings and steel beams, scattered with equipment in various states of disrepair.

Hunter's crouched behind a tractor axle, and the second he looks up and sees me, his entire face shifts—softens, brightens.

"Brought you lunch," I say, holding up the bag.

"How'd you know I was *starving*," he quips, wiping his hands on a rag as he stalks toward me. His eyes are already dark, fixed on me like I'm dessert. Something tells me he's not starving for food . . .

The door clicks shut behind me, and he's on me before I can even set the bag down.

"You're gonna walk in dressed like *that* and expect me to eat a sandwich?" he growls, gripping my hips, fingers digging into the waistband of my shorts.

I grin. "I was making myself a lunch. Thought you might be hungry."

"Oh, I'm hungry all right," he says, yanking the shorts down my legs in one swift, impatient move. Before I can say anything else, he lifts me effortlessly, propping me up on a nearby workbench where he then spreads my legs apart and angles himself between them.

"You sure we have time for this?" I tease.

"No. Not at all. Boys'll be back any minute," he says, dropping to his knees, looking up at me like I'm the only thing he's ever wanted. "But this won't take long."

The next thing I know he's between my thighs, his mouth on my sex, his tongue dragging slow and deep like he's truly famished.

I brace myself on the edge of the bench, gasping, my head tipping back as heat floods every inch of me. His hands are rough, palms spread wide on my thighs, holding me in place, his mouth working me over like he's got something to prove.

He devours me with sharp, precise strokes that make my spine arch, my legs trembling. I bite down on my lip to keep quiet, but it's no use—every flick of his tongue has me unraveling faster than I can hold together.

"Hunter—" I gasp, but he doesn't stop.

He keeps going until I'm breaking apart, the orgasm ripping through me so fast and hard I have to slap a hand over my own mouth to muffle the cry.

By the time I catch my breath, he's standing, wiping his mouth with the back of his hand, grinning like he just won first prize at the county fair.

I re-dress as quickly as I can, tugging my shorts and panties up, barely managing to get my tank top straight when the door swings open.

Three guys stroll in, talking loud—until they see me. Then it's crickets.

"Boys," Hunter says, his voice casual. "This is Wren."

They each nod, eyes flicking between us like they know exactly what they just walked in on. My cheeks flush warm. Hunter stays composed and unbothered with a hint of pride behind his bright blue eyes.

"That's Cal," Hunter says, motioning to the tall guy with a backward hat and a permanent shit-eating grin. "Truitt"—he gestures to a stockier guy with a dark beard and kind eyes—"and that's Levi. He's Cal's cousin. Sometimes he helps out around here."

Levi gives me a polite nod, young, probably late teens, shy smile on his face.

I give them a wave, cheeks still burning but trying to play it cool.

They're rough around the edges, but polite. The kind of farm boys you can tell grew up being raised right, even if they can't hide the knowing glances between them.

Hunter grabs the lunch bag from the counter and winks at me.

"Thanks for lunch," he says, his eyes still eating me alive.

And all I can think about is the fact that I'm standing in a grease-stained shop, my body still buzzing, my stomach still growling. He got his fill, but I'm still hungry—for him.

39

Hunter

The door's barely shut behind Wren when Truitt starts in.

"Jesus Christ, boss," he mutters, grinning like he just saw Santa Claus. "*That's* the girl? No wonder . . ."

"We're neighbors. She brought me lunch, that's all," I say.

Cal chuckles, wiping grease from his hands. "She *brought you lunch*, huh?"

Levi, quiet and polite as ever, keeps his head down, pretending to check the oil filter on the tractor even though he's watching every move I make.

I grab a wrench off the bench like it's business as usual.

Truitt laughs. "So what'd you do to earn that delivery service?"

"Told you. We're neighbors," I grumble, heading back to the rig I was working on. "We do nice things for each other."

"Uh-huh." Cal shoots me a look. "Fellas, do you always look like you ran a marathon after your neighbor stops by? Because I sure as hell don't."

"Get to work," I bark, pointing at the half-assembled engine Truitt was supposed to finish an hour ago. "We've got two planters still torn apart."

They chuckle among themselves, but they listen. Eventually.

Still, I'm off my game for the rest of the day. I can feel her on me—the ghost of her legs wrapped around my shoulders, the sound of her breath catching when my tongue first dragged the length of her slit. I can smell her addictive scent in my beard, faint but unmistakable, and it's enough to keep me hard half the afternoon.

I wish we'd had more time. I wish I could've slowed down, stripped her bare, laid her out right there on the workbench and taken my time making her come again and again until she was begging me to stop.

The things I'd do to her if I had more time.

Instead, I'm dealing with grease and gears, half crazy with want, replaying the sound of her muffled moans like a dirty highlight reel.

I don't know what I did to deserve her visit today, but there's one thing I know for sure—I'm not gonna last long before I find another excuse to see her again.

40

Wren

By the time afternoon rolls around, I'm at Natalie's shop downtown, half helping, half hanging out while she unboxes her latest inventory shipment.

I've been writing so much lately I actually hit my daily word count before noon—*and* I still feel like I've got more in the tank. But instead of draining my creative well dry, I decided to visit Natalie in the name of having some kind of work–life balance.

"Ugh," I moan as I help her unbox a package of linen skirts.

"What?" she asks.

I show her my phone screen. "My ex is still texting me. Doesn't matter how much I ignore him, he's relentless. I don't know what he expects. Hunter told him to stop, and I thought maybe that would—"

"Hold up." Natalie splays a hand in the air. "Back up. Hunter did what?"

I fight the smile threatening to cover my face at the mere mention of his name. "The other night, Hunter stopped by. Nick was texting me, and I mentioned that he wouldn't stop. Hunter had him call me, but Hunter answered and basically told Nick off, then hung up on him."

Natalie stops steaming the skirt on the hanger in front of her, eyes wide. "Wren . . . that's really freaking hot."

I fan myself. "I *know*."

"He's protective of you."

"Yeah. It's weird, right?"

She lifts her dark brows. "Uh, yeah. Very weird . . . for him. He's not like that. He doesn't really care about anyone but himself."

Hearing Natalie say that makes my heart beat a little faster. It's a kind of confirmation I didn't need to hear, because it's only going to make me want him even more than I do—and I'm trying not to.

I want the physical with him.

That's safe and fun.

I don't want to get attached.

"Okay, seriously," Natalie says, pulling a stack of denim jackets from a box. "What's going on with you and Hunter? Has anything changed?"

I peel the tape off another box. "Nothing's going on."

Natalie gives me a look that says she knows I'm full of shit. "You sure about that?"

I shrug, playing it down. "We're just neighbors who visit each other once in a while. That's it."

She shakes her head, smirking. "You know he punched Cole Benton in the face, right?"

I blink twice, then squint. "*What*? When?"

She wrinkles her nose, like she's trying to remember. "I don't know—last week, maybe? I'm guessing it had something to do with what Cole said to you that night at the Turtle."

I stare at her, that little fact rewiring my entire brain.

Hunter—grumpy, levelheaded, avoidant Hunter—punched someone . . . for me.

I don't know whether to feel flattered or furious.

He could've gotten arrested—or worse, Cole could've pressed charges.

I don't say anything more to Natalie about it, but when I leave her shop an hour later, the first thing I do is text Hunter.

ME: I just heard a rumor you punched Cole Benton in the face. Anything you wanna share with the class?

A minute later, the dots bubble up.

HUNTER: No idea what you're talking about. Probably just another one of those small-town rumors.
ME: Uh huh.
HUNTER: You know how people talk.

I roll my eyes and reply:

ME: Thanks again for yesterday . . . a girl could get used to that if she's not careful.
HUNTER: Just doing my job.
ME: Your job is to give me orgasms?
HUNTER: Who else is gonna do it?

I laugh under my breath, thumbs flying.

ME: Bold of you to assume I don't have options.
HUNTER: Are those options battery operated by chance?

He's right and he knows it. I bite my lip, grinning like a teenager.

We keep texting all afternoon—him teasing, me pretending not to take the bait, though we both know I'm hooked. This is a side of him I haven't seen before—playful, cocky, but not in an arrogant way, like he knows he has my attention and he's enjoying it.

I'm enjoying it too.

Probably too much.

I know I'm playing with fire, and sooner or later I'm going to get burned, but for once I don't care. I haven't felt this alive, this seen, since

I don't know when. It's a drug. It's addictive. And it consumes every last piece of me.

By the end of the day, I'm still thinking about him—his mouth, his hands, his texts—and I stare at my phone for a full ten minutes before I finally type something out. It's been hours since his last message, and I'm jonesing for another fix.

ME: You hungry?

I hover my thumb over the send button, warring with myself, but then I press it anyway.

Three dots appear almost immediately.

HUNTER: Depends. What's on the menu?

I bite my lip, smiling.

We both know he's not talking about food.

41

Hunter

I hate texting. My fingers are too damn big for these tiny little letters, and the voice-to-text feature thinks every word out of my mouth is a curse or a command. But every time my phone dings, I grin like a teenage idiot.

I've probably read every text Wren sent today a dozen times. More than that, if I'm being honest. It's been a while since a beautiful woman blew up my phone for any reason other than asking for help fixing something. And none of them made me feel half the way Wren does. Electric. Wired. A man in hot pursuit.

I scrub the grease and grime from under my nails, shower off the day's work, and clean up. Fresh jeans. A black T-shirt. The boots stay—I'm still me.

By the time I pull up to her place, the sun's starting to hang lower, streaking the sky in oranges and pinks. Atticus is in the corral, riding Sugarplum in lazy circles, singing to himself.

"Hey, cowpoke," I call. "Why don't you head in? About time to eat."

He waves, beaming, his boots sticking straight out the sides of the pony before he slides off. I need to adjust those stirrups again.

Inside, Wren's finishing up dinner, the house warm and cozy, smelling like garlic and something I'd probably eat three plates of if given the chance—only because it'd put a smile on her face and let me spend even more time with her.

"Hi, neighbor," she says, tossing me a glance when she peeks out from behind the fridge door. "Atticus, please go wash up for dinner."

There's a box on the counter, worn cardboard with peeling tape, filled to the brim with dusty old toy tractors and miniature combines.

"Atticus found these on the top shelf of his closet," she says when she notices me looking. "They look ancient."

I walk over, peering inside. The second I see them, I feel the color drain from my face.

I know these.

The green John Deere 4020 with the chipped paint. The bright red International Harvester grain truck missing a wheel. I had the same ones as a kid—until they got lost when we moved.

Or so I thought.

Because that's my name, scribbled in faded Sharpie on the bottom of one.

I'm trying to think of what the hell to say, how to even begin explaining this weird twist of fate, when there's a knock at the door.

Wren frowns.

"You expecting someone?" I ask.

She shakes her head, then strides to the door. A moment later she returns to the kitchen, Will Cunningham and his wife, Trish, in tow.

Trish smiles apologetically. "We were in the area, thought we'd stop by. Hope we're not interrupting."

Wren glances back at me with a wince that implies she had no idea this was going to happen. I shrug and smile, giving her a look that implies this is par for the course with small-town living.

"You guys wanna stay for dinner?" Wren asks. "We were just about to eat. Plenty to go around."

"We don't want to impose . . ." Trish says, looking to Will.

"I do." Will rubs his belly and takes a seat at the kitchen table. "I'm starving. What are we eating?"

Dinner is . . . pleasant. Awkward but pleasant. Will talks my ear off about the farm and various pieces of John Deere equipment before asking if I've upgraded to the new 8RX yet or if I'm still holding on to my older models. I humor him, mostly because he reminds me of every retired farmer who thinks the latest technology is witchcraft but still wants to know all about it.

Wren watches us interact, sipping her wine, eyes shimmering with amusement like she can't believe I'm putting up with this.

Afterward, we all head outside. The sun's lower now, horizon bleeding gold and orange, and Atticus hops back onto Sugarplum, looking like he's found his entire purpose in life. He's probably gone in about a hundred circles already. He needs to give that poor old mare a break.

Will and Trish say their goodbyes, hugging Wren, waving to me. Will tells me we'll have to get together soon and talk "real farming" without the women interrupting. I just nod.

Once they're gone, Wren exhales. "Sorry about that."

I wave her off. "It's fine. They're nice people."

She leans against the porch rail, staring at the sunset. "They're going to grill me tomorrow, though. Wanting to know what you were doing here, having dinner with us."

I smirk. "What are you gonna tell them?"

"No idea." She shrugs. "Good thing they think pretty highly of you."

"Yeah?"

She glances sideways at me. "They were happy to hear you were going to be my neighbor. They said you were a good man . . . and I'm starting to see why."

She says it so easy, so matter-of-fact, but it hits me square in the chest. People say a lot of things about me in this town, and they always find a way back to me, but this is the first I'm hearing of someone calling me "a good man."

Wren returns her gaze to the amber sky.

I want to kiss her right now. The way the sunset paints her skin. The way the wind teases her hair. The way her lips are stained a deep shade of purple from the wine.

She's glowing. Peaceful. Happy.

For a moment, everything feels right.

This feels right.

Like it's exactly where we're both supposed to be.

Like our entire universe conspired to bring us to the here and now.

She looks up at me, catching me staring, but she doesn't look away. She holds my gaze, something soft and curious in her eyes.

And all I can think is—

How do I get this look for the rest of my life?

42

Wren

It's Saturday, and Atticus is back at his grandparents' for the rest of the weekend, living his best life. I'm pretty sure he'd move in with them if I let him—he's got free rein, unlimited snacks, and all the grandparent spoiling a kid could want.

I'm supposed to meet Natalie for another girls' night later, but the dress I'm wearing is . . . more revealing than I'd usually go for. She picked it out for me the other day at the shop and practically begged me to wear it tonight. I didn't want to be rude. Plus, it really *is* cute. Baby blue, sleeveless, fitted in all the right places, the hem hitting just above mid-thigh, making my legs look longer than they actually are.

My mind wanders to Hunter, wondering what he'd think of me in this.

I bite my lip, imagining it driving him wild.

I'm almost done with my hair and makeup when the urge hits—the itch to write. I can't *not* scratch it, not when the words have been coming so easy lately.

I abandon the bathroom counter, dash to my office, and grab my sunflower notebook, paging through all the scribbled letters I'll never send, until I find the last one. Then I crack open my laptop and start tapping out a frenzied sex scene for *Unsent Love Letters*. Before I know it, an hour's gone and I've got not one but two new chapters down.

I've still got two hours before I have to meet Natalie.

Perfect. More time to write.

I'm just about to start another chapter when there's a knock at the door. I glance at the clock, frowning. Natalie's not supposed to pick me up, and my parents learned after last time not to show up without calling first.

Peering out the bay window, I spot Hunter's white pickup.

My heart leaps into my throat at the sight.

When I greet him at the door, he's holding a small stack of mail, but his eyes are already on me—dragging down my body, lingering on my legs, my hips, the way the dress hugs and exaggerates my curves. His jaw ticks, his nostrils flaring slightly like he's trying to rein himself in. But the more I study his expression, the more I don't think he's turned on so much as he's bothered by the sight.

"Did you get my mail or something?" I ask, playing coy.

"What's the occasion?" The tone of his question reminds me of a protective father. I realize now that he probably thinks I'm going on a date.

"Girls' night out." I spin in a circle. "It's a little much for the Tipsy Turtle, but—"

He doesn't let me finish.

Instead, he steps forward, wraps an arm around my waist, and tosses me over his shoulder like I weigh nothing.

"Hunter—what are you—"

"You're not going out looking like that," he mutters, carrying me up the stairs. "Not until I've had you first."

My stomach flips, a breathless laugh catching in my throat as I swat at his back. But it's useless. He's all muscle and determination, and before I know it, he's kicking my bedroom door open and tossing me onto the bed.

I bounce once, breathless, flushed, staring up at him.

His eyes are dark, hungry, devouring me.

"You can't do this to me," he growls, crawling over me, his hands sliding up my bare thighs until he reaches my panties. "You answer the door looking like a snack, and you're going to get eaten. I'm sorry, but I can't let you go out looking like this, not without me dripping out of you, reminding you no one else can give you what I can."

I grin. "You sound jealous."

"I am."

"And a little possessive."

"You bring it out in me, honey." His lips curl at one side. "Don't act like it doesn't turn you on just a little."

In my thirty-nine years, I've never had a boyfriend be jealous or possessive of me, and I always thought those traits would border on creepy. But not with Hunter. It amplifies his sexiness.

And it only makes me wetter.

He kisses me, hard and deep, his hands moving under my dress, dragging it up my hips until it's bunched around my waist. His mouth moves down my neck, sucking a mark just above my collarbone, claiming me with bites and nips.

"You have any idea how good you look right now?" He breathes his words against my skin.

I shake my head, dazed, wanting, wishing I could cancel my plans and have a night in—with him.

He sits back, his hands gripping my waist, pulling me onto his lap. I'm straddling him, the dress pushed up, nothing between us but my panties and his jeans. His rough hands roam, palms skimming my thighs, my hips, my waist. He traces every curve like he's memorizing them.

"You're so fucking beautiful. You have no idea," he says, his voice thick. "I could come just looking at you."

I shiver, his words sinking into my skin, wishing I could hear them for the first time all over again.

He pulls down the bodice of my dress. His gaze drops, drinking in every inch of me. His fingertips trace the stretch marks on my hips before tending to the soft curve of my stomach.

My eyes follow his hands . . . My tiger stripes now feel more illuminated than ever. It isn't like he hasn't seen my body before, but under the golden lamplight of my bedroom, they're on full display. Without thinking, I rest my forearms over them.

He moves them immediately and drinks me in along with a long, slow breath and a steady gaze.

"I hope you know," he begins, fingers ghosting over the lines, "that I fucking love these. Not only is your body a work of art, it brought a life into this world. You're a woman in every sense of the word and it drives me crazy."

I bite my lip, watching him, my chest tightening at how reverent he looks—like I'm some masterpiece he's been waiting his whole life to see. The first time Nick saw them, he had a micro-visceral reaction. When I pointed it out, he assured me they didn't bother him, but his eyes told a different story. After that, he only ever wanted to make love in the dark. If only I'd put it all together earlier . . .

Hunter's hands are everywhere—rough and insistent, like he can't decide where to touch first. The hem of my dress is still bunched around my waist, my panties now pushed aside. He palms my hips like he owns them, like I'm his to ruin, his to devour.

And then he's between my thighs, the heat of his mouth demanding, reverent.

I fall back on my elbows, my breath catching as his tongue drags slow, delicious strokes that make my legs tremble around his shoulders. He holds me open, his grip commanding and steady, like he wants to make sure I don't squirm away—not that I'd ever dream of it.

"Hunter," I gasp, my hips tilting toward him, chasing the friction.

He groans against me, the sound sending a vibration straight through my core. I'm already close, already aching, and he knows it.

He flattens his tongue, teasing the spot that makes me shudder, then pulls back just enough to look up at me.

"You taste so fucking good," he whispers, lips glistening. "I think you should cancel your plans and let me spend all night right here, between your thighs, working this gorgeous fucking pussy."

His words are gasoline on an already burning fire.

He dives back in, hungrier this time, his tongue circling, his mouth sucking just right. My body tenses, the orgasm inching closer, faster, and I can't catch my breath.

"God—Hunter—just like that—" I breathe.

My body tightens, the pressure snapping as I come hard against his mouth, my back arching, a strangled cry slipping out before I can stop it.

He doesn't let up—not until I'm trembling, too sensitive, pulling at his hair, begging him to stop.

When he finally rises to his feet, his grin is smug, his eyes dark with heat.

"I'm not done with you yet," he says, voice thick. "We're just getting started."

I don't argue. I crawl to the center of the messy bed, discarding what's left of my now-wrinkled dress and panties, my skin flushed, my wetness still throbbing. I watch as he strips, his body all sharp lines and solid muscle, every inch of him chiseled like he was built for hard labor—and for me.

He climbs onto the bed, his hands roaming my thighs, my hips, my stomach. He traces the faint stretch marks there, too, his touch gentle, his eyes locked on mine.

Hunter murmurs something that sounds like pleasure, his thumb brushing one of the lines.

I swallow hard, my throat tight. No one's ever looked at me like this before. Like every part of me—every so-called flaw—is something to behold.

"You're so goddamn stunning, Wren," he says, his gaze worshipful. "Every inch of you. Every freckle. Every scar. Every curve. Every mark. Every angle. Every line."

His words make me dizzy and warm. I pull him close, kissing him deep, tasting myself on his tongue. He pins me, pressing me into the mattress, his body heavy and hot, his cock hard against my thigh.

"Condom," I whisper, breathless.

He reaches for his wallet on the nightstand, tears one open, rolls it on. Then he's between my legs, his eyes never leaving mine.

I wrap my legs around his waist, urging him closer.

He pushes into me slow, inch by inch, until I'm stretched full, gasping at the perfect pressure, the perfect fit. We stay like that for a beat—still, connected, eyes locked. The air between us is thick, charged, like we're both waiting for the other to say something, to break the spell.

But there's nothing to say.

I feel it in the way he moves—slow, deep, intentional. Like he's savoring every second. Like he's making a memory.

He thrusts deeper, hitting that spot in front of my cervix that makes me cry out, and his hand clamps over my mouth, his eyes darkening.

"Gotta stay quiet, honey," he murmurs, his forehead pressed to mine. "Don't want anyone hearing you like this."

Despite it just being the two of us for miles and miles, his words make me wetter, my body clenching around him, desperate for more. He moves faster, his hips snapping, his hand still over my mouth, his other hand gripping my thigh, holding me open wide so he can go deeper yet.

I'm close again, the tension building, my body burning. He feels it, too—I can tell by the way his thrusts get rougher, more urgent, his breath ragged against my ear.

"Come for me," he commands in a low growl. "I want to feel you pulse around my cock."

Just like that, I do—hard and fast, my body shuddering beneath him, the orgasm tearing through me like a wave I can't outrun. He follows with a guttural groan, his body tensing, his hips stuttering before coming to a complete stop for a few seconds.

When it's over, he collapses on top of me, both of us breathless, our skin damp, hearts racing.

We stay like that for a long time—tangled, sweaty, quiet.

Eventually, he rolls onto his side, pulling me with him, his arm heavy around my waist, his lips pressing lazy kisses to my shoulder.

"You've ruined me," he mutters against my skin, "for anyone else. I hope you know that."

Same—only I don't tell him that.

He pulls me tighter.

For a while, there's nothing but the sound of our breathing, the chirping of the crickets and bullfrogs outside, and the steady thrum of his heartbeat against my ear.

I've never felt more wanted, more desired in my life.

He holds me close for what feels like forever, his hand stroking my hair, his lips brushing my temple.

I never want this to end—but I know too well that all good things always do.

"You're addictive," he says, still catching his breath. "Every time I get a piece of you, I want even more."

I smile, letting his words soak into my desert-dry soul. I hope he means it, but odds are he's just a man saying what men say when they're basking in the afterglow of an intense bedroom session.

Still, I allow myself to enjoy it—carefully.

We stay tangled in each other's arms for a while, neither of us moving, both of us pretending time isn't ticking by faster than we want it to.

I'm half tempted to text Natalie and cancel, just so I don't have to leave this bed.

My head is on his chest, his hand lazily tracing circles on my back, when a thought pops up and won't leave.

"Hey," I say. "Those old toys . . . from the other night. The ones Atticus found in the closet."

His hand stills.

I lift my head, catching the shift in his expression—softening, clouding. He stares at the ceiling for a beat, his jaw tightening like he knows exactly where this is headed.

"Those were mine," he says, voice low. "Mine and my brother's."

I blink, sitting up a little. "Ben?"

His gaze flicks to mine, surprised. "How'd you know?"

I push some hair out of my face. "I saw some drawings. In the closet in Atticus's room. They had his name on them."

He lets out a breath, like the memory's settling heavy on his chest.

"You grew up in this house, didn't you?" I ask, gently.

He nods.

"That why you wanted this land so bad?"

His eyes drift to the window, the fields stretching wide and endless under the afternoon sky. "Yeah."

I almost tell him I'm sorry. That I didn't know. That I wouldn't have bid on the place if I'd known what it meant to him. But I bite my tongue because he's not done. His eyes are somewhere else—years away, distant but vivid.

"I was sixteen. Ben was twelve," he starts, his voice steady but faint. "We were outside . . . right down by the river that runs past the back of the property. Ben was messing around, skipping rocks, doing whatever he could to get my attention."

He pauses, his lips pressing thin.

"I didn't pay him any mind. I had a girl over. My first real girlfriend. Big deal at the time, I suppose. At that age, I was more interested in her than my kid brother. She wanted to go sneak around behind the grain bin . . . so I went."

I can already feel an ache boiling in my chest because I have a feeling where this is going, but I don't interrupt.

"When I came back, he was gone," Hunter says, staring hard at the ceiling. "At first I thought he just wandered off to chase frogs or something. Then I heard screaming."

His voice wavers, just barely.

"The current was strong that day. Fast. We'd had a lot of rain that spring. I saw him bobbing . . . going under and coming back up. Flailing. Screaming."

He swallows hard, voice tightening.

"I kicked off my boots and jumped in. My girlfriend ran for help. But the water . . . it was too fast. Too damn fast. I couldn't get to him."

His eyes turn glassy and he goes quiet, too quiet.

I remain in this silence with him, my chest tight, my pulse hammering.

"We didn't find his body until the next day," he finally says, barely above a whisper. "Five miles downstream. Washed up on some riverbank."

I swipe at my eyes, tears I didn't even realize were spilling over.

"Hunter," I say, my voice breaking. "I . . . I can't imagine how horrific that must've been."

I think about the day he pulled my son from that river. The fury in his eyes, the way he snapped at me, the way his hands shook. It all makes sense now. Every piece of it.

"My mom couldn't bear to stay here after," he says, staring blankly ahead. "Too many memories. Too much tragedy. Every time she looked at the river, it reminded her of what it stole from her. Wasn't long before my parents sold the place to Rich Sanders for dirt cheap, and we moved to the other side of town. Away from the river."

He shakes his head like he's still pissed about it, all these years later.

Knowing what I now know about Hunter and the kind of man he is, I imagine this is why he owns all the riverfront land in the county . . . he wanted to do what he could to keep that water from stealing another life.

"I always told myself I'd buy it back. Despite everything . . . this land, this house—it reminds me of Ben. Every inch of it. It's all I have left of him." His voice is soft, reverent. "It's sacred ground to me."

I press my lips tight, willing myself not to cry harder.

"Before my mother passed, she told me she regretted selling it. She said she was too heartbroken to think straight at the time. But she wished she'd never let it go. I promised her I'd get it back someday." He turns to me then, eyes heavy but kind. "Then you showed up."

My heart aches at the way he says it.

"I didn't know," I whisper.

He nods, a faint, sad smile pulling at his mouth. "I know you didn't."

Without thinking, I throw my arms around him, holding him tight, burying my face in his neck. He smells like skin and warmth and something distinctly him.

For a while, neither of us says a word. We just hold each other, the weight of the past sitting with us while the comfort of the present wraps itself around us like a warm blanket.

In this moment, he doesn't feel like a friend with benefits or the moody farmer next door.

He feels like a complicated, misunderstood, beautiful man who's trying everything in his power to win me over . . . and I fear it's starting to work.

43

Hunter

The Jasperville County Fair's in full swing by the time we get there, and Atticus looks like his brain might explode from the sheer number of food stalls, lights, and rides spinning in the distance.

"Can I get that? And that? And that?" he asks, pointing at everything.

"Whatever you want, kid," I tell him.

By the time we've made one lap around the fairgrounds, I've got him loaded up with a corn dog in one hand, cotton candy in the other, a deep-fried Oreo stuffed in his pocket, and a giant cheese curd on a stick that his mother's graciously carrying.

"Gonna need to roll him out of here by the end of the night," Wren jokes, shaking her head.

We pass the midway games, and I let him play every single one—basketball, ring toss, that rigged game where you shoot water into the clown's mouth. Fifty bucks later, he wins a neon-green stuffed frog that's almost as big as he is.

"You're spoiling him," Wren says as I pay for a midway ride pass so he can go on anything he wants.

"He's having the time of his life," I say, watching Atticus run toward the Ferris wheel. "He'll be fine."

"If he throws up in your truck on the way home, I'm not cleaning it up."

I laugh. "You haven't lived until you've puked up corn dogs on the way home from the fair."

We wander a bit, watching Atticus from a distance as he bounces from one ride to the next, his face lit up like the Rockefeller Plaza tree at Christmastime. Wren stays close to my side, her arm brushing mine now and then, and every time she does, it sparks something warm beneath my skin.

Once again, all feels right, like this is exactly how it's supposed to be. It's a feeling I can't quite put into words, I just know that it's everything I never knew I needed and I'm going to do everything in my power to make sure it never fades.

We're heading toward the Ferris wheel when I see him.

Cole Benton.

He's standing with a girl half his age clinging to his arm, dressed like someone trying too hard to look grown. She looks exactly like the kind of girl who'd fall for his payroll offer—impressionable, too naive to understand how the world works, too insecure to not fall for someone like Cole.

Wren sees him a second after I do, her body tensing beside me. "Ugh. He's shameless. How old is she? She's got to be nineteen, maybe twenty at the most."

"That's his MO," I say. "Pluck some girl out of the crowd, promise her the world, treat her like shit, then pay her off when she's too ashamed to admit what he is."

Wren watches him, her eyes hard. "She looks like a baby. I wish I could warn her."

"He likes them that way," I say, my jaw tight. "Inherited his daddy's half-billion-dollar operation, lives like some Midwest playboy. Private jet and all. But the thing about money—it doesn't buy you class. Sure as hell doesn't buy you a personality."

Unfortunately, Cole spots us too. He waves, grinning like the asshole he is, and stumbles toward us, beer sloshing out of his cup with each unsteady step. How any women find this attractive is beyond comprehension.

"Well, well, well," he slurs. "It all makes sense now. The farmer and the smut writer. Isn't that a Hallmark movie or something?"

I stare him down, my fist clenched. Wren holds my arm tight, as if she can read my mind.

He smirks, turning his unfocused attention to Wren. "*This* is who you turned me down for? Hunter fucking McCrae? Could've been me, sweetheart. I'm a whole lot more fun than this stuck-up prick. Man's got a corncob permanently shoved up his ass."

His eyes drag down Wren's body, slow and shameless, like he's picturing every way he'd ruin her if given the chance—and he does it in front of his girl, who either doesn't notice or is too passive to care.

I clench my fists tighter, watching the Ferris wheel rotate, counting the seconds until Atticus is back on solid ground. We can't leave yet, not without him.

Cole grins wider, interpreting the delay as an invitation to stick around a bit longer.

"So," he says, swaying slightly, "is *he* the inspiration for your next dirty book? Gonna write about the broody farmer who plows his fields *and* his neighbors?"

I step forward, eyes hard. "Did I not make myself clear the first time, Benton?"

He chuckles, throws his hands up. "What are you gonna do, McCrae? Punch me in front of all these people?"

He points behind me, and I glance over my shoulder, where a county deputy stands by the ticket booth, watching the crowd, chatting with some locals.

"You and I both know you're not gonna go to jail over me," Cole taunts. "You love your little operation too much. You'd never leave it in someone else's hands."

Little.

It's a dig, meant to needle me, but I know better than to bite. I've got more acres under management than Cole could comprehend if he weren't too busy blowing his inheritance. At least I manage my farm myself. He wouldn't know where to start if he tried.

I stare him down, quiet, composed, because I learned a long time ago—men like Cole want a reaction, a show.

I'm not giving it to him.

But I promise myself this—his day's coming.

44

Wren

Natalie's picking at the last of her sandwich across my kitchen table, her leg tucked under her like she's settled in for a while. It's an easy afternoon—Atticus is at the local arts and crafts fair with my mom, the house is quiet, and the windows are open, letting in a breeze that smells like cut grass and sunshine.

I tell her about the county fair. About Cole. About the beer, the slurs, the way Hunter's entire body tensed like he was a split second from decking him in front of half the town.

Natalie just shakes her head, sipping in a breath of air through a straw-sized hole in her mouth. "Those two have had bad blood as long as I can remember."

"Really?"

She nods, taking a drink of her iced tea. "Cole's a few years older than us. Went to school in the next town over, so you wouldn't know him. But he's always been that guy. Even back then. Sleazy. Textbook womanizer. Married three times. Trades in a girlfriend for a newer model every year, just like he does with his truck."

I grimace. "Charming."

"You dodged a bullet. But Hunter? He must really like you if he's standing up to Cole like that. Cole's got a lot of money and pull around here. He knows everyone. If he wanted to ruin someone's career or reputation, he could."

I pick at the edge of my napkin, the knot in my stomach tightening. "I hope that doesn't happen. Not because of me."

"Hunter can handle himself. Anyway, speaking of Hunter." She leans forward, eyes bright. "How's the book coming? You writing your ass off or what?"

I smile, unable to help it. "Okay, for the record, it's not *about* Hunter, but it's definitely inspired by him."

"Ooooh." She lifts her brows. "Inspired how, exactly?"

"Not like *that*," I say, laughing. "Just . . . he's solid. Reliable. Always shows up when I need him. Even when I don't, he finds a way to make himself useful. And Natalie, he's *so* good with Atticus."

She watches me, that knowing glint in her eyes.

"I used to think words were everything," I admit. "That's what I do, right? Words. But with someone like Hunter . . . he shows he cares by doing. By showing up. I never knew how good that could feel until him."

Natalie sniffs, squinting. "I thought it was strictly physical between you two."

"It is," I say without pause. "That's all it's supposed to be."

She grins. "Sure, okay, yeah. He's punching people for you and charming your kid and you're gushing about how romantic he is, but go on. Tell me more about how he's just your fuck buddy."

I sigh, leaning back in my chair. "You have good points. I'll give you that. I don't know what we are or if we're even anything. But right now? He's treating me like a queen. And I'm just . . . trying to enjoy it . . . while also waiting for the other shoe to drop."

Natalie rests her chin on her hand. "That's smart. Because you might be eating out of the palms of each other's hands now, but it *will* drop. It's Hunter McCrae. That's what he does. He loves and leaves. Rinse. Repeat. But in the meantime? Have fun. Have fun on behalf of all the Jasperville County women who have tried—and failed—to get a front-row seat with that man."

"I don't know why he's so taken with me," I say. "I've seen the way other women look at him. The butcher. The baristas. I've been trying to figure out what's so different about me."

She studies me, looking just as perplexed as I feel. "Yeah, I'd love to know too. He's always had a type. Brunettes. Exclusively brunettes. The small-town-prom-queen, girl-next-door kind. I swear all his exes have fit that mold."

"I feel like you're describing yourself."

Natalie cackles before rising from the table and putting her dishes in the sink.

"I hate to end this conversation, but I need to get back to the shop," she says, returning to kiss my left cheek. "I'll text you later."

I walk her out and return inside. The second the door closes behind me, the house feels too quiet.

I think about everything Hunter's done since I moved here. Getting me unstuck from the mud. Bringing me a generator during the blackout. Saving Atticus from the river. Teaching him to ride Sugarplum. Helping with dishes. Telling Nick off. Defending me against Cole Benton—not once, but twice.

Worshipping my body like no one ever has before.

And then there's the way he looks at me.

The way his eyes soften when I talk.

The way his voice drops when he says my name.

He makes me feel things I thought were dead inside me, things I didn't know I was capable of feeling in this lifetime or at this point in my life.

The thought of it all being temporary—the idea of him waking up one day and deciding he's done—makes me physically sick.

I press a hand to my stomach, swallowing the nausea that creeps up my throat.

I'm playing with fire. I'm going to get burned. It's only a matter of time.

My entire life, I've been strong.

But I don't know if I'm strong enough to handle the day that other shoe finally drops.

45

Hunter

It's late when I pull into Wren's drive, the lights in the house dim except for the porch light I'm pretty sure she leaves on when she wants me to know she's home.

She texted earlier—Atticus is down for the night. You coming over?—which is basically a polite version of a booty call. And yeah, I'm not stupid. I'd never turn that down. But I'm still working on more than that. I'm working on her. On *us*.

I stopped and grabbed a bottle of her favorite wine on the way—something sweet and fruity I can't pronounce, but the lady at the store swore by it. It wasn't cheap, either, but this woman's worth it. I'd slap down my last nickel if it made her happy.

When Wren opens the door, she's wearing this linen thing—gauzy, loose but barely there. She looks like a dream, like something out of one of her own books.

"Brought you something," I say, holding up the bottle.

She grins, stepping aside to let me in. "Bribing me with wine?"

"I like it when you're a little tipsy. You're easier to throw around, like a little rag doll," I say with a wink.

We don't even make it to the couch before she's pulling me to her, kissing me like she's been starving for it all day.

"You're sure Atticus is asleep?" I ask.

She nods, voice light. "Out cold."

That's all I need to hear.

I back her against the wall and take her mouth with mine—slow at first, just enough to make her gasp, then deeper, rougher, until I feel her melt against me. One hand fists in my shirt like she needs to hold on. The other slips under the hem, nails dragging against my stomach.

I tug her chin up and look her straight in the eyes. "I've been thinking about this all damn day."

My hands slide up her thighs, gripping her ass as I lift her. She wraps around me like she's done it a hundred times before—legs tight at my waist, mouth against my neck. I carry her through the living room, past the kitchen, up the stairs and straight into her bedroom, where I toss her onto the bed like a man done pretending he doesn't want something.

She scrambles up onto her elbows, a coy little smirk on her juicy lips. "You gonna take your boots off, Tractor Daddy?"

Her nickname makes me smirk for a split second. But her playfulness has a time and a place. I'm here to do some serious damage . . . of a specific variety.

"Eventually." I was so eager to get her up here I hadn't thought to do that.

She laughs, but it dies the second I crawl over her.

I yank the linen nightgown over her head. No bra. Perfect fucking breasts, nipples already pert. My mouth is on her a second later, kissing down her chest, dragging my tongue over soft skin, biting just enough to make her squirm.

Her hands thread into my hair, and I can feel the tension already brewing in her body, which only serves to make my cock harder than it already was.

I work the elastic waistband of her pink lace panties down, mouth following the path—kissing, biting, teasing her thighs until she's whispering my name like a prayer.

"You wet for me already?" I slide two fingers over her slit.

She whimpers. "Hunter . . ."

"You want me to stop?"

She glares down at me. "Do you want to get punched?"

"Tiny and ferocious. I fucking love it," I say, dark and low. "That's my girl."

I drag my tongue through her folds, and she arches off the mattress. I take my time—slow, deliberate licks, holding her thighs open, teasing her clit with just enough pressure to make her curse me and beg in the same breath. She grabs the pillow behind her head like it's the only thing anchoring her.

And when I feel her about to break, when her legs start shaking and she's whispering please, I pull away.

I watch as her eyes snap open.

"Hunter," she pants, desperation on her warm breath. "I swear to God—"

"You'll come when I'm inside you," I say, standing and peeling off my shirt. "And not a second before."

I drop my jeans, kick off my boots, and climb over her again.

"Wait." She places a palm against my chest. "I want the boots on."

"They're dirty."

"I know." She slams her mouth against mine, nails dragging down my ribs. And that look in her eyes? It's not just hunger. It's trust. It's vulnerability. It's surrender. It's a woman who wants me exactly the way I am.

And it's going to be my undoing.

I waste no time sliding my feet back into my boots, lining my hips up with hers, then plunging into her with one deep thrust.

She moans—loud and guttural—and I curse under my breath before clamping a hand over her mouth.

"Fuck, you feel good, honey," I purr into her ear. "Tight. Wet. All mine."

A few more thrusts and she's not just wet, she's soaking.

I grab her wrists and pin them above her head, hips rolling slow and deep, watching her face as I drive into her again and again. Her mouth falls open. Her eyes flutter closed.

"No," I tell her. "I want you looking at me."

She opens her eyes and stares right into me like she's afraid of what she might find but also afraid to disobey.

She should be.

My control slips a little when she clenches around me, gasping as I push harder, faster, until her legs are trembling and she's whisper-crying out my name like it's the only word she remembers.

I feel her fall apart beneath me, and that's all it takes.

I bury myself to the hilt and release every last drop I have with a low grunt, resting my forehead against hers, still holding her hands tight above her head like letting go might wreck me.

For a while, we don't move.

Just the sound of our breathing in the dark.

Eventually, I roll to my back and she curls into me, both of us naked under her soft white quilt, her head on my chest as her fingers trace lazy circles along my stomach.

"I'm a hopeless romantic," she whispers.

I don't say anything.

"I write about love for a living," she adds. "So I know how it's supposed to feel. And I know better than to expect it from someone who's never promised it."

I tense beneath her, but she keeps talking, soft and slow.

"I'm having a lot of fun with you . . . but just so you know, I don't need anything from you, Hunter. I've learned not to need things from people who can't give."

I stare at the ceiling. My chest is tight in a way that has nothing to do with exertion.

A woman said something like that to me once, years ago. She was trying to play hard to get. Make me chase her. Prove something.

The more she acted too cool to care, the more I knew she felt the exact opposite.

But from the moment I met Wren, she's not been one to play games. She's brutally honest, unafraid of the kinds of topics that make most people uncomfortable. She's unapologetically herself. I believe what she's saying . . . except it only makes me want her more.

I want to say something. Tell her she's wrong. That I *can* give her more. That I *want* to. And I *plan* to.

But I don't.

Because I can't shake the feeling that maybe she's right.

Maybe I can't.

I've never been able to give anyone all of me. Not the women before her. Not even the ones who waited years for a fraction of what I gave her tonight.

I disappointed every single one of them.

But Wren?

God.

I don't think I could live with myself if I broke her heart.

"What are we doing?" she asks.

I glance at her, playing dumb because part of me wants her to take the lead on this. I've never been good at talking about my emotions, especially when they're terrifyingly out of my control.

"What do you mean?" I ask.

"This." She gestures between us. "If we keep doing this, someone's going to catch feelings."

I give her a slow half smile, brushing her hair back from her face. What I really want is to tell her "Too late."

She tilts her head, studying me. Sometimes I think this woman can read my mind. It sure feels that way when she looks at me like this.

I kiss her bare shoulder.

She goes quiet, directing her eyes on the ceiling like she's sorting through a million complicated thoughts at the same time.

"I don't like sneaking around," she says after a couple minutes of silence. "But I also don't want Atticus getting attached or confused. Maybe this isn't a good idea."

I trail my hand along her hip, teasing the curve until she squirms just a little. "I don't know what it's gonna take to show you I'm serious about making you mine. I don't care how long it takes. But I'm not going anywhere."

She watches me, suspicious but softening. "How do I know you're not just telling me what I want to hear?"

"Honey, I barely have time to get all my work done in a week. You think I've got time to play games?"

She laughs quietly, shaking her head. "Then how do you keep managing to make time for *me*?"

I kiss her cheek, then her jaw, before moving lower. "Because I always make time for the things that are important to me."

She melts a little, sinking into the bed, curling into my side with her head in the crook of my arm. We stay like that, the quiet humming between us.

After a while, she speaks up again. "I want to understand your . . . reputation."

I glance down at her. "Yeah?"

"Tell me about your exes. All of them. I want a full postmortem."

I let out a slow breath, eyes on the ceiling. I really don't want to do this, but if it means she might give me a chance, so be it.

"Some of them, I can barely remember," I begin.

I give her the rundown. The woman I dated casually for a few months, who started driving by my house late at night long after we ended things. The woman before that—wanted a baby with me even though we were more off than on, and I never once told her I loved her. She was sweet and kind, but her desperation made me feel like a means to an end.

"Before her," I add, "there was a local woman. Owned a boutique. You might've gone to school with her. Prom queen back in the day.

Peaked in high school. Never quite got over it. Still thinks she's a big fish in a small pond."

Wren sits up, eyes wide. "Natalie Dinsmore?"

I wince. "Ah, so you know her."

"That's one of my oldest friends. We've been hanging out."

I rub the back of my neck. "So she's the one filling your head with stories about me?"

She doesn't answer, just stares at me, her mouth pressed tight.

"Natalie meant nothing," I tell her. "We dated a little over six months. She wanted to move fast—marriage, babies, the whole thing. But I wasn't feeling it. I kept hoping maybe I'd catch up, maybe the connection would show up, but it didn't. There was never a spark. It was always surface level, performative. I never really felt like I knew the real her."

Wren is quiet, contemplative.

"She seemed . . . desperate. Her clock was ticking, early thirties, ready for the next chapter whether I was or not. She didn't get my humor. She hated my long hours. Always starting fights about me not making enough time for her." I shake my head. "It was never gonna work, so I ended it. I didn't want to waste her time."

Wren watches me, her expression unreadable.

"She didn't take it well. Tried for months to get me back. Blew up my phone every day. Left me crying voicemails. Texted me big, long paragraphs. She must've been more attached than I thought. Took her a few years to get over me—least, that's what I've been told."

I meet her gaze, my voice steady. "It's in the past, Wren. It means nothing. You need to know that."

She shakes her head slowly. "I'm not upset about that."

"No?"

She looks down, frowning. "I'm upset that Natalie never mentioned it. We've talked about you multiple times. Why wouldn't she tell me?"

I don't know, but I've got a bad feeling that answer isn't gonna make this easier.

46

Wren

I planted sunflowers near the river this morning. Not for me, but for Ben—technically for Hunter. I wanted him to have a place to go to "be" with Ben, a memorial of sorts. I thought maybe this might be a way to quietly heal a part of Hunter. I think about the way his eyes turned glassy and his voice broke as he told me the story. It was as if he was still there, the moment fresh in his memory. Having to stay off the land for decades after Rich Sanders bought it must've been difficult for him, but I want him to know he's welcome here anytime he wants.

I don't quite have a green thumb yet, but I thought, too, this might resonate with Hunter because the soil, the sun, the seasons—that's his language.

Sunflowers seemed like the obvious choice, not just because they're stubborn and resilient but because they're always turning their faces to the sun no matter how heavy their heads get. My grandmother once told me sunflowers symbolize loyalty, adoration, and longevity—things, I imagine, that defined the bond between Hunter and his brother.

When these eventually grow and bloom, Hunter will have a place to visit that doesn't require words, apologies, or explanations. A place that isn't sterile or grave-like but living, breathing, and growing. Something beautiful rising in a place where everything went dark. A reminder that life always goes on, even in places where death once stood.

My hope is that with enough time, this will be a place where Hunter can come to unburden himself, to forgive himself—because I know he still blames himself for what happened, even if he didn't say it.

The dirt is still under my fingernails, my knees a little sore from kneeling too long, but I don't care. It'll take months for the flowers to grow—maybe longer if the soil doesn't cooperate—but I love the symbolism of it. A stretch of tall, unapologetically bright flowers in a place that's carried nothing but darkness and grief for too long.

There's a weeping willow nearby, its branches sweeping low like they're mourning something too. But I think the sunflowers will brighten the space. I've already decided I'll add some colorful wildflowers—blues, pinks, purples. When it all fills in, it'll be like sunshine surrounded by the soft chaos of color.

I'm going to order a bench too. Something solid and weatherproof, something to last all year round because grief knows no season.

Hunter's done so much for me and for Atticus. He's shown up again and again, never asking for anything in return. I want to give him something back. Something meaningful.

Back inside, I'm folding Atticus's laundry in his room, the repetitive task soothing in a way I didn't expect. But even as I match his tiny socks and stack his folded shirts, my mind keeps circling one thing like a vulture: Natalie.

Why didn't she tell me about Hunter? About their history? Especially if he broke her heart like he said. If it took her *years* to get over him, why wouldn't she have mentioned it? We've talked about Hunter plenty of times. It would've been easy to slip it into conversation, even casually.

Unless she didn't want me to know.

Unless she's still not over him.

Either way, it's bizarre, and I don't like how it sits in my gut.

I think of Reese—not my oldest friend, but my truest, bluest friend. She'd have never kept something like this from me.

I finish putting the laundry away, still thinking about it, still chewing on the discomfort. Afterward, I head to my office, ready to knock out another chapter or two while the house is still quiet. But when I start digging through my desk for my notes, the sunflower notebook—the one I've been writing in every night, the one where I've scribbled plot ideas and sensory details from every night with Hunter—is *gone.*

I stop in my tracks, jerking open every drawer twice before flipping through stacks of paper. Next I sprint upstairs to check my nightstand and dresser drawers. I check every inch of the kitchen. Every shelf in the living room. The entry table. The laundry room.

Nothing.

My pulse hammers, stomach dropping. I've had that notebook by my side constantly. If that gets into the wrong hands—Hunter's hands—I'll be humiliated. My most intimate thoughts about him, my hopes, daydreams, fears, insecurities, and hard truths are all laid out bare on those pages. Unpolished. Unfiltered. Raw. Vulnerable.

I imagine him poring over those writings and walking away with the notion that I'm some lovesick romance writer with a schoolgirl crush. Now he thinks I'm sexy, independent, intriguing. If he reads my writings? I'll come across as someone who's so desperate for love she started idealizing a complete stranger from the very first meeting.

I'll lose him.

I'll lose him for good.

And if Natalie finds it? All those personal details about the things Hunter and I have done . . . will be public fodder. He's a private man, and I can think of no bigger invasion of that privacy. Not to mention, I can only imagine Natalie spinning it like I'm using him for literal inspiration when I'm only drawing inspiration from the way he makes me *feel.*

Panic claws up my throat. I can't breathe. I tear the house apart, room by room, checking and rechecking. Under beds, behind cushions, in the laundry basket. I even check the car, despite knowing I haven't taken it out of the house.

Still nothing.

I rack my brain. The only people who've been here in the last few days?

Natalie and Hunter.

But Hunter didn't go near my office. He was with me the whole time he was here, barely let me out of his sight. Natalie, though . . . she took a couple of bathroom breaks. We even hung out in my office for a few minutes as she paged through my paperbacks in search of one to take home.

I don't want to believe she'd do something like that. But who else would have? Who else *could* have?

I sit at my desk, staring at the empty spot where my notebook should be, a hollow ache opening in my chest.

Regardless of who has that notebook—Hunter or Natalie—no good could possibly come of this.

47

Hunter

I'm fixing a gearbox at a bin site when my phone buzzes in my pocket. I wipe my hands off on a shop rag, check the screen—local number, one I know well.

Bill Porter—an old, retired farmer I've been negotiating with for months over that 220-acre parcel south of the river. We finally agreed on a price last week—a damn good one for me, better than I expected. He's been working with his lawyer to get the paperwork drawn up.

"Bill," I answer. "Good timing. I was gonna follow up this week, see how the paperwork was coming."

There's a pause followed by a raspy exhale on the other end.

"Hunter, I'm callin' to let you know the deal's off the table," he says.

I straighten, frowning. "What?"

"You heard me."

I press the phone tighter to my ear. "We settled on a number. You said you were moving forward."

"Yeah, well . . . I'm backing out of the deal."

"That doesn't make sense. Why? What changed?"

Another pause. I hear his breath rattle through the line, like he's debating if he wants to say it.

"You're not who I thought you were," he says finally. "That's all I'm gonna say."

I grit my teeth. "Bill, what are you talking about?"

"I ran into Cole Benton the other day. He told me how you assaulted him."

I close my eyes, pinching the bridge of my nose. I should've known Cole wasn't gonna let that go quietly.

"He also said," Bill continues, his voice going lower, "you're datin' some . . . well, some woman, the kind of gal a man wouldn't take home to his mama."

I bark a humorless laugh, shaking my head. "You believe everything that drunk son of a bitch says?"

The irony of this whole thing isn't lost on me. In fact, it infuriates me. Cole's painting me in a negative light, and Bill's turning a blind eye to the fact that Cole's exactly the kind of man Bill wouldn't do business with.

I can't say I blame Bill. In his old age, he doesn't have time for drama, avoids it like the plague, and he knows damn well Cole could make or break anyone in this town. Cole's got so much money it wouldn't surprise me if he offered Bill seven figures cash *not* to take the deal.

"I'm just tellin' you what I heard, Hunter."

"And I'm telling you it's a hell of a lot more complicated than that."

"Maybe so," Bill says. "But I'm almost eighty years old, son. I don't need complicated."

I swallow my frustration, trying to salvage it. "We've been working on this deal for months. You're gonna throw it away over gossip?"

There's a beat, and then Bill says, "Cole offered me twenty percent more than what you were gonna pay."

And there it is. Just as I suspected.

I clench my jaw until it burns, staring at the concrete floor like it's personally offended me. "I'm disappointed, Bill. I thought you were a man of your word."

"I am. But I'm also a man who knows a better deal when I see one."

I don't tell him he's wrong.

We hang up, and I stare at the dead screen in my hand, rage simmering under my skin. This is Cole's doing. Retaliation for being rejected, for getting embarrassed in public. He's got money, power, and no one to keep him in check. That makes him dangerous, especially in our little farming community, where word spreads fast and everyone's a friend *and* a competitor at the same time.

Cole is the worst kind of man. And he's not going anywhere—he's a goddamn local fixture, sitting on tens of thousands of acres like some spoiled prince wearing his daddy's crown.

A truck door creaks open, and over walks Cal, wiping sweat from his brow. I hadn't heard him pull up. He isn't wearing his trademark smirk and he doesn't have some witty, smart-assed line for me. He simply gives me a look like he's about to deliver more bad news.

"Just drove past the Highland farm on my way here," he says. "Corn was just starting to sprout, but the leaf buds? They're turning yellow already."

I frown. "That can't be right."

"It's the whole field, boss. It's like someone sprayed everything with bleach or something. I dunno. Never seen anything like it."

I nod, putting the pieces together. "Cole."

Cal's eyes narrow. "Cole Benton?"

In addition to inheriting his father's massive operation, the man owns an aerial ag business. Planes, helicopters, crop-dusting, spraying. If someone wanted to sabotage a field without setting foot on the property, that'd be the way. And if he does it in the middle of the night? With a helicopter? It'd go by virtually unseen, especially the Highland farm. It's miles from the nearest house.

Cal shakes his head. "Why the hell would he do that?"

"Because he wants what I have."

Cal scratches his temple. "Land?"

I shake my head. "No. He wants Wren."

He lets out a low whistle, chuckling under his breath. "Women are not worth it, man."

Normally I'd agree with him. But I think of her smile, the way she laughs when she's trying not to like me, the way she looks when she's naked and happy and completely unguarded.

"This one?" I say, silently plotting how I'm going to deal with this obnoxious waste of human space. "She's worth it."

48

Wren

While Atticus sits at the table, devouring a bowl of cereal, I scroll through my text messages, half-awake but already restless.

Nick hasn't messaged in a few days. That alone feels like a gift from the universe. Still, I can't relax. I keep expecting his name to pop up, like a snake lurking in the grass.

Further down, Natalie's name flashes across my screen.

NATALIE: You around today? Want to meet up?

I don't respond. I can't—not yet. I'm still trying to wrap my head around the fact that she and Hunter had a history and she never breathed a word of it.

I keep flipping back and forth in my mind—there has to be an explanation. Maybe it wasn't that serious? Maybe she didn't think it was relevant? But according to Hunter, it was serious to her. She wanted marriage. Babies. A life. It took her years to get over him.

And she never told me.

The longer I let that thought sit, the worse it feels. I can't just hang out with her like nothing's changed, like I don't know there's a giant unspoken secret between us. But I don't know how to bring it up either.

I leave her on read and toss my phone onto the couch.

After Atticus finishes his cereal, I poke around the house again, turning over every pillow, pulling open every drawer. Searching for that damn sunflower notebook. Still nothing. It's like it vanished into thin air.

But the pit in my stomach says otherwise.

"Mom?" Atticus pipes up, wandering into the living room with his favorite stuffed dog. "When can we see Hunter again?"

I look up, caught off guard. "What makes you ask that?"

"'Cause it's been a while." He plops onto the couch, clutching his toy. "And I like him. He's fun. And he makes you happy when he's here. I like when you're happy, Mom."

I smile softly, sitting beside him. "He *is* fun."

"I wanna ride in his tractor," Atticus says, eyes wide. "You said he has a tractor. Can I? Can I ride in it?"

I hesitate. I'm not going to tell him that Hunter *has* been around, just . . . not during daylight. I'm not ready to explain the arrangement we have—the one I keep telling myself is just physical, even though my heart is starting to argue otherwise.

"We'll see," I say, standing to grab my phone.

I call Hunter. He answers on the second ring.

"Hey," I say. "I've got a little boy here asking when he can ride in your tractor."

Hunter chuckles on the other end. "Good timing. I'm just mowing some grass ways today. You can bring him out if you want."

"Really?"

"Yeah. I'll drop you a pin as soon as we hang up. He can ride in the jump seat with me."

I glance at Atticus, already bouncing on the couch. "Okay. We'll head out soon."

Hunter sends the location, and Atticus insists on packing a backpack. He fills it with fruit snacks, juice boxes, a toy truck, and his lucky coin—some rusted thing he found behind the barn the other day. His excitement is so pure, it makes my heart ache a little—both happy and nervous.

Happy because he's so eager to see Hunter.

Nervous because the lines between all of us are blurring, and I'm not sure how much longer I can keep pretending we're not well on our way to becoming *something*.

Something messy.

Something dangerous.

And maybe something real.

The butterflies in my stomach take a nervous turn. The last time I let someone this close to us, we both got burned. The thought of that happening again makes me recoil, makes me hold my breath until it physically hurts.

"Come on, Mom, we gotta go!" Atticus bounces on his heels, his shoelaces untied and his smile almost wider than his face. "Hunter needs me in the tractor. We can't keep him waiting. We've got a lot of work to do."

I grab my purse and keys and chase Atti out to the driveway, barely able to keep up with him.

If this blows up in my face, if Hunter breaks my heart . . . I'll get over it.

If he breaks my son's heart? I'll never forgive him.

49

Hunter

Atticus is riding shotgun in the tractor's jump seat, chattering my ear off like he's been saving every thought in his head just for this moment.

"What's that button do? What happens if you push that lever? What's that sound?" He bounces in sync with every bump in the field.

I explain what I can, pointing to the display screens, the throttle, the controls that move the batwings, even though I'm just mowing today—not exactly the most glamorous farmwork. But to a kid, everything is magic when you're sitting this high off the ground.

"When we get to fall," I tell him, "this whole field? We'll be out here with combines. Harvesting all the corn. My favorite time of year."

His eyes get big. "I wanna do that! Can I do that?"

"You can ride with me if you want," I say, grinning at his excitement. I remember being that age. Riding with my dad and grandpa in a combine was always the highlight of my fall—more exciting than Halloween. "When you're older, maybe you can be my grain cart operator."

"What's that?"

I explain how the grain cart keeps the combines running by unloading on the go, how it's the most important job in the field next to running the combine itself.

"And if you're really good at that," I add, "when you're older, I'll let you run a combine."

He lights up like I just promised him a trip to Disney World. "Really?"

"Really."

I watch him take it all in, staring out the window like he's imagining it already.

I always thought I'd have a son someday—a little boy who'd love farming as much as I did. A kid to teach everything to. Someone to take over the land, carry on the McCrae name, the legacy.

Funny how life doesn't always play out the way you picture it.

"How's your mom doing?" I ask him. We've texted a few times this last week, but every time I think I have a spare minute to sneak in a visit, something comes up. Our schedules haven't synced up in a minute, and it's killing me.

"She's happy now," he says, digging into his backpack for a snack.

"Yeah? How come?"

"'Cause she's writing again."

That makes me smile. "She told you that?"

He nods, mouth full of goldfish crackers. "She's working on a new book. It's about a farmer."

My hands freeze on the wheel for just a second, palms dampening. A flicker of something sharp cuts through the warm haze of the moment.

She's writing a book about a farmer?

I clear my throat. "She say what kind of farmer?"

He shrugs. "A regular kind."

The kid's five. He's not going to be much help in this department.

I stare ahead, watching the mower eat up the rows of grass, dust kicking up behind us. Wren *did* promise me she wouldn't write about us—about me. She swore anything personal stayed between us. But now I'm wondering if I've just been one long research project. If she's been cataloging every touch, every kiss, every private, stolen moment—for the proverbial plot.

I shake it off, refocusing on the field in front of me. Still, the doubt sticks to my ribs like a meal I can't digest.

50

Wren

I wait until after I've dropped Atticus off at day camp before I finally muster up the nerve to walk into Natalie's shop.

The place is quiet for a Monday morning, her new inventory displayed neatly in the front window, and the smell of some fancy candle burning in the corner. She looks up from behind the counter, visibly surprised—but happy.

"Hey, stranger," she says, smiling.

I didn't come here to waste time.

"Why didn't you tell me you dated Hunter?" I ask, my voice level, even though my pulse is kicking up. "Why didn't you mention he broke your heart? That it took you years to get over him?"

Her smile falters, but she recovers fast. She shrugs, brushing it off with a casual wave of her hand. "Because that was over a decade ago, Wren. I'm over it. I didn't see the point in beating a very dead, very old horse."

"We've talked about him a lot," I press. "Multiple times. Why wouldn't you at least mention it?"

She crosses her arms, her face unreadable now. "Because, like I said, it's in the past. It's irrelevant. What would telling you have done? Would it have changed anything? No. It only would've made things weird, and

I didn't want you to think about any of that when you're . . . enjoying your time with him."

I say nothing, because she has a point—but that's not the issue.

"I told you everything else I knew about him," she adds, her tone sharpening just slightly. "That he's a heartbreaker. That he leaves women worse off than he found them. I was trying to protect you without injecting myself into it. I was trying to be a good friend."

I want to believe her. I really do. And maybe she's right. Maybe dragging up ancient history would've just made things messy. But still . . . it gnaws at me. It feels like a lie of omission.

And then I think about the notebook.

I hesitate because I know how it's going to sound, but if I don't ask, it'll drive me crazy.

"Hey," I say carefully, "this is probably nothing, but . . . the other night, when you were over, did you see a notebook sitting in my office? Small, sunflowers on the cover. The pages are all crinkly."

Her brows pinch. "No. Why?"

I swallow. "Because it's missing. I've been looking for it everywhere."

Her eyes narrow, defensive. "What are you implying? That I stole some random notebook off your desk when you weren't looking?"

I wince, heat flooding my cheeks. "No—I mean, I was just wondering if you saw it, that's all. I haven't been able to find it since."

She scoffs. "Maybe Atticus took it?"

"He knows better. He doesn't touch my stuff in there."

She stares at me, frowning. "Okay . . . well . . . who else has been over?"

I hesitate.

And that's when she asks, "Hunter?"

I pause. Come to think of it, I haven't heard from Hunter since the tractor ride with Atticus. It's been days. I figured he's been busy—it's planting season—but it's not like him to stay silent this long.

I shake my head. "No . . . I don't think he's even been in my office."

Natalie watches me carefully, like she's trying to read my mind.

I sigh. "Sorry. That was awkward. And I don't mean to accuse. It's just a very important notebook. I need it for the book I'm writing. It's a big deal that it's just . . . disappeared."

She softens, stepping around the counter to hug me. "It's fine. You've been through a lot this last year and you're going through a lot now. I get it. No hard feelings."

We hug, we smooth it over, but when I leave, I don't feel any better.

If anything, I feel worse.

On the drive home, I text Hunter.

ME: Hey, you free tonight?

Normally he replies within minutes. Sometimes seconds.

But hours pass. Evening falls. The text is still sitting there—delivered, not read.

By the time I go to bed, it's still that way.

He swore he wouldn't play games.

Guess he lied.

Maybe one of these days I'll stop falling for all those pretty words that come out of men's mouths.

51

Hunter

I'm standing in line at the coffee shop the next morning, bleary-eyed and barely human, when I hear my name in that sharp, chirpy voice I'd recognize anywhere.

"Hunter McCrae," Mrs. Harrison beams from a table near the window. "Is it true?"

I glance over, lifting my chin in greeting. "Morning, Mrs. Harrison."

She grins, chin tucked, like she's been waiting for this. "Is it true you're dating that author in town? The one who writes the *dirty* books?"

I rub the back of my neck, chuckling under my breath.

"They're not *dirty*," I say. "They're very tasteful."

Her brows shoot up like she's not convinced, but she's thoroughly entertained. "Okay, fair enough, but are you dating?"

"I've . . . spent some time with her," I admit carefully, because around here, anything you tell one person is circulating countywide by sundown. "She's a good neighbor."

"Mm-hmm," she hums, her eyes twinkling before she goes back to her hazelnut latte.

I step forward in line, still irritated from everything I've been carrying lately. Cole's stunt with the Highland field, the sabotaged land deal . . . and then there's the *notebook.*

Atticus gave it to me in the tractor the other day, just pulled it out of his backpack like it was no big thing.

"Found this in my mom's office," he said. "She's been teaching me how to read this summer. She said since she writes books, she wants me to be a good reader. I saw your name on all the pages. I thought you might wanna read 'em."

I didn't open it right away. I wasn't sure I wanted to.

But curiosity got the better of me that night.

I needed to know how she felt about me, how she really felt. Because I've been dying to have that conversation with her, antsy to move things forward and stop dancing around in this gray area.

So I read it.

And it was filled with *everything*. Sweet notes, her hopes, her worries, things she never said to my face. And then there were the detailed logs of us—of our nights together. What I did to her. What I said. How I made her feel. And alongside those? Plot notes. Chapter outlines. *Book material.*

A farmer romance . . .

There it was, in her own handwriting—proof that this was *all for the proverbial plot* after all.

I'm still stewing when the door swings open and in walks Natalie—one of the last people I want to see for a myriad of reasons, but lately she's at the top of my list due to all the things she's been filling Wren's head with about me.

I've seen her around town plenty since we ended things. Usually we're ships passing in the night, barely a nod, maybe a polite wave. But this time, her eyes lock on me and she makes a beeline for the line where I'm standing.

She slides in behind me, her perfume as familiar as it is suffocating.

"Hi," she says, like she's trying to sound casual. "How've you been?"

I glance back. "You tell me. You've had a front-row seat, apparently."

Her brow arches. "What's that supposed to mean?"

I turn fully, facing her. "You could've told Wren you dated me. She confided in you about me and you sat there playing dumb."

Natalie crosses her arms, her mouth twisting into a half smirk. "Our dating history is irrelevant, Hunter. I told her what she needed to know—that you're a serial heartbreaker. You've got a reputation, and I thought she should be prepared. I was just trying to be a good friend."

I stare at her, jaw tight, but she's not done.

"Apparently she didn't take my advice—or she didn't care—because now she's writing a book about you." She watches for my reaction.

I don't give her one.

And I don't tell her I already know.

"She says it's *not* about you, but come on. Isn't that what authors always say? *'Any resemblance to real people is purely coincidental.'* But we both know that's bullshit." She sniffs a laugh, waving her hand through the air. "God, that's so cringey. And how embarrassing for you, right? Everyone's going to know who it's about."

Again, I don't reply.

"She told me herself you're literally her inspiration," she adds, voice syrupy and cutting. "But maybe it'll work out because you're both kind of just using each other. I'm just glad one of your conquests is actually going to get something out of her time with you other than a broken heart."

She's desperate for a reaction, but she's still not getting one.

The line inches forward, but I'm done with this conversation. I grab my coffee when it's finally my turn and head out without another word.

I need space. I need to think. Because right now, I don't know what to think.

I'm sitting in my truck a minute later, my coffee untouched and my window rolled down because the air in the cab is too thick to breathe. Natalie Dinsmore struts out a few seconds later, her iced latte in hand, hips swaying as she walks. She's parked next to me. I keep my eyes trained ahead, avoiding her as best I can, but she stops by my open window like it's some kind of invitation.

"You know, maybe this makes me sound petty, but you're finally getting a taste of your own medicine, and I kind of love this for you," she says, wearing a smug smirk that only serves to discredit most of what she's saying. People like Natalie don't change. She's as jealous and insecure as she's ever been. "Also, you know she's still texting her ex, right? He blows her phone up all the time. If you ask me, she's still not over him. She says she is, but . . ." Natalie sips her drink. "Anyway. Nice to see you, Hunter. Enjoy being book material while it lasts."

Wren's still talking to Nick? After I warned him off? And she didn't tell me? Was she not comfortable asking for my help?

This, along with the notebook and Wren's insistence that we should just keep things physical, is starting to make sense now. She never let me in—not as deep as I thought she did. She kept things from me.

From the start, I secretly worried I wasn't capable of meeting her depth.

But I thought she was giving me a chance.

Turns out she was keeping me at an arm's length the whole time—same as I did to her in the beginning.

I never saw this coming, but then again, that's what makes love dangerous: You never do.

52

Wren

I can't stay in this house a second longer.

Every time I pass a window, I catch a glimpse of the lodge on the hill—Hunter's house, looming over me like a shadow I can't escape. And every time I see it, I feel everything all over again. Anger. Sadness. Confusion. That awful ache that settles in my stomach and just sits there.

I haven't written a single word in days. Every time I sit down, my head floods with *him*. His mouth on mine. His voice in the dark. His promises. The way I feel every time I'm around him, calm and at ease, like nothing could go wrong as long as he's by my side.

I stuff my laptop and notebook—a *new* one the color of maraschino cherries, because the sunflower notebook is still missing—into my bag and drive into town, aiming for the coffee shop. Maybe a change of scenery will shake something loose.

I'm pulling into a spot across the street when I catch them.

Hunter.

And Natalie.

They're outside the coffee shop, him in his truck, her standing beside him, deep in conversation. Natalie's grinning, laughing, her hand brushing his arm like she has every right to touch him. Hunter's head is down, too far away for me to read his expression.

I don't get out of the car. I stay there, frozen, watching, slumped down behind my steering wheel while my heart sinks lower with every passing second.

Hunter told me Natalie meant nothing.

Natalie said Hunter was ancient history.

I believe him.

But he's listening to her, hearing her out.

And the longer I watch, the sicker I feel.

What if Natalie lied? What if she took my notebook, showed it to him, spun some story about me being unstable or obsessed? About me *using* him? She could've convinced him I was exploiting him for the sake of some stupid book. She's clever enough. Petty enough.

And now, maybe she's using it to worm her way back into his life.

My blood runs cold at a different thought—one of her not spinning a narrative that I used him as book material. Instead I imagine her poking fun at my "teenage girl diary," maybe pointing out how pathetic my confessions are and using my rawest, most vulnerable emotions to paint me in a cringey light.

Whatever she's saying to him about my notebook, it's out of context—and that's a thought that chills me to the core.

I'd give anything to see his face right now. Does he look annoyed? Bothered? Is he eating this up? Laughing along with her? A hundred scenarios fill my mind, none of them ideal.

I'm still spiraling when my phone vibrates in the cup holder.

Another text. I hold my breath, unreasonably hoping it's from Hunter.

NICK: I'm coming to Colton Valley.

I stare at it, dread sinking low in my gut. Before I can overthink it, he's calling.

I answer. "Don't. Don't come here. You're not welcome here."

"Wren, please," he says, his voice low, urgent. "Hear me out."

"There's nothing you can say to change anything," I snap. "You've done enough."

"I'm not trying to change anything. I just want to apologize to Atti," Nick says. "That's all I want. That's what I've been trying to do this entire time. I know I blew it with you, I know you don't owe me the time of day, but I feel awful about what I did to Atticus. Let me tell him I'm sorry. I at least *owe* him that."

I blink, caught off guard. I never expected that. But the way he says it, I can tell—this has been the real reason he's kept contacting me. He wants closure. Or maybe absolution.

Atticus *is* owed that.

I swallow, hating how uncertain I feel. But the words slip out anyway.

"Fine," I say. "But that's it. Nothing more. You show up. You apologize to him. And then you leave. Understood?"

"I understand," he says quietly. "Thank you. I'll be there tomorrow night around seven."

"Six," I say. "Atticus goes to bed at seven thirty."

"Sure. I'll be there at six."

I hang up, toss the phone in the passenger seat, and sink back against my seat, exhausted.

Natalie outside the coffee shop. Hunter leaning out his window, talking to her. Nick on his way back into my life, if only for a moment.

I thought moving home would simplify things.

But all I've done is get tangled up in more of a mess than I ever imagined.

53

Hunter

I've been up to my neck in small projects all day—tinkering, repairing, organizing shit that doesn't actually need organizing. The kind of work that keeps my hands busy but my mind just as restless. Doesn't help that I ran into Natalie this morning. It seemed to set the tone for a day that was already well on its way to being shitty.

The music's blaring loud enough to piss off the dead, but it still doesn't drown out my thoughts of Wren and that goddamned notebook.

It's been days since I've seen her. Days since she texted me, asking if I was free that night. I didn't answer. Not because I didn't want to—but because I didn't know what to say. I didn't want to brush her off, and I didn't want to pick a fight. But pretending it wasn't a big deal? That'd be a lie.

And lying isn't in my nature.

I keep replaying my conversation with Natalie at the coffee shop. The way she said Wren's writing some book about me. About *us*. She made it sound like the whole thing's been one long exercise in research. Like I'm just the broody farmer prototype she needed to round out her plot.

And then there's Nick. Her ex, still circling like a vulture, still texting her.

Natalie was quick to remind me of that too.

I remind myself—this is Natalie we're talking about. Desperate Natalie. The same woman who, after we broke up, used to call me six, seven times a day. When I stopped answering, she faked a damn car accident to get my attention. Claimed she hit a deer. I didn't buy it, but I still called her back because I thought she was hurt, and it was the right thing to do.

She used to be beautiful. Back in the day, she had that queen bee glow, always the prettiest girl in the room. Always got what she wanted. She thought she'd have me in the bag. When I proved to be a challenge, when I didn't fall into line, when I ended things . . . it wasn't just heartbreak. It was humiliation.

She's still attractive, sure—but her beauty is only skin deep. Peel it back and it's nothing but insecurity, gossip, and fake smiles. Not someone I'd ever build a life with. Not someone I could trust. Her best days are long behind her, leaving a bitter, jealous woman in her place.

I should take everything Natalie said with a grain of salt.

But that notebook? That's harder to shake. It wasn't gossip or hearsay. It was real. In her handwriting. Our nights, our words, our private moments . . . scribbled down alongside chapter outlines and plot beats.

I try to shove it down, keep my head focused on the task in front of me, but by late afternoon I'm spent. Physically. Mentally. Emotionally.

I head home, crack a beer, and step out onto the deck on the back side of the lodge—the side that faces away from the little white farmhouse down the road. Out here, it's just open sky and quiet.

I drop into a chair, the wood creaking under my weight, and stare out at the horizon until the sun starts to dip low. I initially came out here to think, but now that I'm out here, thinking's the last thing I feel like doing. I've done enough of that for the day.

The beer in my hand remains cracked and untouched.

My grandfather always used to say too much thinking and not enough doing was the worst way to solve a problem, so I dump the beer over the railing of the deck, head inside, and grab that notebook.

54

Wren

I've been sitting at my desk for over an hour and all I have to show for it are three sentences—not even good ones.

I backspace the last line and sigh, dragging the curtains shut to block the view of the lodge on the hill. It helps a little—not seeing his house—but only barely. The imprint of it is still there, in my mind, every time I close my eyes. Knowing he's so close yet so far away at the same time has been eating me alive.

I can't stop thinking about this morning, seeing Hunter and Natalie conversing outside the coffee shop, a little too close, talking a little too intently. I'd almost bet money she's spinning a web about me using him for my book, telling him how inspired I was by our rendezvous. Sabotaging any remaining chance we could've had to make a go of this. I'd bet even more money that she downplayed Cole Benton on purpose, hoping I'd nibble at his cheap attempt to reel me in, her knowing damn well what kind of person he is.

Regardless of what Natalie did or didn't say at the coffee shop, Hunter's been ignoring me since *before* that run-in. Whatever Natalie said probably just cemented whatever narrative he'd already been writing in his head.

It's over. Done.

It was fun while it lasted.

And hey, I've got half a book out of it, so it wasn't for nothing. That's the only real way to salvage the pain of all of this going belly up. It's the only spin I can put on it that doesn't feel like a hot knife gliding into the center of my heart.

I'm mid-sulk when Atticus tiptoes into my office, still in his dinosaur pajamas, his hair sticking up like a haystack. I tucked him in an hour ago.

"Hey, what are you doing up, buddy?" I ask, glancing at the clock. "It's way past bedtime."

"I heard a funny noise," he says, rubbing his eyes.

"This is an old house, kiddo. It makes funny noises all the time."

He shuffles closer, his face scrunched. "I'm sad."

I swivel my chair to face him fully. "Why?"

"'Cause Hunter doesn't come around anymore."

The words hit me square in the chest, but I force a smile. "Hunter's really busy, baby. He runs a big farm. A *huge* one. He'll come visit when he can."

"But when will that be?"

I swallow, searching for an answer that won't break both our hearts. "I don't know."

His face falls. "When I was in his tractor last week, I asked him to come over more. He promised he would."

That *does* break my heart . . . clean in two, but what really bubbles up is anger—scorching, searing.

Hunter didn't just break a promise to me—he broke one to my son.

"He probably just got busy," I say, trying to soften it. "That happens sometimes."

"Maybe I can ride Sugarplum up to his house," Atticus says, hopeful. "Then he'll have to see me."

"You know you're not allowed to leave the corral with Sugarplum," I remind him. "We've talked about that. Now back to bed, mister."

He yawns, rubbing his eyes again. I scoop him up, his weight warm and familiar against me as I carry him back to bed. I tuck him in, brushing his hair off his forehead, lingering and watching until he finally drifts off.

When I get back to my office, I stare at my phone, debating whether to text Hunter. Maybe ask him what the hell his deal is. Why he lied about not playing games. Why he'd let Atticus down so easily.

But I stop myself.

Nick is coming tomorrow. And I'm already dreading that. I don't have the energy for both of these men *and* their bullshit.

After this, I'm done.

I'm done wasting my energy on people who don't deserve it. Done chasing. Done pleading. Done apologizing when I've done nothing wrong. Done breaking promises I made to myself. Done compromising my standards for the promise of something that always turns out to be smoke and mirrors. Done downplaying my needs and wants to make myself more palatable for someone.

If it's just me and Atticus the rest of my life, so be it.

I deserved better. Atticus deserved better.

I'd rather be alone than settle for less ever again.

55

Hunter

I'm sitting in my living room, the house dead quiet except for the creak of wood settling and the occasional low whistle of wind against the windows. The notebook's in my lap—her notebook—and I've been flipping through it for the past hour.

The first time I read it, I was pissed. Seeing everything I thought was just between us written down, some of it explicit as hell, mixed right in with plot notes and chapter outlines. I felt exposed. Played. Used like a damn fool.

But tonight, I'm calmer. Less . . . reactive.

Trying like hell to give her the benefit of the doubt.

I read slower this time. Really read. Not just the sex. Not the observations about the way I move or what I say in the dark when it's just the two of us.

It's the other stuff.

The letters to me.

The confessions about her ex, the emotional scars he left behind.

Her fears and vulnerabilities.

Her hopes and dreams.

The ache she tries so hard to cover up.

The way she describes grappling with all the conflicting feelings I stir up in her.

The entries about how hard it is to do this life alone, but how she's done it anyway, because what choice does she have?

There's a page where she writes about independence like it's her religion, but then right under that, like a whispered secret—she writes *I think I could need him if I let myself.*

Some pages are stained. Like she was crying when she wrote them.

I'm starting to think this wasn't a gimmick or some cold, calculated thing.

It's just her, being a complicated human like the rest of us.

I close the notebook, my thumb resting on the weathered cover, and lean back in my chair.

I'm done spinning my wheels about this. Done listening to other people.

I need to go talk to Wren—hear it straight from her. Let her explain—or yell at me or slam the door in my face. Hell, I probably deserve that much for going radio silent on her, for keeping her at arm's length when she let me into her world without much hesitation.

But I'm not doing this guessing game anymore.

I need to know once and for all . . . was any of this real?

56

Wren

Nick should be here any minute.

I'm in the kitchen, trying to prep Atticus—gently, cautiously—for what's about to happen. Not that I have the right words for this kind of thing. There's no parenting manual for *ex-fiancé shows up to apologize for ghosting your kid.*

"He's just coming to visit for a little bit," I tell him, smoothing a wrinkle from his T-shirt. "Just to say a few words, okay?"

Atticus lights up. "Is he moving in with us? On the farm?"

I shake my head, swallowing the lump that rises. "No, baby. He's not moving in. He just wanted to see you since he didn't get to say goodbye before, that's all."

Atticus frowns, but he nods. I can tell he doesn't understand—not fully—but he's trying to. Trying to wrap his little brain around the grown-up mess he was subjected to.

Then I hear the crunch of tires on gravel and peek out the front window.

There it is. The shiny black BMW. Classic Nick. A fresh haircut, a designer shirt that probably cost more than my monthly utilities, tailored pants, and that signature cocky confidence he always wears like cologne. He didn't get dressed up like this for my five-year-old.

Thinking about how I used to find this attractive makes me want to throw up in my mouth a little.

Atticus runs ahead of me, bursting out the door just as Nick steps out of the car. Nick barely gets a foot on the driveway before Atticus barrels into him, and Nick scoops him up like they do this every weekend.

"Whoa! Look at you!" Nick laughs, spinning him around. "You're getting huge!"

Atticus beams, babbling excitedly, already pulling Nick by the hand. He drags him all over the property—the river, the gazebo, the barn, Sugarplum. Nick plays along, pretending to be impressed, though I can tell he's just following the kid's lead. That's the thing about Nick—he's always been good at performance.

At one point, Atticus tugs on his sleeve. "Can I show you the house?"

"No, honey," I call from behind. "Nick isn't staying long."

Atticus pouts but doesn't argue. Eventually, we circle back to the driveway, standing beside the front passenger door of Nick's car.

Nick crouches and lifts Atticus onto his hip, settling him there like he weighs nothing.

"Hey, buddy," he says gently, "I wanted to tell you something important."

Atticus stares up at him, wide-eyed, all ears.

Nick clears his throat, glances at me—like he's searching for the right words—but I don't help him. This is his mess to clean up.

"I wanted to say I'm sorry," he tells Atticus. "I'm sorry I couldn't be your dad. I really wanted to, I did. But . . ."

He looks at me again, then back at Atticus.

"Your mom and me . . . well, sometimes adults figure out they're not meant to be together. And when you're older, maybe you'll understand. And maybe we can talk more about it then. But for now, I wanted you to know I think you're the coolest kid I've ever met, and I'm so proud of you, and I know you're going to do amazing things with your life."

Atticus looks down, his little hand clutching Nick's collar. He doesn't cry, but I can see the sadness swimming in his eyes. The whole moment—Nick's unexpected kindness, Atticus's reaction, it moves me to tears, but I blink them away before they have a chance to fall.

"Okay," Atti whispers.

I cross my arms, hugging myself. There's nothing left to say. Nothing that'll make this easier or cleaner.

I'm waiting for Nick to get going when I hear it—the low rumble of a diesel engine, the distinct hum of tires on gravel.

I turn my head just in time to see Hunter's big white truck barreling toward my house, kicking up dust like he's a man on a mission.

Of all the times for him to show up . . .

57

Hunter

I pull up the drive faster than I should, gravel kicking out behind me, my pulse pounding harder with every foot closer to that obnoxiously shiny BMW.

I barely kill the engine before I'm out of the truck, door slamming shut behind me.

Wren's by the driveway, standing stiff, her arms crossed, eyes heavy with something between exhaustion and guilt. And then there's him—*Nick*, I'm guessing. Dressed like he's about to walk into a board meeting. No one dresses that way unless they're trying to impress someone, and the only person around here for him to impress . . . is Wren.

I gesture sharply in his direction, my eyes locked on Wren. "Really? *Really*?"

Nick looks slightly confused, his brows pulling together like he's not sure what the hell he walked into, or maybe he's wondering if this is the man who answered Wren's phone that night and told him off. But before I can say anything else, a small blur shoots across the gravel.

Atticus.

He runs straight for me, his face beaming, and before I can process it, he's got his arms around my waist, looking up like he's been waiting for me to come back home.

"I *knew* you'd come back!" he says, his grin infectious. "Hunter, this is Nick. He came by to say he's sorry he couldn't be my dad."

I freeze, my jaw still tight, but the fight's bleeding out of me already. I glance at Nick, who suddenly looks sheepish. Small. Maybe even embarrassed. A fish out of water if I've ever seen one.

I bend down and scoop Atticus into my arms, settling him on my hip. He wraps his arms around my neck, his head resting there like it's the most natural place in the world.

My eyes find Wren again, but she's not meeting them. She looks caught—like a deer between two trucks speeding at full tilt. Her gaze flicks between me and Nick and Atticus, her mouth tight, saying nothing.

Nick clears his throat, shifting awkwardly. "I should get going."

He looks at Atticus. "Be good for your mom, all right, buddy?"

Atticus nods, and Nick climbs into his car, the engine purring like a satisfied cat as he pulls back down the drive.

I watch the taillights until they disappear around the bend.

Wren walks over, gently lifting Atticus from my arms without looking at me.

"We're going inside," she says flatly. "It's getting late. I need to get him to bed."

I step forward, my voice low. "It's only six thirty."

"It's been a long day," she says, her eyes finally meeting mine, but they're guarded. "Did you need something?"

I open my mouth, but nothing comes out. I knew what I was going to say—until I saw her ex-fiancé here. Then all I saw was red. All I could think about was what Natalie said about Wren not being over him. For a moment, it appeared it might be true.

All the things I came here to say took a back seat. Now Nick's gone and she's trying to do the same.

Wren watches me another beat, her eyes hollow, and then turns away, carrying Atticus up the porch steps and through the front door.

I stand in her front yard alone with my thoughts and all the things I came here to say—but didn't.

58

Wren

Atticus has his head on my shoulder, half-lidded and yawning, but his mouth keeps going. A thousand questions spill out, barely a beat between them. "Why did Nick have to leave so soon? Why was Hunter mad? Where did Nick go? Is Hunter mad at *me*? Will Hunter come back? Can we ride Sugarplum to his house tomorrow?"

He gets extra chatty when he's tired, but tonight it's worse than ever. Seeing two of his favorite people show up one after the other—it's lit his little brain on fire. Every question breaks my heart more than the one before it because I don't have any good answers.

I press my cheek to his hair, rocking him gently as I sit on the edge of his bed.

"Hunter's not mad at you, baby," I whisper. "I promise."

"But he looked mad," Atticus mutters around another yawn.

I debate telling him Hunter is mad at me, not him, but it's late and his curious mind is too young to comprehend this complicated of a dynamic anyway.

"I promise he's not mad," I assure him, leaving it at that.

That seems to satisfy him for the moment, and his eyes droop heavier with every turn of the page in the book I'm reading, my voice as low and slow as I can make it. It still takes twenty minutes, but eventually he's out cold, soft snores puffing from his lips.

I sit there for a minute, too drained to move, staring at the ceiling. Everything feels heavy, as if my life is collapsing on top of me, slowly, inch by inch.

Seeing Nick earlier—it churned up so much resentment and regret, like the ghosts of every bad choice I've ever made lined up on my front lawn.

And then Hunter's truck barreling up the drive like some goddamn avenger, his face thunderstorm dark, his eyes on *me* like *I* was the villain when he was the one who ignored me all week and then listened to an ex-girlfriend who "meant nothing to him."

It's all too much, too fast, and I can't catch my breath from any of it.

Heading to my room, I change into something comfortable and breathable, my day clothes suddenly feeling suffocating. Then I grab my phone and call Reese.

"Baaaaaabe," she answers. "Oh my gosh, it's so nice to hear from you. What's going on?"

I picture her in her favorite fuzzy robe, pausing some Netflix show and putting a bowl of popcorn aside to give me her undivided attention. It's a heartwarming visual that also sends a painful stab to my chest because it reminds me of how much I miss her.

I begin to say something, but my voice breaks.

"What? What is it?" she asks. "Are you crying?"

"No," I say, sniffling.

"Don't lie to me, Wren Jensen." Her voice is stern. "Spill it. Now. Or I'm coming to your house immediately."

"I wish you would actually," I say with a pained laugh. "I miss you."

"I miss you too. I've been waiting for a formal invitation. You told me how beautiful this property was and how you had a spare room and then . . ."

"I've been a little . . . preoccupied." I dab my nose on the back of my hand. "And you know you don't need a written invite. You're welcomed here anytime. You know that."

"Yeah. I just like teasing you. But seriously, what's going on? Why are you calling me this time of night, pretending like you're not crying?"

I perch on the end of my bed and spill everything.

When I'm finished, she tells me she's coming to visit as soon as possible—that she just has to clear some things off her work schedule. This puts a smile on my face for the first time all night. I head to the bathroom, splash some water on my face while she updates me on her latest work drama.

By the time I finally make it back downstairs, I expect the house to be quiet. I expect the driveway to be empty. But through the front window, I see the silhouette of a man still sitting on my porch swing, the wood creaking faintly under his weight.

He's still here.

He never left.

I roll my eyes so hard it hurts, my exhaustion giving way to irritation.

He isn't moving, he's just staring out at the dark.

Waiting.

For *me*.

"Reese," I say. "I have to let you go."

"Everything okay?" she asks.

"Yeah," I say, though I don't quite believe myself.

We hang up and I head outside.

"You have *some* nerve," I snap, crossing my arms, my voice sharp. "Showing up here like this. After ignoring me. After lying to me and my son. After breaking promises you swore you'd never break."

His head turns, his eyes finally finding mine, calm in that infuriating way like nothing I'm saying is news to him.

"I believed you, Hunter," I push on, my throat tightening. "I actually thought . . . I let myself think you were different. And now I just feel like a fool. Again. Because you're just like the rest of them."

"I never lied to you," he says, grounded in his signature stoic confidence. He reaches into his back pocket and pulls something out. "But *you* lied to me."

My heart stutters when I see it—the sunflower notebook.

I snatch it out of his hand without thinking, my fingers clutching it tight like it might disappear again. "*You're* the one who stole this?"

"No," he says evenly. "Atticus gave it to me that day in the tractor. Had it in his backpack."

I blink, stunned. "Atticus?"

But . . . he knows better. He knows he's not allowed to take things from my office, let alone *this*.

"Why would he do that?" I ask.

"He said my name was all over the pages and he thought I should have them."

My cheeks burn, my skin hot. "They were written to you, but never intended for you to read."

How do I explain it was a journal and a writing exercise in one? If I hadn't also used it to outline the plot of my book, I think he'd understand. But the rest of the content is pretty damning.

I look down at the cover, at the worn spine and smudged pages. My hands tremble, just a little. Because it feels like he's read my *soul*, like I've been stripped bare. My deepest, darkest, most soul-revealing thoughts are in the pages of this book, and he's read them *all*.

"I was just trying to get my spark back," I say, my voice barely above a whisper.

His gaze hardens. "The notes about what we did. About *us*. You using that for a book? Is that all I was to you? Just some research project?"

I shake my head. "Those notes . . . they're for me and only me. I wanted to remember how it felt to be with you so I could convey those feelings onto the page. I don't expect you to understand. The mind of a writer is . . . anyway, those notes represented the feelings I wanted to write about—the raw, honest ones. But the things we did together? I'd never publish something that personal. I'd never betray you like that."

He exhales, jaw ticking. "Natalie said you told her I was inspiring you. That you're writing a farmer romance. Awfully coincidental."

I cross my arms. I *knew* it.

Maybe she didn't steal the notebook, but she attempted to sabotage this anyway.

I'm done with her, but right now, she's the least of my concerns.

"I *am* writing a farmer romance, and you have inspired me," I say, keeping my head high and owning it because I've done nothing wrong, nothing but channel my real emotions into a fictional story. "That's true."

"And she said you've been talking to your ex. After I handled it, why didn't you tell me he was still bothering you?"

I square my shoulders. "Because you've helped me enough and it wasn't your problem to deal with. I don't need you to rescue me all the time."

He huffs, almost a laugh but not quite. "Your letters beg to differ, honey."

I flinch because it's true. And because I *hate* that it's true.

"You said you don't play games," I throw back. "So why'd you ignore me all week? After everything we shared? I thought we were becoming close."

His eyes stay on mine, unwavering. "Because I needed time. Time to figure out what the hell to say to you. Time to cool off so I could talk to you with a level head."

"You couldn't have just told me that?"

He gives me a firm look. "I was too worked up, didn't want to risk saying something I'd regret later on. I've done that in the past. I didn't want to do that to you."

I'm both frustrated by his lack of communication and impressed by his restraint. In a world full of reactive men who lash out and shoot off text messages fueled by pure ego, here's one who waited until he could speak with clarity—because he didn't want to risk hurting me.

"It was a slap in the face," I say, "being ignored by you."

"I was pretty upset," he says.

We bicker some more, circling the same arguments, the same misunderstandings.

"I just wish you'd—" Before I can finish my sentence, he shuts me up with a kiss—hard, impatient, searing.

I'm breathless when he pulls back.

His hand cups my jaw.

Our stares hold hard, steady, with the kind of intensity akin to baring your soul.

"What are we *doing*, Wren? I don't want to keep going rounds with you when at the end of the day we're arguing over the same thing. I don't care who's wrong or right. I just want to be with you, and I know you feel the same, or you wouldn't be standing here talking to me. You wouldn't be kissing me back like it's the last time you'll ever see me again."

I start to answer, my voice thick with frustration, but then his mouth is on mine again, swallowing the words before I can spit them out.

"Get in the truck," he says, pulling back just enough to speak. "We're done arguing, honey."

"No," I say, panting. "I can't. My son's inside. I'm not leaving."

"Who said anything about leaving?" His eyes darken, and his voice dips lower, rougher. I glare at him, chest heaving, about to unleash a fresh round of indignation—but then he walks off, strides to his dusty Silverado, and swings open the rear passenger door. "Get. In. The. Truck."

59

Hunter

The second the passenger door clicks shut, she's all over me—hands in my hair and lips crashing into mine, that soft little sound she makes when I pull her deeper into me.

I grab her hips and haul her onto my lap like I've been starving for this—because I have. I've been *starving* for her. Every inch of her. Every sound. Every taste. Every breathless, desperate touch.

The cab fills with heat fast—windows fogging, breaths quick and heavy like we're running out of time.

I drag my hands under her shirt, palms hot on her bare skin, feeling the curve of her waist, the softness of her back, the little ridges of her spine. She shivers under my touch, her nails digging into my shoulders as I suck at her neck, just below her ear, like I want to mark her—because I do.

She shifts in my lap, grinding against the growing bulge beneath my jeans, her breath hitching when she feels exactly what she's doing to me. My hands don't leave her body, not for a second. I spin her around, pressing her hands against the foggy window.

Her jeans come off with a struggle—too impatient to be careful, too desperate to take our time. My hands are everywhere, squeezing, stroking, worshipping.

She gasps when I sink inside her from behind, her body clenching around me, perfect and warm and so goddamn tight I nearly lose it right there.

"Jesus, Wren," I growl against her shoulder. My hips snap forward, and I give her every inch of me before grabbing a handful of her behind. "I've missed this perfect little ass."

She whimpers, her breath fogging the glass, her palms flat against it as I drive into her, slow and deep at first, savoring every reaction, every little shiver that rolls through her body.

"Say it," I rasp, my hand sliding up her front, palming her breast, fingers tweaking her nipple through her bra. "Tell me you're mine."

She moans, arching her back into me, needy and breathless. "I'm yours."

"Damn right you are."

I move harder now, the truck rocking faintly on its shocks, every sharp thrust dragging a broken sound from her throat. The cab is thick with the scent of us—sex, sweat, heat—the air barely breathable, but neither of us cares.

I fist her hair gently, pulling her head back just enough to mouth at her neck, sucking hard enough to leave evidence. My free hand slides between her thighs, finding her clit, teasing it just enough to make her squirm and gasp.

"Come for me," I mutter against her ear. "Come on, honey. Show me how bad you want it, how much you've missed it."

She cries out, legs trembling, her body convulsing around me as I fuck her through it, chasing my own release with every desperate thrust. I swear under my breath when I hit the edge, spilling into her with a groan, my head falling to her shoulder, sweat slicking my back.

We stay like that for a moment, bodies trembling, breaths tangled.

Eventually, I pull back, our skin sticky and damp, and we fumble for our clothes—half-clothed, hair a mess, skin flushed. We climb out of the truck, the cool night air biting at our overheated bodies.

I pin her against the side of the truck, kissing her hard, deep, like I'm still starving for her because I am. I'll never get my fill of this woman, not until my dying day.

"You're mine," I tell her, my hands cradling her face. "I've been trying to tell you that from the start."

I brush my thumb across her kiss-swollen lips, my eyes locked on hers.

She looks at me like she's still catching up, like she doesn't know if she wants to kiss me again or slap me for being this intense. I like that. I like her fire. I've missed it.

"I really hate to leave you like this, but I've got an early morning," I tell her, still reluctant to let her go, "but I'll be back tomorrow. You have my word."

I kiss her again. "And the day after that. And the day after *that* . . ."

She smiles softly, something simmering behind her eyes that looks suspiciously like hope.

Before I leave, I reach into my jacket pocket and hand her a folded note.

She looks at it, one brow raised. "What's this?"

"Just read it later."

She gives me that wary, curious look but tucks it into her pocket.

"Also, I'm taking you out on a date," I add. "A proper date. This Friday. Pick you up at seven."

With that, I climb back into the truck, my body still humming from her, and drive off into the night, already counting the hours until I can see her again.

I'm not just falling for this woman, I'm plummeting.

There's no going back after this.

She's got me.

I'm not going anywhere.

I'll be her happily ever after if it takes me the rest of our lives.

60

Wren

I'm still flushed and raw when I get back inside, the air cooling the parts of me that still feel his touch—his hands, his mouth, his weight. I should shower. I should sleep.

Instead, I pull the folded piece of paper from my pocket.

It's crumpled a bit, the corner bent, the words McAninch Seeds stamped faintly at the top in green ink, like it was scrap paper he grabbed in a hurry. His handwriting is small, almost messy, the kind of penmanship you have to squint to understand—like every letter was written with impatience.

I sit at the kitchen table, the light low, the house dead quiet, and I unfold it carefully.

And I read.

> Wren,
>
> I'm not great with words. Never have been. Never been good at saying how I feel. But I figured I'd start with what I thought the first time I saw you. I thought you were trouble. The kind of trouble a man like me doesn't walk away from. I thought you were beautiful—so beautiful it almost made me mad. I thought

you looked like you'd burn a man to the ground if he got too close, and I guess I was right because here I am, writing a letter like I'm twenty years old.

I love your fire. I love that you're independent. That you don't need me. But I also love that sometimes it feels like you might want me anyway.

After reading your notebook, after trying to understand where you were coming from, I realized I'd be a damn fool to let you go. Because you're still the same person I thought you were.

No one's ever fought for you, Wren. But I will. Because that's what you deserve.

I've lost a lot of things in my life. A lot of people I can't get back. But I can't lose you. Not when it took me 42 years to find you.

You're a one-in-a-billion woman—the kind that doesn't come around twice in one lifetime.

A few months ago, I didn't know you existed. Now I can't imagine my life without you in it. I want to do this with you. I want a relationship. I want all of it. I want the next forty years to be the best ones yet—for you, for me, for Atticus.

You're everything I've ever wanted.

Yours,

Hunter

I have to blink through the tears clouding my vision, my hand covering my mouth as my chest caves in under the weight of it. This rough, reserved, emotionally cautious man just bared his heart in scribbled handwriting on seed company stationery, and I'm sitting here like some lovesick teenager, crying over every word.

I press the letter to my chest, closing my eyes.

Because my god, I wanted to hear this.

Because my god, I wanted him to feel this.

Because somewhere deep down, I think I've been waiting my whole life for someone to say something like this to me and actually mean it.

This man has done nothing but show up for me, fight for me, and claim me—with his hands, his body, his actions, and his words.

I always thought moving back home was one of the biggest plot twists of my adult life.

But it turns out that Hunter McCrae is the biggest plot twist of all.

61

Hunter

The shop is extra quiet this morning, the air usually thick with the sound of tools clanking and the low hum of an old radio playing something twangy and familiar. I crank some music so I don't have to sit alone with my thoughts again. I'm in the middle of cleaning chemicals out of a sprayer tank when I hear the door creak open, little footsteps pattering across the concrete.

Then I hear his voice.

"Whoa! Cool!"

I look up just in time to see Atticus scampering across the shop floor, climbing in and out of tractors like he's in a playground built just for him. He's already found a combine ladder and is halfway up before Wren strolls in behind him.

Wren's radiant today—lighter, brighter, like a flower that's finally been placed in the sun and is starting to bloom. Her shoulders aren't so tense. There's color in her cheeks. She looks like she finally got a decent night's sleep, and seeing her like this?

It does something to me.

"Hey," she says, sidling up to me, her arms crossed but her eyes soft. She looks at me through the dark fringe of her lashes with that look—the one that makes me feel like I'm standing there naked, exposed in ways that have nothing to do with clothes. She looks at me like she *sees* me.

"Hey," I say back, wiping my hands on a rag.

She watches me a beat longer, and then: "So you really want to do this?"

I blink, the question catching me off guard. "What kind of question is that?"

She shrugs, but there's a sly grin playing at the corners of her mouth. "Just making sure."

I shake my head, chuckling. "You really asking me that? After everything? Did I not make myself clear or . . . ?"

She holds up a finger. "Some rules first."

I cross my arms, nodding. "Okay."

"No games," she says.

"Agree."

"No breaking promises."

"Easy."

"And no silent treatment."

I grin. "That was one time."

She arches a brow. "One time too many."

"Fair." I smirk. "Anything else?"

She shakes her head. "That's all for now."

Before she can say more, I pull her into my arms, pressing her close, her softness fitting against me like we were made to slot together. She doesn't fight it. She leans into it.

Over her shoulder, I catch sight of Atticus watching us through the window of a tractor cab, his little face squished against the glass, grinning so big he looks like he might explode.

Kid's having the time of his life, I think to myself. And he hasn't even experienced the fun stuff yet.

I could give them the best life. And I *want* to give them the best life. It's the least I can do, considering they've given me something I didn't know I was missing—purpose. Love. Appreciation. A family to come home to every night.

I kiss Wren—deep, long, hard. My hand cups her face, my thumb brushing her cheek like I need to memorize it all over again.

How did I get this lucky?

She pulls back, slightly breathless. "You want to come over for dinner tonight?"

I shake my head. "Nah. You and Atticus come to my place. I'll make dinner."

She laughs. "Oh yeah? What's on the menu?"

"I grill a mean non-grass-fed steak," I tease with a wink. "Just ask the butcher."

She swats at me, laughing that pretty laugh that always makes me feel like I'm the funniest damn man alive.

"I'll see you at six o'clock," I tell her.

"Okay," she says, eyes warm. "Can I bring a side?"

"Please don't."

We share a laugh that somehow feels like home and forever at the same time.

They leave not long after, but not without Atticus asking if he can ride the combine next time. I promise him he can—but not until harvest. I watch them drive off, my chest swollen with something I haven't felt in too damn long—hope.

Whatever chapter comes next, I'm ready.

And truthfully, I'm really looking forward to letting her rewrite the story of my life.

62

Wren

It's Friday night and Reese shoots me a knowing look from my porch swing, one dark brow arched and a smirk playing on her glossed lips. She's already made herself comfortable—crisp white wine in hand, cozy throw draped across her legs, and Atticus curled up beside her with a stack of library books.

"You sure he's not a romance novel come to life?" she asks as a freshly washed white pickup rolls into my driveway, sunlight catching on the chrome bumper like a wink.

My heart flutters. I try to play it cool.

"I'm not even convinced he's real," I say.

Hunter steps out of his truck, and I swear the man's been plucked from a small-town thirst trap calendar. Non-ripped dark jeans. Polished boots the color of sawdust. A red plaid button-down so crisp it probably saw an iron this morning. And cologne. Actual cologne. Not tractor grease, not sun-warmed sweat—cologne. And somehow, his eyes are extra blue tonight.

He moves toward us with long, purposeful strides, and once he gets close, his eyes drag the length of me as a pleasant expression sweeps over his face. I chose this dress just for tonight—one that hugs in all the right places yet still leaves enough to the imagination. And I spent an hour putting curls in my hair, brushing and smoothing them out until I achieved perfect date-night waves.

"You look stunning," he says before stealing a kiss, slipping his hand in mine, and making me twirl.

Reese shoots me a bitten grin, giving her stamp of approval without saying a word.

"You must be Reese," he says, offering his hand.

She takes it, all charm and finesse. "And you must be the one making my best friend swoon like it's her full-time job."

Hunter chuckles, the corners of his eyes crinkling just enough to make my insides somersault.

"Atticus, you be good, okay?" I say, ruffling his hair.

"Aunt Reese and I are gonna build a pillow fort," he tells me, like this is the most serious of life's pursuits. "A big, huge one."

"Just make sure it's still standing when I get back," I say, my voice light as I descend the steps.

Hunter opens the truck door for me, and I swear, if he's not trying to kill me with his dashing good looks, he's trying to kill me with his old-fashioned manners. "Evening, Wren."

"Evening, McCrae."

He leans in once I'm buckled and kisses me—soft but full of intention. Like he's trying to say something without words. And he does. I feel it in every part of me.

"So. Where are we going?" I ask, unable to contain my excitement. Normally I hate surprises. I'm a planner. But handing over the reins to Hunter felt like second nature. When he told me he was taking me on a date and he'd pick me up at seven, I resisted the urge to ask any questions. I've never met a man who led. Who planned. Who took control. So far, Hunter's been doing all of that and more without an ounce of my help—and I'd be lying if I said it wasn't the sexiest thing in the world.

He pulls onto the road, his hand resting casually on the gearshift. "Got a few things planned. Dinner. A drive through the countryside. Maybe some stargazing."

I melt into my seat. The man just said the word *stargazing* like it wasn't the most romantic damn thing on earth.

Like I told Reese before, I'm not sure he's even real.

If this is a dream, I hope I never wake up.

The sun dips lower as we drive, casting long shadows across the rolling fields. He takes me to a quiet little steak house off a gravel road where we grill our own steaks, where no one knows our names, and no one's watching. We talk and laugh over candlelight, and for the first time in years, I feel like a woman—not just a mother or an author or someone who got left behind or abandoned.

I feel *chosen.*

After dinner, he drives with the windows cracked enough to let the summer night breeze slip in, one hand on the wheel, the other reaching for mine. For several endless miles, we pass silos and sleeping cattle and distant porch lights, and I don't want the night to end.

But eventually it does.

It's after ten when he pulls into my drive and kills the engine, but before he can say good night, I turn to him.

"Can I show you something?" I ask.

He nods, squinting and curious. "Lead the way."

We walk hand in hand to the back of the property, the moon lighting our path until we reach the riverbank. The air is soft. Still. The water, dark and reflective while bullfrogs and crickets create an evening symphony.

"It's not blooming yet," I say, stopping beside a small, fenced-off patch of soil, "but I planted a sunflower patch here. For you."

Hunter blinks. "For me?"

"It's a place where you can come and remember Ben. Honor his legacy. A living memorial."

His throat works around the emotion I can see creeping up on him.

"You've never said it outright," I continue, "but I know you carry that loss like a stone in your pocket. Always there. Always heavy. I figured you're a man of the land, so I wanted to speak your language. Give you something that grows. Something alive."

Hunter's quiet for a long moment. Then he says, voice thick, "Growing up, sunflowers were my mom's favorite. Ben and I used to plant them in random places for her. Behind the barn. Beside the driveway. Middle of fields. Around the gazebo. We'd tell her they were wild, like they just showed up one day. She'd always act surprised, but as I got older, I realized she probably knew the entire time. She probably got more enjoyment out of us seeing her happy than the actual flowers. I guess that's a mother's love."

I laugh softly. "Love is really something, isn't it? Sometimes it grows wild, in places you least expect. And sometimes we plant it, hoping that with the right care and conditions, it might just bloom."

He looks at me then, really looks at me.

"You didn't have to do this," he says, voice gravel-soft.

"I know. I wanted to." I drag in a slow breath as I drink him in. "Sunflowers are resilient. Stubborn. Always turning their faces to the sun no matter how heavy their heads get. I thought maybe this could be something beautiful rising in a place where things went dark."

He pulls me to him then, arms wrapped tight around my waist, and rests his forehead to mine. "You always know what to say."

I sniff a laugh. "Words are kind of what I do for a living . . ."

He presses his lips against the side of my cheek, and I deduce that I've rendered him speechless.

"I know this land means something to you," I add. "Which is why I've decided—I want to sell it to you."

He jerks back like I slapped him. "No. Absolutely not. This is your home. Yours and Atticus's. I won't put you out."

"You're not. I just need some time to find us a new place. But this land? This property? It was always meant to be yours. And you made a promise to your mother. Now you can finally fulfill it."

"Wren," he says, tone unflinching. "You are *not* selling me this place. End of discussion."

I open my mouth to argue, but he cuts me off.

"Because I'm not letting you go anywhere. I want you close to me at all times."

The air stills between us.

"I love you," he says. Just like that. Simple. Raw. Effortless. Like it'd been dancing on the tip of his tongue all night—or maybe longer. "I know it's soon, and I know it's fast. But when you find what you've been looking for your whole life, why hold back?"

I don't speak. I can't.

Because I've never been looked at the way he's looking at me now.

Like I'm his obsession and his sanctuary and his entire world at the same time.

And for the first time in my life . . . everything feels exactly right.

"I love you too," I say.

And I mean it.

I wish I could say I've loved him from the moment I first laid eyes on him, but I don't think I did—I think I knew I was going to.

And that's even better.

63

Hunter

The sun's sitting high and lazy above the hills, bleeding gold over the tops of the pines as I kneel next to Atticus near the edge of the barn. A soft breeze carries the smell of damp earth and warm hay, and somewhere in the distance, a hawk cries out over the fields like it's got something important to say.

Kid's got a bent nail in one hand and a hammer in the other, his tongue sticking out the side of his mouth with that level of concentration only five-year-olds can manage. We're fixing a busted slat in the chicken coop—the one a rogue raccoon decided to test last week. Easy work, but good hands-on experience for someone who's been asking me all week how everything works around here. Last night at dinner, Wren mentioned something about getting chickens. I figured this would be a nice surprise for her to come home to after she and Reese are done painting the town red this afternoon.

"Like this?" he asks, squinting one eye shut as he raises the hammer.

"Move your fingers first," I say, and he does—right before the hammer comes down and misses by an inch.

He huffs. "This is hard."

I nod. "Most things worth doing are."

Wren and Reese left an hour ago, buzzing about town and errands and lunch. Reese practically shoved Wren out the door, said something about needing girl time and good wine and probably a pedicure. I didn't ask. Just told her to go and have fun, and I'd hang back with Atticus.

I don't have much experience with kids, but for some reason, every time I see that woman, I get the urge to do whatever it takes to make her smile.

Also, I'd be lying if I said I wasn't having fun.

Didn't expect to like hanging out with him as much as I do.

The kid's funny. Smart. Curious as hell. And polite, too, which tells me Wren's doing a damn fine job raising him. But more than that, he's easy to be around. Doesn't whine. Doesn't expect to be entertained every minute. Just asks questions like he's trying to figure out the world, and maybe I see something of myself in that.

"I think I bent it," he says, showing me the nail.

"Try again," I say, instilling confidence in him the same way my father did with me when I was a kid. McCraes learn by doing, not by watching. We're not afraid to get our hands dirty. Ever.

Atticus nods and holds out his hand. I fish a new nail from the box. He grips it tighter this time, more assured.

I crouch back on my heels, watching him line it up, and my chest gets tight in that way it does when life gives you something you didn't even know you were missing.

Never had a son. Never seemed like it'd be in the cards for me.

But if I could've picked one?

It'd be this kid.

I'd be proud to call him mine.

It hits me then—like it has a few times lately but never this hard—how much I love his mother. How easy it was. How natural. Like breathing. Like gravity.

She just showed up and rearranged everything I thought I knew about myself. Wren with her messy hair and determined spirit and that fierce little boy who looks at the world with fresh eyes and reminds everyone around him that it's okay to take life a little less seriously sometimes.

I fell in love with Wren all at once. Like my heart took one look at her and decided *That's it. We're doing this.*

It didn't take long for me to realize there's no one else out there for me . . . because it's her.

It was always supposed to be her.

It took a long time to find our way to one another, but my god was she worth the wait.

I love the way she talks to Atticus—like he's the most important person in the world. And I envision the three of us together. Wren leaving her hair half up the way she always does, maybe forgetting her coffee cup on the porch railing because she's distracted by the sunrise. I picture her scribbling book notes when she gets a wild idea she doesn't want to lose, lips moving silently while she thinks. I imagine the clink of Atticus's cereal bowl in the sink every morning before he slips on his boots to join me in the shop for the day.

I want it, I want them, and I want it all.

"Hunter?" Atticus says, pulling me back to the moment.

"Yeah, kid?"

"Do you think I could live here forever?"

The question punches me in the chest. He doesn't look up, just drives the nail in with another light tap, tongue out again.

"I really, really like it here," he says. "And my mom is so happy. She smiles a lot more than she used to."

I clear my throat. "I think that sounds like a pretty great idea."

He grins, proud of his work, and I reach over to straighten the board before he hammers another nail.

"She said this barn used to be red," he tells me. "But she wants to paint it white now, to match the house."

I chuckle. This woman could say she wants this barn to be electric yellow, and I'd show up with a five-gallon bucket of paint tomorrow.

"Do you think it'd be weird if I called you my stepdad someday?" Atticus's next question catches me off guard.

I look at him then—really look—and he's not asking for reassurance. He's just curious, like all kids are. But I see the hope in his eyes, too, even if he doesn't know it's there. I think about Nick and the heartbreak this kid's gone through before. Wren would kill me if I filled his head with false hope, but telling him no might break his heart too.

"You can call me whatever you want as long as your mom's okay with it," I say, voice thick. "But I'd be proud if you did."

He nods, like that makes sense, like my answer satisfies his curiosity. "Cool."

We fall quiet for a bit, hammering in a few more nails, letting the warm afternoon settle around us.

"You hungry yet?" I ask.

He shrugs. "A little."

"Your mom said there's some string cheese in the fridge. And chocolate milk."

His eyes go wide. "She *never* buys chocolate milk."

I laugh. Atticus mentioned that day in the tractor a while back that he loved chocolate milk, that it was his favorite thing about day care. I brought a jug with me today just in case. Thought it might make the day that much more special.

We clean up the tools and wash our hands with the hose before heading inside. He kicks off his muddy Converse sneakers by the door without me asking and leaves them neatly by the mat.

In the kitchen, I hand him the cheese and chocolate milk, and he climbs onto one of the barstools at the island and props his cheeks on his hands while he stares at me with the big blue eyes that match his mother's fleck for fleck.

For a split second, though, I see Ben sitting here, staring up at me with his big blue eyes, looking at me this very same way—perfectly content to follow me around like my personal shadow.

I realize for the first time since Ben died and the light dimmed for a long, long time—my life is finally becoming full again. Because love doesn't always knock politely. Sometimes it barrels down your road driving a black Audi, carrying a sunflower notebook, and pushing every last button you have in all the right ways.

64

Wren

Pop music's playing low on the radio, the air smells like summertime, sunscreen, and perfume, and Reese is digging through my glove compartment for gum like she's on a classified government mission.

"Do you ever clean this thing out?" she asks, pulling out an expired insurance card, a Capri-Sun straw, and a Hot Wheels car missing two wheels.

"Does it look like I clean it out?" I shoot her a sideways glance.

She makes a noise in her throat and finally finds a piece of gum. "Victory."

We're winding down Colton Valley's Main Street, windows cracked, sunshine pouring in like warm honey. It's the kind of Saturday that makes the past feel far away. The kind that makes you forget about pain, even if just for a minute. The kind that makes you feel . . . new.

Reese's been here since yesterday and so far she loves it, just like I knew she would. While I know she'll never stop being a city girl who breaks out in hives around too much nature, she's leaning into this visit more than I expected. This morning she fed Sugarplum a carrot and only screamed once.

I slow the car as we pass a familiar boutique on the corner—Natalie's shop. Window display full of flowy floral dresses and overpriced soy candles that nobody buys.

Reese leans forward, peering through her sunglasses. "That the place?"

I nod. She knows the story, and there's nothing more to say.

"Park the car," Reese says, unbuckling. "I'm going in."

I grab her wrist. "No you're not."

Her brows shoot up. "You're seriously just going to let her get away with everything she did?"

"She's not getting away with anything." I glance at the store again. "Natalie's been Natalie since the sixth grade. Miserable. Insecure. Starved for attention. Drama is her oxygen. I'm not giving her a damn thing to breathe."

Reese shakes her head, impressed. "That's . . . awfully big of you."

I offer a wry smile. "I've got more important things to worry about. More important *people* to worry about."

She re-buckles her seat belt, leans her head against the headrest, then says, "I'm proud of you, you know."

"For what? Not throwing rocks at the boutique window?"

"For all of it. For doing the scary thing. For taking the leap. For choosing yourself and that beautiful little boy of yours. For following your heart—even after all the times it betrayed you."

I swallow the sudden lump in my throat. Reese rarely gets emotional like this, but when she does, it always affects me to my marrow in the best way.

"You became the version of yourself you were always meant to be," she says, reaching across the console and squeezing my hand. "And that led you straight into the arms of someone who was truly worthy of you."

I blink out the window, trying not to cry.

Damn Reese and her sentimental speeches.

We grab iced lattes at the coffee shop and head back toward the house. Gravel crunches beneath the tires as we turn onto the long drive lined with trees and budding wildflowers, a place I comfortably and lovingly call home.

In the distance, Atticus and Hunter are laughing together, messing with some fence line next to the acres I'll be renting out next year. And I'm not one hundred percent sure, but from here it looks like they fixed that hole in the chicken coop. My jaw hangs loose. How this man continually shows up for me in all the ways—big and small—is something I don't think I'll ever get used to.

"I still can't get over it," Reese muses.

"Over what?"

"How happy you look."

I glance at her.

Her lips pull into a slow, contented smile. "You don't just look like someone in love, Wren. You look like someone who *is* loved. There's a difference."

And just like that, I feel it again.

That steady burst in my chest.

Love in bloom, growing wildly.

EPILOGUE

Wren

One Year Later

The sky is painted in shades of tangerine and plum, the sun sinking behind the hills like it has nowhere else to be. We're up at the lodge—Hunter's place.

Well . . . *our* place now.

I still call it the lodge, even though it doesn't feel so dark and brooding anymore.

When I moved in earlier this year, I swapped out the heavy curtains for gauzy linen ones, brought in some lighter furniture, added a few vintage rugs and cozy throws, and filled the corners with potted plants and bookshelves. I expected pushback. Maybe even a dramatic protest. But Hunter only walked in, looked around, nodded once, and said, "Finally feels like home."

We're sitting on the porch now, two glasses of wine between us, the sound of cicadas chirping like white noise. Down the lane and across the road, the little white farmhouse glows like a storybook, porch light flickering on automatically with the dusk.

We kept it. Couldn't bring ourselves to sell it. Too many memories for Hunter. Too much magic for Atticus and me. That property is sacred for more reasons than we could ever list.

"I feel like Reese would be an entertaining neighbor," I say, sipping my wine.

Hunter sniffs. "You think she'd actually move here?"

"She's been back four times this year alone. Last time she texted me a picture of a vintage rooster mailbox and said, 'I get it now.' So yeah. I think she might."

"Cal's lease is up in two months," he says, glancing down at the house. "He needs a place."

"Could be fun to watch," I muse.

"Roommates?" he offers, smirking. "She'd eat him for breakfast."

I laugh. "And he'd eat her for dessert."

He raises his glass. "To morally questionable housing arrangements."

I clink mine against his. "To front-row seats."

Inside, the lodge is quiet. Atticus is fast asleep, his favorite stuffed pig tucked under one arm. He spent the whole afternoon mowing waterways with Hunter in the 7600, and he's already counting down the days until harvest. He wants to sit in the combine again. Says driving is his favorite thing in the world.

We've yet to tell him about autosteer.

In a couple months, we'll be living in the hum of combines, late autumn nights, and crop dust that settles like mist.

I'm ready for it.

"Dropped off some paperwork at Glenda's office this afternoon," Hunter says, stretching his long legs out in front of him. "Saw Natalie's shop sign was gone."

I blink. "Gone?"

"Place looked closed. Display window was all cleared out."

"Karma."

He laughs, shaking his head. "You're vicious."

"She's still a miserable human being who tried to come between us. Forgive my lack of sympathy. I only hope with all this time she has on her hands now, she'll have time to reflect on how to be a better person."

"I wouldn't hold your breath on that." Hunter finishes his wine and sets the glass on the railing. "Truitt also said there's a rumor going around about Cole. His last ex-wife reopened their divorce settlement. Turns out he was hiding assets."

"Seriously?"

"Yep. Local reporter did some digging. Got tipped off about shell companies he was using to buy land under fake names. Looks like he's about to lose a big chunk of change. And now no one wants to work with him. He's radioactive."

I smirk. "Funny how that works."

Hunter doesn't say anything, but I know he's thinking what I am. That people like Cole always think they're untouchable—until they're not.

"Ready for your book launch next week?" He changes the subject, and I'm grateful for it. I don't like to linger too long in the past, not when I have so much to look forward to in the future.

"Ready as I'll ever be." I smile. "Mrs. Harrison's book club is throwing me a launch party at the coffee shop. Did I tell you that?"

He grins. "That woman would throw you a parade if you asked."

"I know. The whole town's come around. Even the old guys at the feed store don't call me 'city girl' anymore."

"You've earned your place here. You had it once, just don't let it go this time."

"Wouldn't dream of it."

We finish our wine in silence, the breeze cooling and soft as the sun goes down. Eventually, we gather ourselves and head inside, turning off porch lights and locking up. The house is dim and quiet, wrapped in the kind of tranquility reserved for country nights like this.

I slip into my favorite silk pajamas, brush my teeth, and check on Atticus one last time. He's still sound asleep, arms sprawled wide like he owns the world.

Back in our bedroom, I grab my notebook from the nightstand. A *new* sunflower one Hunter got me when I moved in, something to represent a new start.

I flip to a blank page and start writing—soft, slow words about a man with broad shoulders and a quiet heart.

Hunter walks in, towel slung over his shoulder, skin damp from the shower. He spots the notebook and narrows his eyes.

"You writing about me again?" he asks.

"When am I *not*?" I wink.

He crosses the room and leans down, lips brushing my temple. "Can I read it?"

"Someday," I whisper.

He plucks the notebook from my hands, places it on the nightstand, clicks off my lamp, and climbs in beside me. Pulling me into his arms, he kisses me—long and sure and deep—the kind of kiss that makes my toes curl and my heart remember every reason I'm here.

In his arms, I fall asleep knowing I'll never stop writing about him.

Because I used to write about love.

Now I live it.

About the Author

Photo © 2024 Jill Austin

Winter Renshaw is a *Wall Street Journal* and #1 Amazon bestselling author of contemporary romance. Her novels have sold nearly five million copies all over the world.

Winter also writes psychological suspense under her Minka Kent pseudonym. Her debut title, *The Memory Watcher*, hit #9 in the Kindle store and is currently being adapted for the screen in South Korea. Her follow-up, *The Thinnest Air*, hit #1 in the Kindle store and spent five weeks as a *Washington Post* bestseller. Over the years, the author's suspense work has been nominated for two ITW Thriller Awards and one Shirley Jackson Award. It's been mentioned in the *New York Post* and *People* magazine, as well as optioned for film and television. Her novel *Unmissing* was adapted for the Lifetime network in 2024.

Born in Iowa and a graduate of Iowa State University, Winter still calls the state home, where she resides with her three children. She is represented by Jill Marsal at Marsal Lyon Literary Agency.